The Little Fays in the Air
and Other Tales of Faerie

BY THE SAME AUTHOR

The Exigent Shadow
Don Juan in Paradise

The Little Fays in the Air
and Other Tales of Faerie

by
Catulle Mendès

Translated, annotated and introduced by
Brian Stableford

A Black Coat Press Book

Visit our website at www.blackcoatpress.com

ISBN 978-1-61227-846-9. First Printing. March 2019. Published by Black Coat Press, an imprint of Hollywood Comics.com, LLC, P.O. Box 17270, Encino, CA 91416. All rights reserved. Except for review purposes, no part of this book may be reproduced or transmitted in any form or by any means, electronic or mechanical, including photocopying, recording, or by any information storage and retrieval system, without permission in writing from the publisher. The stories and characters depicted in this novel are entirely fictional. Printed in the United States of America.

TABLE OF CONTENTS

Introduction

The present volume is an addendum to the series of collections and anthologies produced in association with *Tale of Enchantment and Disenchantment: A History of Faerie, with an Exemplary Anthology of Tales*.[1] It is also one of a set of three collections assembling a substantial fraction of the short fantastic fiction of Catulle Mendès (1841-1909). One of the other two volumes, *The Exigent Shadow and Other Strange Obsessions* assembles tales of the *fantastique* dealing with anomalous events and altered states of consciousness that might or might not have supernatural causes, while *Don Juan in Paradise and Other Amorous Fantasies* assembles *contes*, fables and apologues employing supernatural motifs other than the apparatus of faerie.

Mendès' contributions to the French genre of *contes de fées* are marginal because what he meant by the word *fée* is quite different from what the writers who invented the genre in the 1690s, and those who resurrected it briefly in the mid-eighteenth century, meant by it. The *fées* featured in the paradigmatic *contes* by Mademoiselle de La Force, the Comtesse de Murat and Baronne d'Aulnoy, which originated from the Parisian literary salons in the 1690s and spread briefly to Louis XIV's court at Versailles before the genre was abruptly suppressed, were human enchantresses modeled on exemplars taken from Medieval romance, most evidently Mourgue la Faye [Morgan le Fay in Thomas Malory's English translation] and Merlin's protégée and nemesis, Viviane. The label *contes de fées* was, however, translated into English as "fairy tales," introducing a significant confusion, because English "fairies" already had an elaborate literary history, in which fairies were seen as supernatural beings, often minuscule and mischievous.

---

[1] Black Coat Press, ISBN 978-1-61227-838-4.

That imagery had been somewhat revised and lent useful gravitas by William Shakespeare's *A Midsummer Night's Dream*, and Catulle Mendès' *fées* are based in that English tradition rather than the French tradition, much of which was unavailable to him because of its near-disappearance more than a century before he began featuring *fées* in some of his tales.

The only French writer whose work survived the persecution that crippled or destroyed the careers of his inventive contemporaries in the late eighteenth and nineteenth centuries, Charles Perrault, was marginal to and highly atypical of the genre created and developed in the 1690s, and *fées* only feature in about half of his *contes*, thus encouraging and eventually establishing a notion of "fairy tales" in England that was much broader and vaguer in implication than "tales of fairies."

In France a very different notion of the genre was promoted in the last decades of the eighteenth century by Charles-Joseph Mayer's 37-volume *Le Cabinet des fees, ou Collection choisie des contes de fées et autres contes merveilleux* (1786; subsequently expanded to 41 volumes), which attempted to define the genre by assembling almost all of its accessible materials, although it confused the issue somewhat by adding in the "*autres contes merveilleux*": eighteenth-century Oriental fantasies imitative of Antoine Galland's *Mille et une nuits*. Mayer's collection fell out of fashion very rapidly, however, and soon came to be regarded as a museum of exemplars to be avoided rather than models for imitation and further development; Perrault's stories, the only contributions to the genre designed as tales for narrating to children, were retained for that purpose, and encouraged the mistaken notion that the whole genre had been thus intended. The genre had, in consequence, been misremembered, largely unknown and unread for a hundred years when Mendès reintroduced *fées* of a sort into French fiction on a considerable scale, in the 1880s.

The situation had been further confused in France by the importation on the early nineteenth century of the supernatural tales collected in Germany by the Brothers Grimm, falsely represented as examples of Germanic folktales, and those writ-

8

ten in Denmark by Hans Christian Andersen. Neither of those infusions contained *fées* as they were understood by the French inventors of *contes de fées*—even though some of the Grimm tales were adapted, directly or indirectly, from French sources—but they were much better known in France in the latter part of the nineteenth century than any domestically-produced material other than Perrault's, thus helping to promote the mistaken notion, derived from the latter writer's stories, of what the inventors of the French genre had been attempting to do, and what they had actually achieved. It is not at all surprising that Catulle Mendès adopted that mistaken view, almost unthinkingly, and that he elected to draw his own imaginative raw materials from Shakespeare rather from than any native source.

There is, in fact, no evidence that Mendès ever read any of the original *contes de fées* produced in the 1690s, or the pastiches produced in the mid-eighteenth century. One of his earliest tales in that vein was "La Belle au bois rêvant" (tr. as "The Dreaming Beauty" in *Bluebirds*) which is an ironic gloss of the vulgarized abridgement of Perrault's "Le Belle au bois dormant" (usually known in English as "The Sleeping Beauty"), but that does not mean that he had read the Perrault story, synoptic versions of the abridgement having become an element of orally-transmitted folklore long before 1880.

One fantastic tale produced toward the end of his career, "L'Azur, l'or et la pourpre" (tr. as "Azure, Gold and Crimson"), reprinted in his 1904 collection *Le Carnaval fleuri*, contains echoes of the opening sequence of Madame d'Aulnoy's "La Princesse Belle-Étoile et le prince Chéri" (tr. as "Princess Belle-Étoile and Prince Cheri") that may not be coincidental, but Mendès' story is an allegory that does not feature fays, although it warrants inclusion in the present collection as an associational item. There is, therefore, a certain irony in the fact that if one simply tabulates titles, Catulle Mendès wrote more tales featuring "fées" than any other French writer—nearly twice as many as Madame d'Aulnoy—although a purist could easily judge that he wrote no "authentic" *contes de fées* at all.

Seventeen stories featuring *fées* of a sort were collected in Mendès' first collection to consist almost entirely of fantastic *contes*, *Les Contes du rouet* [Spinning-Wheel Tales] (1885; revised in 1888 as *Les Oiseaux bleus*; tr. as *Bluebirds*), along with ten stories that do not feature *fées*. His other collection consisting entirely of fantastic *contes*, *Pour lire au couvent* (1887) contains four stories explicitly featuring *fées*, and several others that warrant consideration as associational items, and there are more than twenty further stories in which *fées* play a significant part scattered through his many other story collections, making a total of at least forty-six—a trifle approximately, as some of those might be deemed marginal, and fays make cameo appearances in a handful of other stories. All of those stories, however—with the sole exception of one of the associational items included in the present collection, the novella *Luscignole* (1892)—are very short, and although Mendès wrote more tales of fays than Madame d'Aulnoy, their total wordage is far less, her stories all being novelettes and novellas.

The brief length of Mendès stories—mostly between 1400 and 1700 words, and some even shorter—is, in fact, the principal determining factor of their existence. It was because an avid marketplace for stories of that length opened up in Paris in the 1880s, for which Catulle Mendès became the most prolific supplier, that he began writing tales featuring his species of *fées* in some profusion as he cast around for any kind of genre that could be fitted conveniently to that short story format, and discovered that whimsical magical fantasies featuring fays, angels, nymphs and/or voluble insects and flowers could be easily adapted to that kind of frame.

That marketplace opened up suddenly because advances in the technologies of printing and paper production made newspapers and periodicals much cheaper to produce in the early 1880s, resulting in a rapid and prodigal proliferation, and consequent fierce competition between them. French newspapers already had a long tradition of "feuilleton fiction," by which a section of one page was ruled off, and the space below it used for serial fiction. Convention had established that the space below a standard feuilleton could accommodate between 1400 and 1700 words of text, and although much of the short fiction published by newspapers in the 1880s was not actually placed beneath the feuilleton, that remained the standard expectation of story length, although Mendès frequently reduced the wordage further in order that his work could be more easily slotted into the limited space available in newspapers that were only four pages long, with the back page mostly taken up by advertisements.

Mendès had begun writing short stories at the very beginning of his career, in 1860, but the works he produced during the next decade were aimed at periodicals of much greater page length than newspapers, which used much longer articles and stories. He was the founder in 1861 of the *Revue fantaisiste*, which followed the then-standard practice of using relatively long feature articles and stories, but as the editor of the periodical, required to fill a fixed number of pages on a regular basis, he routinely had to supply "fillers" of various sorts. Most periodicals employed reviews and short items of non-fiction for that purpose, but Mendès immediately began deploying fictional "character sketches" of a kind that were later to fill three collections entitled *Monstres parisiens* in the early 1880s.

That marketplace was devastated by the economic upheavals following France's catastrophic defeat in the Franco-Prussian War of 1870, and the bulk of Mendes' literary effort in the 1870s went into poetry and work for the theater, but when the technologically-prompted boom began in the 1880s he was ready and prepared to take advantage of it. Again he became an editor himself, for the short-lived geographical periodical *Le Monde Inconnu* and the longer-lasting bi-weekly *Revue Populaire*, both launched in 1882. The latter's chief stock-in-trade was reprinted serial novels, but in both periodicals Mendès employed his expertise in supplying fillers, ini-

11

tially under the pseudonyms Jean-qui-Passe and René Maugéant. Many of them were brief anecdotal sketches of contemporary Parisian life, often featuring Jean-qui-Passe's friend Valentin, who remained the hero of many of Mendès short stories long after the author had abandoned the pseudonym. Mendès soon quit both periodicals, but continued supplying material in the same vein to other periodicals, broadening the scope of his fiction vastly in an urgent quest for variation and originality.

Les Contes du rouet was paired with the parallel collection Rose et noir (1885), which contained numerous fantasies that did not feature fays but laid the groundwork for his series of angelic fantasies, mythological and allegorical fantasies featuring articulate insects, as well as several contemporary stories of revenants and strange delusions. The stories in the generalized collection Lesbia (1886) include eight fantasies, including three featuring fées. Pour les belles personnes (1886) and L'Envers des feuilles (1888) only feature three fantasies each, and many of Mendès' collections features none at all, but La Vie serieuse (1889) has ten, two of which feature fées. Le Confessional, contes chuchotés has six fantasies, three of which have fées. La Princesse nue (1890) has ten, five featuring fées. Les Petites fées en l'air (1891) has twelve, two featuring fées. La Messe rose (1893) has seven, one featuring a fée, plus a portmanteau of fifteen ultra-short tales that includes some mention of the fay-like qualities of their heroine. Le Chemin du Coeur has three fantasies, two of them featuring fees. L'Homme orchestre (1896) has six, one featuring a fée. Arc-en-ciel et sourcil rouge (1897) has two, one featuring a fée. Finally, Le Carnaval fleuri (1904) seventeen, including one fée. The list is incomplete, because some of Mendès collections are not currently available for inspection. The stories in the present collection are arranged in the chronological order of their reprinting in the collections listed above, so they illustrate the development of Mendès' use of fays between 1885 and 1904.

Fées play only a marginal role in Mendès' masterpiece, the novella *Luscignole* (1892), although their presence within the world of the story is admitted; the character featured therein who is called *le roi fée* is a fake, all his "enchantments" being contrived by artificial and mechanical means, and he is clearly a transfiguration of Ludwig II of Bavaria, who was nicknamed the *märchenkönig*, of which *le roi fée* is an approximate translation. *Luscignole* is, in essence, an "anti-fairy tale," in which the fay king's attempt to play the *deus ex machina* role traditionally attributed to good fays fails dismally, thus allowing the story to become a horror story—one of the most horrific ever penned—but it retains a strong affinity with the tradition of *contes de fées*, in terms of its tone and the narrative structure that it reproduces in order to undermine its convention. It has something in common with Honoré de Balzac's tragic requiem for the genre, *La dernière fée* (1823 as by Horace de Saint-Aubin; tr. as *The Last Fay*)[2].

More significantly, however, along with the bulk of Mendès' work in the genre, *Luscignole* has something in common with two tales written by Catherine Bernard for the salons of the 1690s, which Mendès had certainly never read, and even Charles-Joseph Mayer neglected, which illustrate that, from the very beginning, "tales of enchantment" (a far more accurate translation of *contes de fées* than "fairy tales") included a minority of rancorous tales of disenchantment. The symbolism of many of Mendès skeptical tales is very similar to the symbolism of Bernard's "Le Prince rosier" (1696; tr. as "The Rose-Bush Prince"), and so is their fundamental philosophy. Mendès doubtless thought of his own cynicism as a novel adaptation, but it was not, and even the sly lubriciousness that is a hallmark of many his shorter fantasies is similar in tone and outlook to a significant fraction of the second wave of *contes de fées* produced for illicit publication between 1735 and 1755.

---

[2] Black Coat Press, ISBN 978-1-61227-

Even though they feature a different species of fays, therefore, Mendès' belated contributions to the genre have closer affinities with it than he can possibly have suspected, and this volume really does belong, at least as an appendix, to the set appended to *Tales of Enchantment and Disenchantment*; in juxtaposition with *Bluebirds*, it provides a useful illustration of a significant, if decidedly eccentric, phase in the history of the genre.

Considering that Mendès tried so hard, in hundreds of short stories adapted for newspaper publication, to discover new narrative strategies and new patterns of symbolism, it is perhaps surprising that his work in that short format retains a unity and consistency that not only links the stories in the present volume to the other fantastic vignettes featured in *Don Juan in Paradise and Other Amorous Fantasies* but to the vast majority of his fictitious anecdotes of contemporary Parisian life. The key to that unity and consistence is, of course, the qualifier employed in the latter title; Mendès' fantasies, whether they feature fays, angels, nymphs or loquacious insects and flowers, are almost all amorous fantasies. That is not surprising in itself, the only two fundamental topics of story-telling being sex and death, and it was part of the initial prospectus for the genre of *contes de fées* that they are tales of amour, into which the god Eros/Amour was often drafted in the 1690s in spite of his absence from the Arthurian mythos from which the key models of fays were taken.

In the original *contes de fées* the central topic of Amour was fused with the topic of Virtue, the original stories holding up as an Ideal a version of *amour parfait* that is intense, faithful and eternal. The fact that amour in the real world is not like that is the essential tragedy of all *contes de fées*, miraculously avoided, at least by the protagonists, in tales supplied with conventional denouements, but frankly recognized not only in the way that the adversaries of the protagonists behave but in the rare tragic variants, such as those supplied by Catherine Bernard. Mendès is a deliberately subversive writer, even more so than Bernard, not only employing the narrative dynamic of most of his fantasies to insist that amour, in practice, is far from perfect—even in Paradise—but frequently applauding and celebrating certain aspects of that imperfection. Having accepted the inevitability of infidelity, he goes out of his way in many of his stories to compliment and praise it, even though it allegedly inflicts the worst of all imaginable torturers on poor helpless males. However, his attitude is not as far removed from that of the classic writers of *contes de fées* as he might have imagined.

Not unusually for his era, Mendès employs a brazen double standard in his account of sexual behavior, regarding male infidelity as natural, inevitable and fundamentally heroic, while regarding equally natural and equally inevitable female infidelity as essentially treasonous. In his fictitious Paris, serial seducers like Valentin take an allegedly legitimate pride in their success, while deeply lamenting rejection or betrayal on the part of women who are automatically condemned at heartless—a metaphor frequently literalized in his fantasies. His attitude to loose women such as Lise de Belvélize, who are often featured in garrulous conversational pairs such Lila and Colette and Jo and Lo, is markedly different, not because he agrees with conventional morality in disapproving of them, which he is very scrupulous in refusing to do, but because the character of his approval is relentlessly patronizing, regarding their behavior as a kind of charming mischief. It is in that regard that the young women featured in his Parisian anecdotes are sometimes said explicitly to have something of the fay about them. Several of Mendès' *contes de fées*, including two reproduced herein, borrow Shakespeare's Puck as a character, and the majority of his fays, whether benevolent or malevolent, have a similar whimsicality, an eccentric sense of humor that is at best careless and at worst horribly cruel.

There is, however, a double edge to Mendès' cynicism. The impossibility of anyone in his fictitious worlds, whether in contemporary Paris, the remotest "time of the fays," or even after death, ever achieving a lasting *amour parfait* still leaves the chimerical Ideal in place, all the more desirable—after the

15

fashion of the torment of Tantalus—for its impossibility; and the first corollary of that impossibility, so far as Mendès in concerned, is an exaggerated idea of the value of temporary illusion. In his world-view, the fact that amour cannot last, because of the impossibility of fidelity, greatly enhances the sentimental value of its brief "honeymoons"—no matter how few or many there turn out to be in a lifetime—and attaches a precious nostalgia to their memory. For Mendès, the essential angst of existence is not a psychological corollary of the awareness of the inevitability of death but a corollary of the awareness of the evanescence of amour. In his world view, amour is not the only thing that makes life worth living, because there is also poetry, but the subject-matter of poetry, in his view, is the evanescence of amour, so poetry becomes, in essence, a heartfelt expression of his version of angst. There are no happy poets in his work, especially their author.

In many of the stories in which Mendès employs fays as a narrative devices, they are simply employed to emphasize his fundamental conviction with flamboyant and absurdly exaggerated irony, as, for instance in "La Fée Menteuse" (tr. as "The Fay Liar") and "Ce que les fées ne peuvent" (tr. as "What Fays Cannot Do"). Other stories, such as "Les Petites fées en l'air" (tr. as "The Little Fays in the Air") and "Le Prince lys et la vague de neige" (tr. as "Prince Lys and the Wave of Snow") employ a much subtler, far more sentimental irony, the latter partaking of a quirky surrealism that became typical of the last phase of his work. Other vignettes use fays as allegorical devices in themselves, as in "Le Bon almanach" (tr. as "The Good Almanac") or as instigators of allegorical quests, as in "L'Eau, la glace et le feu" (tr. as "Water, Ice and Fire"). Some are straightforward risqué fantasies, such as "Les Souhaits d'une eglantine" (tr. as "The Wishes of an Eglantine") and "Les Solitaries" ("The Solitaries"), the latter offering a slightly surprising moralistic judgment while venturing boldly into the territory of the conventionally-unmentionable.

Underlying all the work, however, is an insistent consciousness that the chimerical nature of *fées* does not render them irrelevant to the precious functions of literature, any more than the chimerical nature of *amour parfait* renders that Ideal irrelevant to the business of real human life. Although the stories collected in the present volume might appear to be frothy and trivial, lacking in real substance or food for thought, that appearance is a trifle deceptive. They are certainly entertaining, and their brevity facilitates quick reading, but they are not as superficial as hasty reading might suggest, and, when considered as a whole body of work, they are greater than the sum of the parts.

The translations of "Les Petite fées en l'air" and La Fée menteuse" were made from a copy of the 1891 Dentu edition of *Les Petites fées en l'air*. All the other translations were made from copies of the collections in which the stories were reprinted reproduced either on the Bibliothèque Nationale website *gallica* or the Internet Archive Digital Library at *archive.org*.

Brian Stableford

The Sufficient Gift

When he was getting old, the prince said to the good fay: "Oh, good fay, how you've deceived me! You promised me that I would encounter in my path, realized in a woman, the prefect ideal for which I was dying of amour; but it is in vain that I have gone forth, first sad and finally weary. I have not found her."

"That is strange," said the good fay, "for I took care to place in your path, and to put within young reach, the purest maidens and the most tender young women. I have reason to be surprised that your dream had not had what was required to be satisfied. But tell me, I beg you, the adventures of your journey, in order that I know how the women who had everything capable of charming displeased you."

"That story," said the prince, sighing, "I cannot tell without reviving very bitter anguish within me; however, since that is your desire, good fay, I shall not hide anything from you.

"I had just reached my sixteenth year when, leaning on the window-sill, I saw the miller's daughter with hair the color of straw, as fresh as a flower and singing like a bird. Oh, what ingenuous eyes she had! It isn't astonishing that the sky was gray that day, since she had all azure in her eyes.

"'Good day, miller's daughter!'

"'Good day, son of the king!'

"And for having exchanged those words, we loved one another. She did not hesitate for a moment, the innocent, to go with me into the nearby wood.

"She sat down next to me on a fallen oak; she left her hands in mine, not forbidding me, in the tender solitude, under the branches full of nests, to respire the odor of the invisible flowers that she had in her hair.

"'Oh, listen,' I said to her. 'How sweetly that warbler is singing.'

"She smiled, laughing; I was mistaken; it was my friend who had spoken. And she told me the most divine things: that no man before me had troubled her indifference; that she had believed, in seeing me, that she had felt a rose blooming in her heart, and that that flower, the rose of our amour, would never fade.

"I blessed you, good fay. At the first step, I had found the desired ideal. And I believed that I was fortunate. But I soon saw that the miller's daughter was speaking to me in that way because I was the son of the king; that what she truly desired was not my lips on her mouth but my crown on her head. I started to weep, disappointed, and I went on my way."

"Prince," said the fay, "you are too subtle an observer. Continue your story, I beg you."

The prince went on: "I arrived in a great city, where there were more beautiful women than in any other place on earth. To tell the truth, they were persons who lacked virtue, who opened their doors and their hearts after very little resistance, but they were so adorably beautiful!

The one I chose—I had four African negroes, of whom I made her a present, take her a coffer full of Brazilian diamonds—welcomed me in an alcove in which I thought, at first, the most beautiful white roses in the world had shed their petals and the whitest snowflakes of the heavens had fallen; no it was because she was lying there.

"Oh, how I loved her! What folly to have adored young women, more ambitious than amorous, who want to marry you because you are the son of the king! I detested the false ingenuousness, the hypocrisy of petty candor; I admired the sublime splendor of the flesh!

"I blessed you, good fay, for no more magnificent, more perfect, more marvelous naked creature had ever abandoned herself in the arms of a lover. I had found a species of ideal, perhaps inferior but ideal nevertheless, and I believed that I was fortunate. But I did not take long to perceive that my mistress, so incomparable, had an almost invisible mark on her beck below the nape of the neck, the color of raspberry. I fled, disappointed again, heartbroken, and I attempted the hazards of the road again."

"Prince," said the fay, "it is necessary not to look at goddesses so closely. Continue your story, I beg you."

The prince went on: "I encountered, I admired and I possessed many other young women. Thanks to you, who had prepared the relays of my itinerary of amour, I saw rosy lips, snowy breasts and streaming golden hair everywhere; but always, at the moment when my desire was about to be divinized in its entire realization, a sensible defect, a flaw, appeared, discouraging my joy and causing me to fall back into the despair of dissatisfaction.

"One who had been married the day before, almost not in bloom, virgin still for having scarcely ceased to be, put her arms around my neck; while opening her mouth under my kiss, I remembered her husband, ugly, aging and going gray; I was horrified before those delicious lips, lips that had touched his, and I fled, as one refuses to pick a flower over which a snail has crawled.

"A poetess, for whom I sang verses, admitted to me, after having pretended to admire them, that she did not understand why I had wasted time hunting such beautiful rhymes, and there was a hiatus in the sonnet that she dedicated to me in exchange. I fled!

"I was smitten with an actress who played bourgeois comedies in I know not what theater of I know not what city. She was exquisite, with all reveries in her eyes and all tenderness in her voice. 'Oh,' I cried to her, 'how I adore you! And how sorry I feel for you in being obliged to play the young woman who marries the engineer in halls hung with cretonne—you, who could modulate so delightfully in the wood near Athens the cooing of the dove that undid the heart of Hermia!'

"She said to me: 'Hermia?'

"'Yes,' I said, in Shakespeare's fairy play." And the name of Shakespeare astonished her, like a noise one has never heard.

"In sum, what can I tell you, good fay—bad fay, rather! You have played mischievously with me. All the innumerable lovers you offered me, alas—virgins or madwomen, wives, poetesses or actresses, all of them!—have desolated me before, during or after the kiss, by virtue of some heart-rending dissonance in the harmony of their charm. And now I have traveled a great deal, and hoped for a great deal, and I am finally weary, and I still bear in my soul the bitter and cruel desire for the ideal coveted in vain."

The good fay remained silent, reflecting. Then, saddened, she said: "You're not accusing me without reason, and I can see clearly that I'm culpable—not in the way that you think, but culpable nevertheless. For while I offered you, to please your dream, the purest maidens and the most tender young women, I forgot to accord you a gift without which perfect joy cannot exist, the gift that makes lovers happy and makes true poets."

"What gift is that?" he said.

"The gift of never knowing, even when it is evident, the imperfection of human beauty, of only seeing what one desires to see: the clairvoyance that chooses instinctively. If you had had that gift, the first maidservant or streetwalker who came along would have been sufficient to enable you to embrace the promised ideal."

The Enchanted Bed

At the corner of the Road of Dreams, near the Crossroads of Chimeras, there is an inn built in Florida rosewood; birds of paradise that dip their feathers in the gilded light of dawn flutter around weathervanes made of two crossed arrows fallen from the quiver of Eros. Under the scattered thatch of the roof, hummingbirds build their nests in the heart of moss-roses. It is an inn where the fays stay, where couples come to request hospitality who have gone astray in the parks of Watteau, mysterious parks illuminated by the misty moon, the celestial whiteness ribboned with radiance.

Puck, the innkeeper, on the seat of an omnibus harnessed to doves, lays in wait for travelers at the arrival of every train, and says to them politely: "Don't fail, noble lords and exquisite ladies, to come to sup and sleep with us, for we have in our larder marmalades of ginger and roses, which produce the most fortunate effects, and the stairways to the rooms are strewn with leaves and flowers so soft that it is a pleasure to climb the stairs barefoot."

But the travelers of either sex pay no heed to that merry banter; they sit down in the serious omnibus drawn by horses, in order to be taken to the Four Nations or the Three Emperors, disdaining the Bohemian hostelry on the Road of Dreams near the Crossroads of Chimeras.

"Puck," I said, "whip your doves. Take care to hitch them to the highest branch of a flowering acacia; don't waste time listening to the nightingales or the warblers in the bushes by the roadside, for I'm in haste to arrive at the inn. I've just married the younger daughter of the Marquis of Srinagar, and today is the first evening of our honeymoon."

When we had arrived, Puck said to me: "Sire, I know too well the regard that is due to newlyweds not to treat you as well as is possible for me. There are only two beds in my inn;

23

you shall have the better one, and I don't think that you'll regret the length of the nocturnal hours in the morning."

On hearing those words, the younger daughter of the Marquis of Srinagar could not help blushing; she gave the impression of a white rose in which a pink eglantine is blooming.

"But you doubtless want to sup before taking shelter," said Puck. "Fortunately, I went hunting this morning; a pâté has been made of Corsican birds with pistachio nuts, utterly appetizing."

"Puck! A room and a bed! Only a good-for-nothing, with a wife like mine, would be hungry for anything but the flesh of a mouth, or thirsty for anything but the dew of lips."

"Very good! That urgency pleases me. I'll take you, then, to a room in which Cleopatra, Queen of Egypt, once slept. You'll find a mysterious, troubling perfume there, which hasn't evaporated."

"What! Cleopatra has slept under your roof, Puck?"

"That she slept I dare not affirm. She came to my inn one evening in spring with a beautiful black slave, whose eyes, so far as I could judge, did not express the intention of an immediate slumber, under eyelids quickly closed. What is certain is that the bed in which the royal transient lay has been endowed ever since with the most active and the most delectable virtue; people believe that they are lying on a living brazier of cantharides."

"You're offending me, Puck! I'm not one of those who need, when the wife is so beautiful, an enchantment that incites them to their conjugal duties. Give me a bed of snow and ice, beaten by the four winds, and provided that the daughter of the Marquis of Srinagar does not disdain to take her place therein beside me..."

"So you're refusing Cleopatra's room?"

"Absolutely."

Puck scratched his ear.

"It's just," he said, "that the other bed—there are only two in my inn—is singularly redoubtable."

24

"Redoubtable?"

"Beyond anything you can imagine, alas. A great misfortune befell me several centuries ago. In steel armor that glittered in the moonlight, fooled by a host of cavaliers, a young woman arrived after a battle to knock on my door as midnight was chiming. She didn't reveal her name, but she resembled a Virgin Mary who was also a Pallas Athene. She slept in my inn, without taking off her breastplate or her leg-guards, until the following dawn, when the trumpets sounded for another battle.

"It was great honor that I could well have done without! Her virginal modesty and warrior rudeness sanctified the bed in which she lay strangely; one can sleep in it, but one can't make love in it. I won't hide the fact that I owe to that fatal bed the discredit of my inn; I can promise the chamber of Cleopatra, but people fear the chamber of the Virgin; the most determined lovers, merely at the sight of my sign, hasten to flee, in spite of the birds of paradise that dip their feathers in the gilded light of dawn and the hummingbirds build their nests under the eaves in the heart of moss-roses.

"If the poor renown of my hospitality continues to spread, I'll be reduced to the most perfect poverty, and I'll be seen beginning on the streets with a lily or a poppy for a bowl, because I won't even have the means to buy a wooden bowl.

"Conduct us to the redoubtable bed!" I cried. "Can't you see how pretty the woman I love is, and the flame that glints between her eyelashes, and the double rosy gleam that flourishes here and there beneath the uplift of her chemisette? By Eros, Puck, I'm curious to test the bed enchanted by the slumber of a virgin."

Puck sighed. "Beware, presumptuous child, of attempting too difficult a proof! Once, a hero armed with a club and accompanied by a queen also asked to enter the virginal apartment. He shrugged his shoulders, believing himself to be sure of his fact. The next morning, Heracles left the inn crestfallen, his head bowed, while Omphale, at the window roared with laughter in the mane of the Nemean lion."

"Take us to the bed," I repeated.

"Beware, presumptuous lover, of not coming out of such a perilous adventure with honor! Another time, a Spanish lord named Don Juan, who was carrying away the daughter of a merchant of Seville in a post-chaise, stopped outside my house. He dared to cross the threshold of the enchanted chamber. The next day, the child, left alone behind the curtains of the bed, wept hot tears for not having been seduced."

"Do you want, to lodge us, hotelier devoid of confidence, yes or no?"

"Follow me, then," said Puck.

But while we were climbing the stairs barefoot over strewn hyacinths and violets, he did not hide the worry into which the temerity of my attempt had cast him. As for the daughter of the Marquis of Srinagar, she did not fail to testify some anxiety herself.

"Oh, my friend these enchantments are sometimes more powerful than we think. Are you quite certain?"

I tried to reassure her by showing her in a mirror the forget-me-nots that she had in her eyes and the red rose that she had on her lips. She turned away, blushing. Perhaps she would have preferred Cleopatra's bed.

Sometime after that—I had had the daughter of the Marquis of Srinagar murdered in order to marry the nice of the King of Trebizond and had replaced that one with the widow of the Emperor of Visapour—I returned to Puck's inn in the company of the Queen of Ormuz, who had quit her twenty provinces and four husbands for love of me.

"Hey, Puck, good hotelier," I shouted. "Have you room in your house for two lovers who are traveling? We'll gladly sleep in the virginal bed."

"Oh, Sire," he replied, "it's very bad of you to mock a poor innkeeper like me. You know full well that, on the night you lay on it with the daughter of the marquis, the bed caught fire from your kisses, and went up in flames so thoroughly that the curtains, the walls and the beams were ablaze, the birds of

26

paradise lit up around the weathervane, and the hummingbirds were roasted in the heart of the moss-roses!"

The Mute Princess

The king's daughter was mute. That misfortune had occurred by virtue of the caprice of a malevolent fay who lived in a pearl amid the coral and the stalactites of a submarine grotto. One cannot imagine anything prettier than Princess Ermelinde; at sixteen years of age she resembled the month of April; her eyes were as blue as forget-me-nots, her mouth as red as eglantines; when she bent her snow-white face over them in order to inhale their odor, jasmines, in a whisper of petals, said: "Oh, how white she is!"

Alas, nothing that exists on earth is perfect; a rose that sang like a nightingale would be too charming. Not only was she mute in the lips, but it was not possible for her to express her thoughts by means of gestures or her gaze. When interrogated, she was unable to make those finger signals, movements of the head and blinks of the eyes that say yes or no; with the consequence that one could no more enter into conversation with her than with a statuette or a doll.

That was a great pity; for, being so exquisite to see, she would certainly have been delightful to hear.

As you can imagine, his daughter's infirmity was a subject of great pain for the kin. He summoned the most illustrious physicians in the world, including a doctor named Sganarelle,[3] who had a great renown for the cure of similar cases, and he addressed the most famous enchanters, but neither science nor magic could render speech to Princess Ermelinde. The good father became increasingly desolate. He finally decided that only the person who had caused the harm

---

[3] Sganarelle is a recurrent character in Molière's plays, who famously masquerades as a doctor in *Le Médecin malgré lui* (1666)

could remedy it, and he resolved to go and visit the fay among the corals and stalactites of the submarine grotto.

There was little appearance that, cruel as she was known to be, she would allow her heart to be softened by prayers and tears; the greatest pleasure of the wicked is to see the sadness and misfortune they cause, but since there was no other recourse than that step, it was necessary to attempt it. The king therefore set forth with a few of his courtiers.

Not without many fatigues and adventures, he penetrated into the fay's mysterious dwelling, where the latter, very small and nestled in her pearl, burst into such laughter on considering him that the pearl shook like a little ringing bell. That was not a good presage for the success of the enterprise; so the new arrivals were no less astonished than pleased when the fay advanced her dainty head and said:

"Well, Sire, you haven't made such a long journey for nothing. I value my reputation much more, as you shall see. Since you desire it, Princess Ermelinde will speak henceforth, like you and me, in all the circumstances of life..."

"Oh, Madame," cried the king, falling to his knees, you are doing me the greatest favor in the world, and there is nothing of which I do not feel capable in order to express to you the extent to which I'm obliged to you."

"But," she continued, still laughing, "in all the circumstances of life...except one."

Coming from a malevolent individual, that reservation was bound to inspire anxiety. The king, full of care, hastened to ask what the circumstance was—the only circumstance—in which the princess would be as mute as before.

His questions were futile, and he had to return home without having obtained any response, for the fay, shaking with laughter, shut the pearl in his face—which is to say, she made it turn around, in such a way that he could only see the closed roundness, in which the orient was scintillating in a mocking fashion.

On returning to his palace, however, the august voyager forgot all dread, so much joy did he experience. The princess talked, talked and talked, in the clearest and sweetest voice that had ever been heard.

She murmured: "My father!"—a word that he had despaired of ever hearing—with such seductive inflections that he felt his heart melt in delight. She said a thousand other pretty, foolish and happy things—all the things she wanted to say. She had kept silent for so long that she had great savings of speech to spend lavishly; she did not fail to do so. Smiling like the flowers, and delighted no longer to be mute like them, coming and going, hopping an skipping from the rooms to the garden and from the garden to the woods, she babbled incessantly, like a chirping bird twittering at a spring.

To shut up was now as difficult for her as speaking had been impossible before. Her maids of honor tried in vain to get a word in; she was the one who said them all; and as soon as the warblers in the bushes began to sing, she interrupted them with a never-ending trill. While she was being dressed, while her hair was being done, while her dancing-master was teaching her the pavane, in the morning, afternoon and evening, at table, at the window, no matter when or where, she talked, and never stopped speaking; by night, while asleep, she spoke in her dreams.

No, truly, whatever the fay had said, she never remained silent. And one day, no longer knowing what to say, she said that she wanted to be married. As you may suppose, the desires of the princess, since she could express them, were orders for the king and all the people of the court. A husband was found for her with whom an empress would be content: young, handsome, from an illustrious family, amorous and covered in glory, and the marriage was made with all imaginable rapidity.

On the day of the wedding the king did not fail to experience some misgivings. The moment of the marriage might be the "circumstance of life" in which Ermelinde would become as mute as before. What a fuss there would be if, at the very moment when the husband took her in his arms and said "I love you," she became quite incapable of responding to that confession by a stammered confession of her own. It is unnecessary, in such a situation, to speak loudly, but it is still necessary to say something, however little and however quietly; it is not only for the kiss that one must open one's lips.

In spite of the apprehensions that it had been possible to conceive, nothing untoward happened, and the victorious expression with which the husband's face was radiant the flowing day was sufficient proof that the princess had said all that it was necessary to say.

Many days went by. The most perfect felicity reigned in the court. History does not say whether the people were as happy as those who governed them, but after all, in their troubles, if they had any, the happiness of their masters must have been a great consolation to them.

The king, entirely given to the pleasure of hearing his daughter chatter, was far from thinking about the disquieting reservation that the fay had made, and the husband of the princess had the joy, to which no other joy is comparable, of possessing a young, pretty wife who was always in a good mood. Furthermore, Ermelinde had at least as many virtues as she had charms; she was not restricted to being as fresh as the flowers and twittering like the birds; she was attached to her duties and faithful to her oaths, not too coquettish and not too frivolous, in spite of her laughter and her loquacity. She did not allow herself to be moved unduly, like so many other women of the royal race, by troubadours who sang tensons and ballads; she maintained the most honest conduct on the days when her husband offered hospitality to passing monarchs or traveling princes, and she never encouraged, by a dropped rose or a missal forgotten on the prie-dieu of the oratory, the ingenuous tenderness of pages who sighed in corners. She had no dearer pleasure than sitting beside her husband in the conjugal chamber, and when the other was distanced from her by affairs of state, the sole amusement she permitted herself was a walk in the orchard or the forest, where she dreamed beneath the branches.

Once, when she was walking, all alone, on the edge of a wood, it happened that a knight passed along the road, searching for adventure, a battle or amour. In those days, paladins showed a great deal of respect for ladies and damsels, but the respect did not go as far as not asking them for some small favor when the opportunity came up. They would have blushed to steal a kiss from a reluctant mouth, but they did not make it a sin to collect one from lips that consented.

The particular knight that was passing along the road, handsome, well made and with fire in his eyes, was more inclined than any other to take advantage of the tender dispositions that the woman one encounters might have. At the sight of the princess, whom he did not know, he cried: "It's necessary to admit that no more beautiful person has ever appeared to my eyes. And, descending from his horse, he continued talking to her. "Whoever you are, learn that I am seized by a great amour for you, you are so young and pleasant. I am not so repulsive myself that people cannot suffer my approach, and since we are both at leisure here, we shall go, if you please, into the depths of his wood, where I will show once more that I am worth no less in amorous battles than murderous combats."

At the same time, took her hands and pulled her, without rudeness. What anger the princess had at those words and that gesture, it would be impossible to say. What, she, the daughter of one of the greatest kings in the world, was being treated thus! At least, the person who had dared to make such an insult would not take long to repent it. She looked him full in the face and was about to confound him with some haughty discourse...

No, she did not pronounce a word—not one! And she did not make a gesture, neither one of those finger signals, nor one of those movements of the head, which say no.

Alas, the circumstance had presented itself in which Ermelinde had to remain mute.

The knight burst out laughing when she did not say a word. "Good! This one isn't grim, and shows no desire to refuse the temporary pleasure."

Then, enlacing her and applying his lips to hers, he took her away silently into the depths of the wood, where he had every facility to prove that he had not lied in boasting of his valor in amorous battles.

Oh, the poor mute!

And that is how the malevolence of the fay who laughed in her pearl was exercised. But she was mistaken, in that the king did not suffer from it, and Ermelinde was its only victim. For, having returned to the palace, the princess refrained carefully, although she had recovered the power of speech, from relating her misadventure; good as she was, she did not want to desolate her husband or her father by the confession of an irremediable misfortune. For fear that they might conceive some suspicion of it by which their happiness might be troubled, she even resolved not to change her habits, and no matter what might happen, she continued to walk on the edge of the woods from time to time, not far from the road where the knights errant passed by.

The Bridal Costume

There was great desolation in the woodland path when it was learned that Vincente was about to be married. And who was desolate? The little flowers, the silky butterflies, and the threads of spider-silk that trembled from one branch to another? You've guessed it.

The little flowers said to one another:

"What! Is that possible? Vincente occupied in cooking bread for her man and the other cares of the household, no longer coming to pick us in the spring hedges?"

"What good will it do us," said the butterflies, "to have wings more brilliant than the robes of princesses, if Vincente no longer runs after us, while we pretend to flee?"

The threads of spider-silk thought: *It's hardly worth the trouble of quivering, suspended between an acacia twig and a lemon-tree leaf, if we to longer have any hope of catching in Vincente's hair as she passes by, singing.*

And with that, it was agreed in the woodland path that all possible means would be employed to prevent the misfortune they feared being accomplished. The fiancé only had to persist; they had very disagreeable surprises in store for him.

You might think that it was not such a terrible conspiracy, but in that you would be mistaken. In those days, threads of spider-silk, butterflies and woodland florets were fays of a sort, and to be at odds with fays is something I would not wish upon you.

The day of the marriage was approaching.

Vincente said to herself: *It's certain that I'm as pretty as the daughter of an emperor, with my yellow bonnet and my fustian skirt, but in sum, it's necessary that I have a more elegant adornment for my wedding night.*

She had a few copper coins in her money-box; she went to the town in order to but suitable attire.

"Oh, that's a pretty bonnet!" she said, stopping outside a milliner's display-window. "How it would suit me, flowery with eglantines so fresh that one might mistake them for natural flowers. But it must surely be very expensive; it isn't made to coif a poor woodcutter's daughter like me."

"In truth," said the shopkeeper, "I've been trying to get rid of it for a long time. You've arrived at the right moment. How much will you offer for it?"

Blushing, Vincente said: "Two sous. Only two sous. I can't afford any more."

"Oh well, take it. I'm not a milliner like the others; what pleases me most of all is selling my merchandise to persons whose beauty can do it justice."

With the bonnet in a cardboard box, the woodcutter's daughter went on her way, very content.

In the widow display of a grand boutique there was a dress that seemed to Vincente to be the most magnificent in the world. It was so silky, so glittery and so vivid that one might have thought that it was made of a great many butterfly-wings sewn together.

"Oh, what a pity that I'm not rich. I'd gladly buy that dress; but doubtless only a demoiselle of the court would have enough money to make such a purchase.

"My God," said the merchant, "I'm not greedy; there's always a means of reaching an understanding with me. Let's see, how much will you offer me for the skirt and the bodice? It's true that nothing similar has ever been seen. It has been cut out and sewn by a couturier who served a apprenticeship with the best dressmaker in Paris."

Blushing, Vincente said: "Four sous. If they were gold, I'd still give them to you, but they're copper, as you can see."

"Take the dress then, for it will suit you marvelously. Only promise me that you'll give me your custom and that you'll recommend me to your acquaintances."

The woodcutter's daughter promised him anything he wished, and went away as happy as it is possible to be. She had one worry, though. A bonnet and a dress are very necessary things, no doubt, but a chemise is no less so. Vincente could feel, not without anxiety, her little body brushed by the fustian of her clothing. Who could think of marrying on seeing her thus deprived? She said to herself, pink with modesty, that it is necessary to have a chemise, in order that it can be taken off.

As she was thinking that, she saw in another shop a light whiteness of batiste and lace, so light and white that one might have sworn that it was woven of spider-silk. As she had gained courage in her previous purchases, Vincente said to a man standing near the door: "It isn't very pretty, that chemise, and I have much nicer ones a home, but I'd make a bargain for it if I could get it for three sous."

The vendor seemed dazzled. "I hadn't hoped for such a windfall," he exclaimed, "And if you like, I'll throw in two amethysts to retain it at the shoulders."

It was thus that Vincente was able to return to her village with a bonnet, a dress and a chemise that would have been the envy of the eldest daughter of a king."

It goes without saying that on the day of the wedding the woodcutter's daughter stimulated strange jealousy because of the fine clothes she had. How had she been able to procure such attire? The bridesmaids discussed it in whispers, with pinched expressions. But the groom, because he was very amorous, paid little heed to the pretty bonnet florid with eglantines and the magnificent dress the color of butterfly-wings. What was important to him was what was underneath the bonnet and the dress; and, leaving people conversing and drinking in the hall of the inn, when night had barely fallen, he drew Vincente to the cottage in which he lived, at a bend in the road.

As soon as they were alone, he said: "Oh, what beautiful hair you have, as blonde as ears of wheat ripened by the sun and perfumed like ripe hay."

And in order to see it better, and to kiss the golden hair, he tried to take off the bonnet. But he could not do it. Was that not a singular thing? With their stems and their thorns, the little flowers clung to the fringes of the ears and the neck.

"Ow! Ow! You're hurting me, my love!" sighed the young wife.

He was not brutal enough to make her suffer already, knowing that it would be necessary for her to sigh, soon, for a better cause, and he did not worry any more about the impertinent bonnet. Another desire occupied him because of the softly inflated bodice, as if it were filled by two living oranges; and, taking her on to his knees, he tried—while she consented, turning her head—to unfasten the dress.

That was quite another story! The fabric, so silky so glittery and so vivid, resisted, refusing to quit the skin and defending itself with all its stubborn fastenings. No, whatever he did, he could not triumph over that dress, too well sewn and determined not to be opened. And yet it had been made in Paris!

Vincente began to exhibit some surprise and anxiety herself. But the husband smiled, for a very natural thought had occurred to him. He knelt down in front of his wife, kissed her, and began, as if unheedingly, a sly ascent of tender fingers.

He uttered a great oath. From the ankles to the hips, a lace chemise more solid than a suit of armor, even though it was as light and white as if it were made of spider-silk, enveloped and embraced inexorably the dainty wife.

In a corner of the cottage, the narrow nuptial bed, partly open, with sheets the color of snow, seemed to be mocking them.

After a full hour—you can imagine the efforts he made—the husband, full of rage and sweating, was in a truly pitiful state. Was it not, in fact a very unfortunate adventure, being so close to his goal, not to be able to reach it? I would like to see what grimaces those who are tempted to laugh at the embarrassment that Vincente's husband was in would make in a similar circumstance. As for the little woodcutter's daughter, without saying a word, she was pulling a face that expressed very well that she was very far from being content.

But a nightingale, which could be seen through the open window, started to sing in a rose-bush, and what it sang was:

"Go on, poor fellow, you're wasting your time; you'll never get to the end of the bridal costume, for it's made of little flowers, butterflies and spider-silk, which are fays, and have a grudge against you."

"Well, I'll avenge myself. I'll go to the woodland path and set fire to it."

"Bah! Other eglantines will flower, other wings will flutter, and the spiders' distaff is inexhaustible. You'd do better to negotiate with your enemies."

"I think, in fact," said Vincente, "that that would be the wisest course."

"What are their demands?"

"Promise not to occupy Vincente in baking your bread and other household chores, and to let her sing her songs, as before, in the forest."

"Well, I swear the oath!"

The little flowers, the butterflies and the spider-silk, knew the husband to be an honest man incapable of breaking his promise, so the bonnet flew away, as if borne by a gust of wind—followed by the dress, and the chemise too.

The Roses of the Blue Garden

Young lads and young lasses, refrain carefully from having a sage mind and a serious heart; but be, in your beautiful season, charming lunatics of either sex. Children, immemorial humankind is a grandmother who has need, in order to be cheered up, of hearing the music of your laughter and the softer music of your kisses. If anyone tells you that it is appropriate to be grave and to disdain joy, do not listen to that dismal counselor; do not listen, either, to the morose individuals who recount the deceits of pleasure and the bitterness of good fortune: the vanity of living.

No, live, ardently and joyfully. Throw songs and bunches of flowers in the face of experience, that senile dotard. Be young, since, in fact, you are. Open your mouths where the kiss of the bee will alight; open your hearts where amours will nest like cooing turtle-doves. Love, love, love! Oh, hasten to love. Do not lost a minute in vain hesitations, for time passes quickly, taking away the opportunity for delights, the possibility of enchantments; and if you delay in plucking the flowering hour, what happened in the times of fays and genii to the youngest of the king's daughters in a realm near Bagdad might happen to you. A song was made of her story:

> *The beauty who wants,*
> *The beauty who does not dare*
> *To pluck the roses*
> *In the blue garden...*

I've forgotten the other couplets; but I will tell you the story of how the princess, in the realm near Bagdad, was punished for having been too sage.

On her fifteenth birthday, while walking along the bank of a river, the princess saw a garden that was the most beautiful and the strangest imaginable. She had never contemplated flower-beds or lawns comparable to that garden; quite apart from the fact that it appeared to be as large as the entire world, it was replete with leaves the color of the sky and florid with blooms that resembled pink flames; and those flowers were so beautiful and so luminous, they exhaled such delicious perfumes, that one might have thought that the hothouses of paradise, carried away by a gust of wind, had overflowed there.

While the king's daughter was ecstatic at such a marvel, a melodious voice like the song of the bulbul said: "Good day, you who are fifteen years old."

Very small, partly emerging from a bush, the person who had spoken thus was wearing a diadem of precious stones, from which golden curls streamed over a brocade coat. It was not difficult to see that she was a fay.

Smiling, the fay continued: "Now, you are of an age to enter the blue garden, where the only flowers bloom that are worth the trouble of being picked. Enter, daughter of a king! Even if you were born of a woodcutter and a washerwoman, the gate would not be closed to you, since you were fifteen years old this morning, at the first trill of the skylark. Enter; don't be embarrassed in any fashion, and don't be afraid that anyone will scold you; make the bouquet that will perfume you all your life, for these flowers, by their true names, are called Tenderness, Kisses and Smiles, and the smallest of them, scarcely opened, which veil themselves with the azure of the leaves, are the Blushes of the first amour."

You can imagine the joy of the princess. All those marvelous roses, she could pick and take away. After thanking the good fay abundantly, she ran recklessly toward the blossoming flames, and was just about to commence picking them, when...

...when a frightful dwarf with a bald head and a white beard, who looked like a tiny old man, stood up in front of her, leaning on a staff, and started speaking to her, while coughing and spitting.

"Well!" he said. "Is it the fashion, at present, for young damsels to run through plains all alone? Are there not in your palace, daughter of a king, maidservants to supervise, linen to arrange in cupboards and pots of jam to put on the shelves of the dresser? I'll wager that you haven't given a thought today to enquiring whether any braid was lacking in your father's royal mantle, and whether your little brother the prince had any socks that needed darning? Go on, go back home, I beg you, and, far from wasting your time picking these flowers by which you're dazzled, go to the kitchens in order prevent the scullions from stealing the wine they ought to be putting in the sauces, in order to drink it."

"But Monsieur Dwarf, the good fay has permitted me..."

"The good fay doesn't know what she's talking about! She has given you very bad advice. Furthermore, know that the roses of the blue garden are not at all what they seem to be. From a distance, I grant you, they seem desirable, but as soon as you have picked them—burning your fingers, because they are made of a terrible fire—you won't fail to curse your audacity; soon you won't have anything in your hand but sad pallors, still devouring. By their true names, these flowers are called Bitterness, Despair and Tears, and the least dolorous are Memories of lost happiness."

You can divine the perplexity of the princess. Who should she believe, the fay or the dwarf? Was it the latter that she ought to obey, or the former? Oh, how smitten she felt with the miraculous flowers! But it might be true that, being so beautiful, they were also fatal.

Not knowing what to decide, she turned back toward her dwelling; she wanted to think about the adventure, and to ask the advice of her nurse—in brief, to take the time to reflect. What was she risking? Tomorrow, or the day after, it would not be too late to go to make a bouquet of the leaves the color of the sky and the flowers of flame; the garden would always be in bloom, near the palace, along the river.

Many days went by. The daughter of the king remained indecisive. She would have given a great deal to put the Tendernesses, the Kisses, the Smiles in the Chinese vases and the Japanese cups on her shelves, and especially the Blushes of first amour, all the exquisite flowers that the lady dressed in brocade had permitted her to pick; but how she dreaded having her fingers burned to ash after picking them, and the appearance in the house of Bitterness, Despair, Tears and Memories of lost happiness!

After a year, more years went by. The father of the princess died and the prince became king. Anxious and unconsoled from dawn to dusk, and from dusk to dawn—for she had never wanted to marry—she had as much to lament as possible, so equally painful did it seem to her to do one thing or the other.

Many a time, leaning on her window sill, she had extended her arms toward the marvelous blue garden in the distance. Alas, she could not get the words of the dwarf with the white beard out of her mind; and she supervised the maidservants, arranged the linen in the cupboards and put the pots of jam on the shelves of the dresser.

Finally, however, one warm summer morning, she said to herself that she could not continue living like that. Abruptly, she decided that she would go, whatever might happen, to make the delectable and redoubtable bouquet. She set forth, all alone, along the river.

Now an anxiety gripped her. What if they were extinct, the beautiful flowers of flame?

It did not take long for her to be reassured; the garden appeared to her, vast and magnificent. It was so luminous, and it exhaled such magnificent perfumes, that one might have thought that the hothouses of paradise, carried away by a gust of wind, had overflowed there.

Full of joy and breathless with desire, the princess was about to launch herself forward...

"Daughter of a king," said the good fay who wore a diadem of precious stones from which golden curls streamed, "you shall not enter the garden where the only flowers grow that are worth the trouble of being picked; and even if you were born of the most powerful emperor of the earth and the queen of a star, the gate would not be opened to you, since too many years have passed since you were fifteen years old at the first trill of the skylark. Look at yourself in the river, I beg you."

The princes leaned over the water; she saw that she had gray hair, that her eyes were like dead cornflowers.

"Adieu, you who are fifty years old," said the good fay, weeping.

Then the daughter of a king let herself fall on to a stone, outside the closed gate, and she lamented, with sobs and tears, at having been

The beauty who wants,
The beauty who does not dare
To pluck the roses
In the blue garden.

Puck in the Organ

Once, Puck had a quarrel with the bees because he had slyly introduced himself into a hive in order to steal the honey from it; the golden insects, drunk on melissa, maltreated him very malevolently with their stings, in a tumult of luminous wings. In truth, Robin Goodfellow did not know where to hide. He made the decision to flee, hanging on to branches, leaping from one blade of grass to another, saying to the birds: "Get out of my way!" crying to the cicadas "Look out! Look out!" and asking the squirrels, who slipped away between the elms, to take him on their back. But the cruel bees did not lose track of him.

He was veritably fearful that he might not be able to escape their wrath when, having arrived in a village street, he spotted a poor young boy, in rags and unkempt, who was playing a barrel organ and asking for alms.

Oh, it was not beautiful music that was emerging from the cracked, discordant and broken down instrument, but Puck was in no condition to pay any heed to more or less agreeable tunes. On seeing the barrel organ he had no other idea than hiding in it in order to escape the pursuit of his enemies. It was no sooner thought than done. A goblin slips easily where the little finger of a little girl could not pass.

Who was caught out? It was the bees, when, rushing in their turn into the village street, they no longer saw anyone except the young boy turning the handle. Very disappointed, they resumed their flight toward their roses and hyacinths, which were beginning to get bored all alone in the gardens, not having their nectar collected.

But then something extraordinary happened. The organ, previously so pitiful, sang the most beautiful songs that could be heard; you might have thought that it was full of nightingales, warblers and early-rising skylarks, it made such melodious laments heard, such light chirpings, such pretty screeches: an entire aviary between four planks.

Where did all that come from? From a caprice of Puck's, who, not knowing what to do inside the instrument in which he had taken refuge, sang to distract himself. Now, no one is unaware that, by dint of listening, from spring until autumn, to the chatter of nests, he has rendered himself more skillful than anyone in the difficult art of charming by means of the voice.

The beggar, at first, was as astonished as it is possible to be; he had never thought his barrel organ capable of such a delightful music; and on the doorsteps, and rapidly opened windows, there were groups of charmed people who could not believe their ears.

"Oh, how pretty that is!"

"Oh, what lovely ballads!"

"One doesn't often feel such ease!"

The most miserly threw copper coins, and silver ones. They would have thrown gold ones if they had had any. The women and the girls even found that the boy was not as nasty as they might have imagined at first. All things considered, his shock of hair was as blond as gilded straw, and his skin must be very white under his suntan; so true is it that one is agreeable to see as soon as one is agreeable to hear. It is via the ear rather than the eye that one enters into hearts.

The renown of the organ player very rapidly surpassed the hamlets and village. There was mention of him in the most magnificent villas, in the greatest capitals; people there wanted to hear him; the enthusiasm was extreme. No harmony delicate and amorous to that degree—for the cooing of doves was now mingled with the twittering of little birds—had yet ravished the connoisseurs. There was no beautiful fête to which he did not come. He deigned to accept invitations, glad to go to the homes of marquises after leaving those of countesses. He had scarcely commenced turning the handle than women began swooning behind their fans.

"Oh, my dear, once couldn't imagine such an enchantment!"

"Doesn't it make one believe in paradise?"

"Personally, I think the angels don't extract such divine concerts from their mandoras or their ectaseons."

He did not find those eulogies exaggerated, growing accustomed to his glory. You would not have recognized the Bohemian child of the roads. He dressed in scarlet satin, embroidered with silver, and wore a crown of gems and fine pearls in his curly hair, for he was no less rich than he was illustrious. Instead of the small change that had been thrown to him before, pages on their knees offered him sequins, ducats, nobles and royals on behalf of their masters, on golden platters; he was begged to take away the platters into the bargain. And the beautiful ladies who obtained the favor of a private audition from him gave him presents a thousand times more precious.

The daughter of the king heard talk of the marvelous musician; she ordered that he be brought to the court. She was not without suspicion, dreading a disappointment; she did not think it possible that he justified his renown. After four measures however, she was invaded by such a rapture that she swore, with a grand passion: "I shall have no other husband than that handsome organ-player!"

That, at first, was not to the liking of the king. A great monarch does not care to accept as a son-in-law a fellow devoid of ancestors—devoid even of a mother and father—who begs on the highway. But, the king having been afflicted by a malady of languor, the physicians declared that he could only be cured by the charm of music; it was necessary to have recourse to the melodious vagabond. Three turns of the handle and the monarch was as well as anyone could desire to be. Then gratitude triumphed over pride; the former beggar married the princess.

You might think that, after that, his glory and his good fortune were at their peak? That's where you'd be mistaken.

Once, when the army departed for the war, he placed himself in the first rank, and the organ launched such furious battle hymns—for Puck remembered having heard soldiers sounding the clarion in the forest—that, in the general opinion, the victory was due to the extraordinary bravery that the music had put into hearts. The people, in their gratitude, did not hesitate; the musician was elected Emperor of the entire country; he had his father-in-law for a vassal.

No reign had ever been so glorious and so happy. In order for the most wretched subjects to be content with their lot, for there to be no despair, no anger and no revolt, it was sufficient for the new master to make a few of his melodies heard.

It was understood that the crown, the scepter and the palaces full of courtiers were only feeble recompenses for such merit. The man who had been an emperor was made into a god; temples of alabaster and porphyry were consecrated to him, always full of incense and kneeling prayers; painted on the walls, above all the altars, there were images of the organ, which was worshiped.

What man ever knew such glory? And with so many triumphs, he had joy, the incomparable joy of playing music, in the evening, for himself alone: a music that made him weep with delight.

Well, said Puck to himself, *it seems to me that I've been inside this box for a long time; I'm beginning to get strangely bored.*

He darted a glance outside, and, on seeing that the bees were no longer there, returned to play on the edge of the wood near Athens, with Monsieur Peaseblossom and Monsieur Cobweb.

The entire city burst out laughing. That was music? Say rather a charivari that would frighten dancing bears. No more discordant racket had ever ripped the ears. It couldn't go on. People couldn't stand it. The god was expelled from his temples, the emperor from his palaces. "Phooey! Phooey! Get out of here, get out, we tell you!" And the riffraff of the kitchens, in order to mock the poor fellow, pursued him, banging their saucepans.

He hoped to find a better welcome among the marquises and the countesses who once swooned behind their fans, but as soon as the first notes they said: "Uh oh! What does this mean? Personally, I thought that all the local cats had been let into the house."

Then the valets threw him into the street, not without having ripped his fine clothes and stolen the money he had in his pockets.

Desperately, he returned to the villages where people had once thrown him copper and silver coins, where the girls had formed groups on doorsteps, in the ecstasy of listening to him. Scarcely had he started to play than the peasant women fled, blocking their ears; it was stones that they threw at him.

Then he understood that it was all over for all the glories and the joys. He let himself fall by the roadside, ragged and unkempt, as in the old times of misery, without any other hope than death, all the sadder because, if he turned the handle of the organ, a shrill sound emerged that, alas, even desolated him.

And I thought, in telling this tale, of the tender or sublime poets, inspired for a long time because they had an amour in their soul, of the glorious poets who now languish, alone, dreamless, in forgetfulness, no longer even able to draw a consolatory lament from their hearts—their cracked, discordant, broken down hearts, from which the beautiful music has flown away, along with the amour.

The Narcissus

There was a great desolation throughout the realm because the daughter of the king was going to die of starvation.

What! Of starvation? A princess! Was there no more livestock in the meadows, game in the forests, vegetables in the fields or fruit in the orchards? Or were there no more cooks in the kitchens? What catastrophe had occurred? How could it be that someone so noble and so rich had lacked even what the peasant in his cottage and the beggar on the road rarely lacks: a morsel of bread?

Well, yes, she had as much bread as one could wish, and cakes too, the most sugary in the world; it would have been sufficient for her to make a sign to have put on the table before her the most flavorsome meats, the most delicate venison, and little peas as fresh as dewdrops, and violet velvet peaches and golden oranges. But that princess could not eat the foodstuffs that sustain men and women; the fays, when leaning over her cradle, had decided that she would be nourished uniquely on newly blossomed flowers or the butterflies that alight on them.

Now, two weeks before, such a storm had ravaged the gardens of the realm, smashing and overturning the green-houses, that it was absolutely impossible to discover an eglantine petal or a cactus-flower calyx. No, there was not a single hyacinth in the flower-beds, not one jasmine, not one daisy, not one foxglove, not one tulip in infantile apparel, nor, in the hedgerows, a single branch of may-blossom. As regards butterflies, it had been a long time since the squalls had carried them all far away, no one knew where, to unknown lands, where they were now probably falling like a debris of snow-flakes, sad and dead.

The consequence was that the princess was in the most pitiful state imaginable; she was paler than the palest flowers, a single one of which would have been sufficient to save her.

She would certainly die if her fast were prolonged for a few more days; and as she had a rather bad temper even when she ate her fill, you can imagine the quarrels she had with her ladies in waiting when they came into her regal bedroom without bringing her the smallest floret of the fields or the woods.

I said—and I had reason to say it—that the entire realm was in desolation because of the imminent death of the princess. You would not have recognized the king, who had gone gray in a matter of days; and the ministers, the chamberlains and the majordomos were pitiful to see, because it would have been truly unbefitting for the majordomo, the chamberlains and the ministers to exhibit a good humor when the Head of State had reason to be chagrined.

But the most sincere, the most violent despair, was in the heart of a little page, for he had adored the princess hopelessly, for a long time. The thought that she would be a dead person plunged him into such distress that it would have enabled the tigers of the woods and the rocks of the mountains to know mercy, if there had been any rocks and tigers there to see him.

It was not that he had anything to praise in the clemency of the princess. Quite the contrary, No description could give any idea of the cruelties she had employed in regard to that little page, who was in her service. As soon as he sighed, she laughed. As soon as he approached her, in the evening, to render her some office, she did not turn away, which would have been charitable, but looked him in the eye, sat down and said to him: "Good, good, come here; it's time to go to sleep; take my stockings off, if you please." Then she drew away, with her demoiselles, who never failed to laugh, also being cruel. But they were excusable, not being loved by the poor boy.

So much barbarity did not prevent him from being the most tender of lovers; if anyone had told him that the princess was not as gentle as the lambs in the meadow, he would have reddened with rage and they would have had to reckon with him.

As soon as he learned that the daughter of the king was wasting away because of the storm that had carried away all the flowers and all the butterflies, he did not hesitate for an instant. He started running around the realm, searching for roses, lilies, daises or no matter what, for the repast of the person he loved. But he did not find any!

Someone said to the princess "Does Your Highness know that the little page has departed in the hope of picking you a breakfast?"

She smiled disdainfully. It seemed that she would breakfast regretfully on any flowers that the little page brought her, and she said: "Oh, how hungry I am!"

Meanwhile, he was running all over the realm in quest of flowers, descending into ravines and climbing the steepest slopes, and he hoped that perhaps he would find, between two rocks near the glaciers, the mysterious flower of the Alps, very small and very blue, which might prevent the person he loved from dying.

But no, even on the highest summits, there was not a single flower, so formidable and furious had the storm been. He came back from all his efforts with the anguish of failure.

"I foresaw that," said the princess. "It's truly ridiculous to entrust the care of royal persons to such children."

Then, on learning that she had proffered those cruel words, the little page felt his heart constricted and torn, as if a vulture had swooped down, claws open, on that little red bird. Since she had the double inclemency of being ill and not being grateful for the efforts of the person who wanted to cure her, he resolved not to live any longer, as she was dying. He ran to a nearby spring, which was very clear and very deep, in order to throw himself into it.

He arrived on the water's edge. After having looked to see whether any lotus was flowering there—for one lotus would have been sufficient to cure the princess—he leaned over wanting to fall. However, he hesitated, for it is sad to die when one is still so young, and when there are so many beautiful women in the world.

A thought occurred to him.

He had read in old books that a young man, by virtue of mirroring himself in water, had become a flower. Why should such a fate not be permitted to him? As a flower, he could be eaten by the princess, and the princess would be saved.

He leaned over the spring and gazed at his image; he looked at it for a long time, and finally let himself fall...

And he had scarcely fallen into the water when one of the princess's demoiselles, who had been prowling around the bank on the lookout for a moment, picked a narcissus made of the page: a pale narcissus that had just opened.

The storm having ended, the narcissus put the princess in a state to wait for the daises to flower again in the meadows, the tulips in the flower beds and the hawthorn in the hedges. However, she was scarcely satisfied, and she said, while biting with her beautiful teeth the petals that, according to what she had been told, were the page himself, who had died for her and been resuscitated as a calyx:

"Yes, yes, one has to eat! But truly, it isn't very good, this flower."

The Three Dresses

Although she was barely fifteen years old, the daughter of the King of Mataquin was nevertheless thinking about the pleasure that might find in the love of a handsome prince. One morning, when her chambermaids were combing in front of the mirror the very long hair that she had, she happened to mention that she would like very much to be married. Doubtless there was something inconvenient in that confession; it is not befitting for young women to declare their secret thoughts so openly; on the day when such frankness ceases to be blameworthy, it will not take long for us to be deafened by the voices of a large number of spinsters, ugly or beautiful, old or young, going about the streets crying: "A husband! A husband!"

However, the fay Holda, who was the godmother of the princess, did not hold a grudge against her because of that desire so carelessly revealed; she was an indulgent fay, in spite of not being entirely exempt from malice. The doors of the bedroom having opened by magic, she was seen to enter, pompously dressed, all smiles; six little negroes, who must have been African pygmies, were carrying three coffers behind her, and those coffers were the most beautiful in the world; the first was nielloed silver, the second fine gold, and the third made entirely of gemstones.

"Bonjour, my goddaughter!"

"Bonjour, my godmother!"

"So it's true, then, that, as impatient as the little eglantines that are chagrined to remain as buds, you're in a hurry to have a husband?"

"It's true that I wouldn't have any reluctance for marriage if I were offered a husband such as I desire, and to say everything, in a word, similar to the young prince who sometimes appears in my dreams."

"What is he like, this prince of whom you dream?"

"Oh, one couldn't see anyone as charming as him."

"What else?"

"First of all, he's dressed with all possible magnificence and in the best possible taste."

"Well-dressed sons of kings are not rare in the surrounding regions.

"He has, in his youthful face, lips as fresh and rosy as a rose damp with dew."

"There's no lack of princes with lovely mouths."

"He has in his blue eyes such a profound and infinite softness that when one looks at them, one imagines that one is seeing the whole sky through two diaphanous sapphires."

"Hmm! Hmm!" said the fay. "Eyes of that sort are scarcely common; you might perhaps have difficulty finding similar ones. Fortunately, as I'm good, and as I don't want you to risk repenting of a choice you've made, it will be permitted to you to marry three times; it'll be diabolical if, out of three husbands, you don't encounter one who suits you perfectly."

"What! Three times!" said the princes, blushing.

"Not on the same day! You'll be careful to put suitable intervals between your three marriages. In any case, although so many marriages are permitted to you, they aren't imposed on you; nothing prevents you from holding on to the one that satisfies you. But in sum, you can attempt three proofs, and that's why I've brought you these three coffers. In one of them, which is nielloed silver, there's a dress made of white satin and lace, which you can put on for your first wedding; in the second, which is fine gold, a costume has been placed the color of the sun and the stars, which you can put on to delight the second husband; and the third wedding dress—the most beautiful of the three—is contained in the third coffer, made entirely of precious stones.

Sometime after that, the nephew of the Emperor of Golconda cane to the court of Mataquin to ask for the hand of the king's daughter, whose beauty was renowned throughout the countries of the earth. Never had it been given to anyone to see a prince as magnificently dressed as him! On satins that seemed made of luminous snow, on muslins as light and pink as dawn clouds, he wore an embroidery of pearls, rubies, beryls and carbuncles, which formed flowers of flame.

The princess, dazzled, made no difficulty about marrying the nephew of the Emperor of Golconda. She took the dress of white satin and lace out of the nielloed silver coffer, and put it on with pleasure for the nuptial ceremony.

But it did not take her long to perceive that a beautiful costume is not an advantage that can make others dispensable. When he was in a dressing-gown in the mornings her husband no longer had anything that resembled the young prince she had seen in her dreams. Where were the young fresh lips, where were the eyes as profound and as soft as the sky?

Gradually, she became very morose, remaining in her chamber all day long, weeping in the corners, with the consequence that she had all the difficulty in the world manifesting an appropriate affliction on the day when she was told that the nephew of the Emperor of Golconda, who was a great hunter, had been devoured by lions in the mountains.

When she had worn mourning for more than six months, the princess began to tell herself that nothing obliged her to remain a widow; and she felt her heart tenderly moved by the sight of a young knight who had just arrived at the court and who had triumphed over the most valiant combatants in a tourney. Not only did the gentleman in question wear superb garments, but in his fresh face he had lips as pink as a rose moist with dew. The princes could not contain her joy when she learned that the knight had the intention of marrying her! She consented immediately to that new hymen.

She took out of the fine gold coffer the dress the color of the sun and the stars, and put it on delightedly for the ceremony.

But it did not take her long to perceive, in spite of the sweetness of his kisses, that it is not sufficient to be well dressed and to have a mouth as fresh as flowers to make the happiness of a young woman as demanding as her. No, that husband was also not the one who had appeared to her in agreeable dreams; he did not have soft blue eyes similar to diaphanous sapphires.

She was chagrined by day and despairing by night, unhappy beyond anything that can be imagined—with the consequence that it was necessary for her to make a great effort not to smile through her tears on the day when she was told that the knight, who was a great seeker of adventures, had been killed by an evil magician in an enchanted forest.

A year passed without the princess giving any thought to another marriage; the first two proofs had been too painful for the whim to take her to try a third. She told herself that she would never find a husband similar to her chimera, and her dreams were melancholy. But one evening, when she was walking in an avenue of the royal park, she saw, coming toward her in the twilight, a young man more handsome than any other. Was he veritably a mortal, or some angel descended from paradise? He seemed to be clad in starlight; his mouth was like a rose, but a rose so beautiful that one would not have been able to find one like it in any garden on earth, and when he was very close to her, he had in his blue eyes such a profound and infinite softness that she imagined that she was seeing the sky through two diaphanous sapphires.

Oh, this time she had finally found the husband she needed! He was there, similar to the delectable apparition of dreams; when he said, in a voice softer than the glide of the wind over a stream: "Beautiful princess, would you like to be my wife?" she felt invaded by such a languor that she thought she might die of delight.

On the day of the nuptial ceremony she opened the third coffer, which an entirely made of gemstones, in order to take out the third dress, the most beautiful of all.

But in the coffer, there was a strange dress: a dress that was a shroud.

Then the princess started to weep, understanding that the moment had come to die. Seized by a sudden illness she rendered her soul before nightfall. She was wrapped in the shroud and laid in the coffin of gemstones. For no one can possess, down here, her chimera realized; it is not on earth that princesses marry princes who have, at the same time, magnificent clothes, lips like flowers, and eyes in which the blue infinity of the heavens smiles.

Courage Recompensed

Little Acidalie, who was the daughter of a woodcutter, had certainly heard it said that happiness exists, but she had no idea where she might find it; assuredly, it was not in the paths of the wild wood where she often walked in the company of her father, her shoulder curbed under thorny faggots, barefoot in the brambles or the stones; and she did not know either of what it was made, although a secret instinct advised her to believe that it had the appearance and the fashions of a handsome young man with a very proud gaze and a very soft smile, dressed, like the son of a prince, in pink or blue satin embroidered with gold or silver.

"What!" she said, one summer morning when she was sitting on the edge of a road in the forest. "Am I destined, then, never to know happiness? However, I was sixteen years old last month; if it delays much longer in manifesting itself, it won't want me, because I'll be an old spinster."

She was desolate, with so much dolor that the pebbles of the path were moved by it, which is a very rare thing, because pebbles are ordinarily not very compassionate; they are more inclined to ill humor, because people are always treading on them, without it being possible for them to complain.

Little Acidalie never ceased to be chagrined. Fortunately for her, there was a good fay not far away from there, in the process of presiding over the marriage of a glow-worm and a firefly. As soon as the ceremony was over she turned toward the woodcutter's daughter and said to her:

"Come on, little one, don't despair of your fate. Happiness is never closer at hand than when we suppose it to be far away. Only look on the other side of the road. Do you see that young hunter who is smiling in his sleep under a large flowery rose-bush? That's the king's nephew; although he has never seen you, he is thinking about you in his dream. Cross the road, go quickly, and sit down next to him. As soon as he wakes up he'll put his arms around your neck and he'll take you to his palace, where you'll be the happiest of princesses."

With that, the good fay disappeared.

As for Acidalie, she did not budge at first, so ecstatic was she. No, no, she would never have believed that something could exist on earth as pretty as the young hunter asleep under the flowery braches. At the thought that he might embrace her, that he might take her with him, she felt faint with joy. But she only wasted a little time in those agreeable ideas, and, tucking up her fustian skirt in order to run more rapidly, she hurried toward the happiness that awaited her on the other side of the road.

Alas, in that forest there were not only good fays, there were also bad ones. It resembled life somewhat, in which evil exists alongside good. A bad fay, therefore, who was in the process of presiding over the divorce of a male and female butterfly, turned toward the little girl and stopped her with an imperious gesture.

"It's necessary not to hope," she said, with an angry expression, "that things will work out like that. What! It's sufficient to take a few steps to attain happiness? That would be new and curious! But then, there wouldn't be anything milder than the fate of men and women! I don't intend that it should be thus. As for you, child, learn that you're not at the end of your troubles. It isn't today or tomorrow that you'll be the happiest of princesses in the palace of the king's nephew."

"Oh, Madame, are you so wicked? What displeasure can the contentment of a poor girl like me cause you? Furthermore, I have nothing to fear from you, since the god fay has told me to cross the road, no power can prevent me from doing that."

"It's true that a fay can't go against the will of another fay. But the one who is protecting you omitted, in the haste of her mercy, to specify the fashion in which you were to get from one side of the road to the other. Go on, hurry up! Run, if you can, but look up there, very high, at that trembling thread of spider-silk, light, almost invisible, which extends from an oak to an elm. It's over that that it's necessary to pass, in order to cross the road."

And when she had said that, the bad fay disappeared, not without a snigger that frightened the nests of the forests; even the twitter of a blackcap warbler suddenly fell silent, like the babble of a spring ceasing in a single frozen drop of water.

At first Acidalie did not want to believe in her misfortune. She resumed running: a vain attempt. A mysterious power maintained her on this side of the road. It was impossible to take a step forward; she could not even extend her arm toward the happiness that was smiling in its sleep, so close at hand, under the rose-bush.

Then she started to weep. What! It was possible? It was true? She would not soon sit down beside the hunter, until he woke up? He would not take her, in order to make her his wife, into the magnificent royal palace?

She raised her eyes, moist with tears, toward the thread of spider-silk that went from the summit of the oak to the highest branch of the elm: so slender and delicate alas, ever ready to fly away on the breeze. A wren could have broken it with a thrust of its wing; it would have required an exceedingly light butterfly to alight upon it without breaking it. If Acidalie, after having climbed the tree, entrusted the tip of her toe, barely, to that quivering nothing, she would fall on to the pebbles and break her bones on them; she would be found there, dead, covered in blood.

Well, no matter, in spite of the impossibility of success, in spite of the certain death, she would attempt the only way that was offered to her to reach the happiness that was so close, and yet so far away. Yes, very small, very frail, often weeping because of a bee-sting, she would have the courage to brave dolorous death!

She climbed the oak, going, from branch to branch, reached the leafy and murmurous crown, and leaned over the thread. Oh, how fearful she was! How she was trembling! But she only hesitated for a moment.

"You who are asleep, with a smile on your lips, under the roses, handsome young man, dear happiness, adieu, adieu!" she said. "I don't know you, and I'm dying for love of you. Adieu! I'll try not to scream as I fall, for fear of frightening you; may the sound of my fall be light enough not to wake you from the dream in which you're thinking of me!"

Then, resolutely, she advanced; and you doubtless imagine that she fell through the air toward the stones?

Not at all. After having touched the frail moving whiteness, she was changed—doubtless by the good fay, and it was the worthy recompense of her bravery—into the tiniest of ladybirds, who very quickly ran along the thread on her slender feet, from the summit of the oak to the highest branch of the elm.

After the crossing, however, the little creature became a young girl again. She sat down beside the hunter under the blooming rose-bush, and the king's nephew put his arm around her neck, saying: "You're even prettier than my dream. Would you like, little woodcutter's daughter, to be a princess in my palace?"

For, as an old woman's spinning-wheel hums, it is in vain the jealous powers try to deprive us of joys that are due to us; if one has courage enough to merit the support of good fays, one never fails to attain the happiness that awaits us on the other side of the road.

Vain Betrothals

It was in one of the first Aprils of one of my former lives, in the middle of a flowery meadow traversed by a path of trodden glass. I saw a pink and blonde child coming toward me, and I understood immediately that, as long as I lived, I would never be able to love another. What was strange and charming is that she did not resemble any of the young girls that I had already encountered, but she was exactly similar to those I saw night and day in my dreams.

She went back and forth, stopped and resumed her course in the flowery meadow; it was like the zigzags of a bee. Sometimes she bent down and put her hands under the grass; it was evident that she was picking daisies and buttercups. But I pretended to misinterpret her gestures and, approaching her, I said:

"Is this the thing that you have lost, and for which you are searching, young damsel, walking in the fields?"

At the same time, I offered her a slender silver ring that I had taken from my finger; I had had it made a month before by the court jeweler for the fiancée that I could not fail to have soon.

Imagine my surprise.

"Precisely, Monsieur," she said, "I was searching for that ring."

And, taking it with a movement swifter than the flick of a swallow's wing, she put the ring on her left hand; then she escaped, running and skipping, and disappeared in the distance, behind the willow grove. I was alone in the field. I might have believed that I had been dreaming if the perfume of young tresses had not remained in the air, and if the florets she had touched had not flowered more delectably than cassolettes when spikenard, amber and iris has been renewed therein.

As I was the young prince of a magnificent realm in those days, I had it proclaimed to the sound of clarions by my heralds clad in red and green, like Brazilian parrots, that my heart and my throne belonged without contest to the woman who brought the slender silver ring back to me. You can imagine what a stir there was throughout the country; there was not enough room in the hostelries for the young women who rendered to my capital from towns and villages, mountains and valleys, attracted by the hope of being queen.

Some were daughters of noble families. Illustrious and pompous, in robes of yellow samite or nacarat velvet, lying in litters carried by African negroes; others were the daughters of bourgeois, more simply dressed, who came by coach, but behind them one saw, in wheelbarrows, large sacks full of coins; they hoped to please by the offer of those riches, for no one was unaware that I had odiously dilapidated the State finances in order to put golden spurs on my fighting cocks and pearl necklaces on the turtle doves of my aviary. Beggar-women also arrived, walking barefoot.

Even the minister on whom the mission was incumbent to discover thefts and pursue thieves—I had appointed to that post a very old blind man, deaf-mute since birth and lame in every limb, for it is necessary that dishonest folk can live and buy silk scarves for the beautiful women they love—nearly perceived the depredations exercised on merchants of jewelry; every ring was stolen from every silversmith's shop, so much were my subjects, even those who had bare fingers, yearning to please me. But among so many rings, I did not discover the slender silver ring give to the vanished child, and among so many daughters of marquises or merchants, shod in golden brodequins or the dust of the roads, I did not encounter the pink and blonde child that I had encountered one morning in April in the middle of the flowery meadow traversed by a path of trodden grass.

Full of dolor, I handed my crown to one of my relatives, who had always desired it; very probably, he would not have taken long to murder me in order to put himself in my place; dressed like the vagabonds of the roads, staff in hand, I started traveling the world, searching for my fiancée.

It would take too long to describe all the countries I traversed. I sat down in the snow and I slept under flowers. I saw seas vaster and bluer than the sky, infinite gilded sands, so luminous that one might have thought they were made of star-dust. But neither in the pale North nor the flamboyant South, nor in cities nor in oases where young women chatted around wells with clay pitchers on their shoulders, was it given to me to see again the child of the flowery meadow who had my slender silver ring on her ring finger; with the consequence that one evening, after many days, many nights and many years, already very old, my heart despairing and my head bowed—my gray-haired head under my large mendicant's hat—I fell upon atone at a bend in the road and lamented in these terms:

"What! It's certain, then, that I shall never find you again, you who are the only one would have loved, the only one I love. Oh, how many beautiful women, with soft eyes and tender mouths, smile at the kiss and do not reject it! But it is in the desire for your lips and you that I languish bitterly. I am the bee with a single rose, the butterfly with a single lily. Alas, that lily and that rose are refused to me henceforth, and I am, in gardens full of flowers, as in gardens devoid of flowers."

And all evening, I desolated thus at the bend in the road.

From behind a clump of grass, a very tiny fay emerged, who said to me: "Well, poor man, it isn't on earth that one rediscovers the one who is like the chimera of the first month of April. But console yourself; you will see her one day, even more delightful than she appeared to you. She will come to you, with the sweetness of a walking dream, and you will kiss the dear betrothal ring on her finger."

"Where, then, will this happiness be offered to me?"

"In Paradise," said the fay.

"And when will I be able to enter Paradise?"

"When you are dead," she said.

I cried that I would like nothing better than to die, and the sooner the better. She went in quest, in a bush, of a pale little calyx on which there was a drop of dew.

"Drink this pearl," she said. "As it is a very violent poison, you will die right away."

I drank the pearl, and I died, and I woke up again—how brief death is!—in a country so delightful that I had never dreamed of its like.

In clouds of liquid gold and flame, amid pale blue vapors that trailed in the air like the caresses of scarves, angel spouses passed in front of me, two by two and hand in hand, and they seemed so happy that I was already fainting with intoxication and thinking that their happiness would soon be mine. For the fay—the little fay of the clump of grass—had certainly not deceived me. Pink and blonde, I would see the child of the flowery meadow coming toward me, the silver ring on her finger, and we would be joined, hearts and wings, in the hectic delights of eternity.

I waited; she did not appear.

I saw a magnificent cortege in the distance, in fumes of light, in which hyacinth and crimson robes were streaming, heading toward an edifice reminiscent of a diamond church. I divined that a wedding was about to be celebrated, and I hoped with a quivering impatience for the hour of my celestial marriage.

But my fiancée did not show herself. I was not unduly worried, however. Fays do not lie. It was only a delay. Doubtless my promised bride, a little coquettish, was finishing knotting some auroral cloud around her neck or adjusting a crown of stars on her head. It was not possible that I alone would remain without a wife in the immense hymen of the heavens.

And I asked an angelic couple who were going to join the nuptial cortege: "What is happening, pray? Has the young girl to whom I gave me slender silver ring not yet arrived in Paradise?"

They looked at me compassionately.

"Alas, yes, poor man, she has arrived, but you will not see her come to you, pink and blonde, as in the flowery meadow, for Our Lord God has found her so pretty that he has taken her for himself, and it is her that he is marrying, over there in the diamond church."

The Enchanted Ring

Three rich and handsome young princes, one named Félibien, the second Roland and the third Aymeril, were traveling on horseback through all the countries in the world, followed by a numerous retinue of servants and baggage carts. A chance encounter in a hostelry had rendered them friends; they were traveling together.

Why were they traveling? To study at close range the power and the laws of different nations? To render themselves more worthy of reigning when the kings, their fathers, who were powerful monarchs descended from the throne into the sepulcher? You have said it. But Prince Félibien and Prince Roland were nor accomplishing their long pilgrimage without annoyance; they were bitterly envious of Aymeril, their companion, who was always in a good humor, and never ceased to sing along the road verses that he had made up for his friends, or songs that his nurse had taught him.

Once, when all three of them were sitting in the arbor of an inn at midday, waiting for their horses to be given something to drink—in a few minutes they would resume their route, toward a large city where they wanted to arrive before nightfall, Félibien said: "It's necessary to believe, my dear Aymeril, that you don't love any beautiful person amorously, for, far from your lady, you would not be as joyful as you are."

"I am inclined to think," added Roland, "that the sonnets and ballads with which you amuse the little birds in the bushes only say tender lies; they were made at hazard in anticipation of an amour that might come to you, but has not come."

Aymeril smiled without responding.

"For myself," said Félibien, I am languishing strangely, because the only woman I love is waiting for me, more than a thousand leagues away, in a castle where she has no other pleasure than the sight of her aged husband, which has never appeared to be a sufficient distraction to a young woman."

"For myself," said Roland, "if I'm in pain, it's because of the daughter of an emperor, to whom I've engaged my faith and who is astonished, in the morning, when she wakes up and comes to lean out of the window of her tower, not to find on the sill a bouquet of wild lilies that I had the custom of putting there every night, hoisting myself from stone to stone at the peril of my life.

Aymeril was still smiling.

"It's certain," he said, finally, "that you have a great deal of which to complain. But you would be wrong to think that I'm not as smitten as you might be. Oh, if you knew how I adore her, the one by whom I am loved! Only, on departing for a long voyage, I was careful not to leave her in her dwelling, tower or castle, and I brought her with me."

The other two princes replied: "You're joking, I think. If you had her with you, we would have seen your lover—unless you keep her hidden in one of your trunks, pierced with holes, or she's disguised as one of your pages."

"She isn't hidden in a trunk; I'd be too afraid that she'd be inconvenienced by the jolts of the cart; she isn't disguised as a page, because dressed thus, people could see her legs, of which I'm very jealous."

"Where is she hiding then, pray?"

Aymeril hesitated to respond, but as they continued to interrogate him with great persistence, he said: "In the stone of my ring."

You can imagine how that assertion made them laugh. A woman in the stone of a ring was something impossible to believe. He loved, then, a lady or a demoiselle as enormous as a mite or as colossal as a flea? She must have hair as long as the invisible down of flowers, and when she walked, in full dress, in the pathways of a garden, the giantess was doubtless afraid of being crushed by a passing ladybird.

Aymeril responded in vain that they did not understand, that everything is possible for the power of certain fays to whom he had rendered great services; they did not case laughing and they said: "Come on, come on, it's a joke; tell it to others, companion!"

It was too much; in the end, he lost patience and decided—with was an imprudence—to show them that they were wrong not to believe him. He raised his left hand, on which the ring was, lifted the stone with his fingernail, and as soon as he put his lip to the narrow opening, a living figurine emerged therefrom, so tiny as to be scarcely visible—which, growing, inflating and filling out, soon became a young damsel clad in silk and gold, the most beautiful in the world!

Putting her arms around Aymeril's neck, she said: "What is your pleasure, my dear lord?"

The surprise of the two incredulous princes was greater than can be expressed, and increased further when, under a breath from her friend, the damsel diminished, became very tiny again, and disappeared under the stone, which closed of its own accord. But for the moment, at least, there was no more mention of that prodigy, for the servants came to say that the horses had been sufficiently watered and that it was time to resume the route.

Even when they had recommenced riding, Félibien and Roland did not say a word to Prince Aymeril, but, somewhat apart, they talked to one another in low voices. Although they had not been shown the mysterious inhabitant of the ring for very long, they had remarked that she was very pretty and seductive in her rich garments, and that anyone who could do with her whatever he wished would not worthy of pity.

"Yes, but to succeed in that wouldn't be easy," said Félibien.

"Really! Are you so scantly inventive?" replied Roland. "What would be difficult about introducing ourselves into our companion's room tonight, as soon as he goes to sleep, and removing the ring from his finger?"

"Without waking him?"

"One sleeps profoundly after a long day's journey. And when we have the ring in our possession I think that we'll easily be able to lift the stone, and, by means of a kiss—for I saw clearly how Aymeril did it—cause the dainty creature, so well-dressed and pleasing, to emerge.

"Oh, the kiss isn't what embarrasses me."

Talking thus, they agreed to attempt the enterprise. It was a very wicked plot. Not only would they be felons in regard to their friend, who had never done them any harm, but they were also being unfaithful, Félibien to the lady who was waiting for him in a castle a thousand leagues away, with no other pleasure than the sight of a husband already old, and Roland to the emperor's daughter who was lamenting, leaning out of the window of her tower, not finding there the flowers of old. Alas, the world has no lack of bad princes who obey their desires without worrying about the torment of others, and there was nothing astonishing in that.

As for Aymeril, not having heard anything, unaware of the plot being woven against him, he was riding without anxiety, sometimes looking at the azure or the clouds, sometimes putting the ring close to his mouth and singing a long in a low voice in order that the little captive would not be too bored in her narrow jail.

They did as they had said. When the servants were in bed in the hostelry chosen for the night and Félibien and Roland supposed hat their companion ought to have been asleep for some time, they introduced themselves, without making a sound, into the chamber that had been reserved for him. Everything was silent and dark. The light respiration of the young sleeper was scarcely audible.

Félibien, who had good eyes, saw something gleaming; that had to be the golden ring. He felt it, cautiously. Yes, it was, in fact, the ring, on the finger of a hand that was hanging outside the bed. He removed the jewel, very slowly. Then he whispered: "I have it; let's go."

You can imagine the contentment of the two traitors when they had returned to their apartment after the success of their enterprise and they considered the precious stone by the light of a candle, the dwelling of such a lovely person!

There was nothing more to do than make her emerge. Roland took charge of that facile task. He lifted the light gold lid with his fingernail and put his lips to the opening...

A dread gripped them. What if the damsel was not in the ring? What if, by night, Aymeril liberated her in order to sleep beside him? In his place, that is what they would not have failed to do. They had not thought of that possible snag. Perhaps they had penetrated slyly into a room, following the conduct of perfect thieves—them, gentlemen and princes!—for nothing.

They were immediately reassured. The damsel was inside the ring! Or rather, she was no longer more than half-inside, for she was coming out. In the semi-darkness of the apartment they saw delicate fabrics of silk and gold growing, swelling and filling out. Oh, the pretty spectacle! They were already breathless, thinking about the joy they would have in a little while, when the dainty creature, grown to full size, would put her arms round the neck, first of one and then the other, saying: "What is your pleasure, my dear lord?"

They did, indeed, feel a caress on their necks, like a sliding sleeve...but only a sliding sleeve.

No, there was no arm under the fabric! And, putting their arms around the robe of silk and gold, the realized that it too was empty.

At the same time, in the other side of the wall, there were reawakened sounds of kisses and laughter.

You can imagine how crestfallen they were. What had happened, then? The just punishment of their treachery. Aymeril, every night, did not fail to have the liberated damsel lie beside him, as they had already deduced, too late. But then, why the garments rising from the ring? Well, because the far-sighted captive had the custom of getting undressed under the stone at dusk, even before being invoked, in order to please her lover sooner.

The Solitaries

In those days there were two tiny fays who loved one another with all the tenderness imaginable. One, who was not as tall as the blades of grass in the meadow, was named Muguette; the other, who needed to stand on tiptoe in order to look over a wild strawberry plant, was named Liseron.

Nothing was more impossible than encountering Muguette without Liseron, except encountering Liseron without Muguette, so much pleasure did they find in one another's company. They were seen together everywhere: on the edge of the forest of Broceliande when the morning round dances of the Good Ladies brushed the heather where the dew dripped in prismatic tears; in the clearing of the wood near Athens, among the games of the sylphs who go up and down, like sweeps in a chimney, in Bottom's ears; and on the shore of the distant sea, where one embarks in skiffs made of a nutshell or the armor of a scarab for the isles of Avalon.

And many a time shepherds bringing flocks back to the fold in the evening, or knights in silver armor going through the solitudes in quest of enchanted princesses, heard a little sound rising from behind the bushes, so vague and so light that they thought that it was two rose petals brushing together as they fell into the moss, but it was the sound of the kisses that Liseron was giving to Muguette, and Muguette to Liseron for those friends kissed one another on the mouth.

Far be it from me to think of approving, no matter how odorant and rosy their lips were, of a familiarity so contrary to propriety. In accord with the majority of moralists, I believe that femininities, even very compassionate and much inclined to prompt abandonments, ought only to concede the delights of which they dispose to virile vanquishers; those two fays were quite wrong not to reserve their kisses for prowling sylphs and robin-goodfellows, who, after all, are very pretty in their small stature, but what do you expect? In those days, the sylphs, and the pucks too, were very occupied in courting the daughters of the earth; they were almost never seen mingling with the matinal or nocturnal dances on the edges of woodlands.

Now, I ask you—respond, quivering lovers, frantic embracers of swooning nudities!—is not the culpable employment of two adorable mouths more worthy of pardon that the inutility of their deplorable unemployment would be? Anyway, what can I tell you? Facts are facts; one cannot change things that are accomplished; excusable or not, the two dainty fays set a bad example. But how well they set it! With what pleasure, never relenting, always renewed! Your heart could fail to be softened—while reserving the judgment of your indignant conscience—if you could have seen them, on the leaf of a plane tree, their little arms hugging their little bodies in the hectic spilling of their hair, longer than the gilded down of wild thistles. There was, as the poet puts it, charm in the crime.

But providence does not authorize reprehensible ecstasies to be uninterrupted. Liseron and Muguette were too happy to be happy always. This is the adventure that disunited them.

One evening, when they were looking for a shelter—the calyx of a flower, a cleft in a birch tree or a pretty mossy gap—for their exquisite sin, they found themselves in the presence of a lily that was the whitest of lilies and a rose, also white, that was the most admirable of roses, although a little frayed by overly insistent provocative friction of lovesick butterflies.

"Oh, the beautiful lily!" said Muguette.

"Oh, the beautiful rose!" said Liseron.

"It's in that lily that we'll sleep," said Muguette.

"No," said Liseron, "it's in that rose."

With that, they quarreled, one holding out for the rose, the other for the lily. Crazy fools that they were! What does the bed matter, if one is sure of not sleeping? And they knew full well, from experience, that in whatever couch they nestled, they would not close an eye, except beneath parted lips. But like women, fays have these fits of nerves, which they cannot always control.

"In the rose!"

"In the lily!"

They stamped their feet, clenched their fists, and showed all the anger that can animate two little creatures that a daisy could rush by falling on them—with the result that the adventure had a very unfortunate denouement.

"I'll sleep alone in the lily, then," said Muguette.

And Liseron said: "Then I'll sleep alone in the rose."

Then, without losing an instant, they hoisted themselves up along the stems like children climbing a greasy pole, each toward one of the calices, and disappeared, Liseron into the rose and Muguette into the lily, pulling the petals of the chosen alcove toward them as one closes a door or curtains.

You might smile and say: "Right! That caprice won't be of long duration," but that's where you would be wrong. Persistent in their obstinacy, they refrained from renouncing bitter sulks; the little couple, that night, were flowers apart!

Although they were annoyed, at first, on their own, the desire took them more than once to admit their errors and exchange pardons; at least, that is what I am led to believe. But they had proud souls even though they had tender hearts, and, unshakably—I am scarcely exaggerating—each of them maintained herself in the solitude of her lodging.

In temporary lodgings one cannot do otherwise than dream; even fays have to obey poets. Certainly, they dreamed. What reverie haunted them, made of memories and hopes, in the sway of the odorous hammocks, counselors of languor? Could they prevent themselves thinking, in spite of sulking, Liseron about Muguette and Muguette about Liseron, and rediscovering, in the chimeras of semi-slumber, the sweetness of the kisses once heard by the young shepherds descending from the mountains and the knights in quest of enchanted princesses? Or, authorizing themselves by the quarrel to venture as far as infidelity, did they imagine—long forgotten and having

74

acquired, in neglect, the perverse charm of the novel and for-bidden—the caresses of some brutal sylph they had once re-jected?

The breeze would try in vain to deny that, fully occupied that night in following through the air and kissing in passing the veil that a nun in a nearby monastery had just thrown over the windmills and bell-towers, it neglected to sway the branches, the florescences and the grass; and yet, the lily in which Muguette was nestled, and the rose in which Liseron was nested were shaken throughout the nocturnal hours by a almost turbulent back-and-forth movement; it is therefore in-evitable to believe that that motion came from an internal agi-tation!

And it cannot be denied that before morning, in the gray brightness not yet reddening of the dawn that does not want to be born, when they descended toward the grass, they revealed in their slow movements a delightful fatigue of amorousness finally extinct, which only consents to live in order to await the house when it will die again. The eye of the last star, which was about to fade away in the melting of the darkness saw their little eyes, also little stars, ringed by brown languors.

Having no honest reason to give for their lassitude, they seemed delectably weary; even an observer would have been able to remark that Muguette, in wanting to pick a strawberry, and Liseron, in wanting to pick a cob-nut, had an awkward-ness in all their little fingers that allowed the cob-nut and the strawberry to fall, and testified to mysterious fatigues.

They saw one another, but they pretended not to see one another. They recognized one another, but they pretended not to recognize one another. Alas, had a single desert night suf-ficed to convince them that solitude has charms and spells of which the most passionate real hymen, even culpable, cannot equal the delights? Had they, so rapidly, arrived at understand-ing—oh, the unfortunates, albeit fortunate!—that any retalia-tion, perfectly delightful as it might be, cannot be anything but the melancholy aftermath of divine desire, that no joy exists except on the condition of not existing?

Sensate seekers know full well that the void is the only garden in which the miraculous flower of total satisfaction blooms and that "Nothing" is the true name of the terrestrial paradise.

Henceforth, Muguette and Liseron, who had so ardently sought and found one another, avoided one another; not only did they no longer express any tenderness to one another, but they did not even display anger; in the evenings it was with absolutely sincere indifference that they passed so close to one another, Muguette to climb into her lily, Liseron to climb into her rose...

Oh, young people of the century in which I live, you will render me the justice that I did not counsel you, in commencing this story with the sinister denouement, to follow the example of the two little amorous fays who joined one another behind the bushes in order to exchange kisses whose sound imitated that of two petals rubbing together. I criticized the culpable lovers of the forest of Broceliande or the wood near Athens; I wanted to direct you away from the wrong path.

But know this: even the crime from which I have turned you away would be less frightful than the one to which Muguette and Liseron abandoned themselves, for having quarreled one evening. Whatever propensity that damsels and ladies experience to model themselves on queens or fays, refrain from following the example of solitary sinners. Love your fiancés with full hearts, O virgins; love your husbands and your lovers with full mouths, and full arms, O young spouses; even resign yourselves, if necessary, if some abominable slope inclines you that way, only to get up blushing from the chaise-longue where you have obliged the insistence of a detestable friend; but in any case, do not consent to the infernal and paradisal solitude of chimeras.

Let your chaste beds, O virgins, never have any resemblance to the pale lily in which Muguette enclosed herself, and never, O wives and lovers, let your less ingenuous beds have the slightest rapport with the slightly frayed rose in which Liseron enclosed herself. Do not be the sisters of those frightful little fays. Do not steal your lips from living lips, do not reserve yourself for absences, for the sin that one commits only has the excuse of the joy one gives. If you follow the miserly and jealous example of Muguette in her flower, and Liseron in hers, you will be cursed by all the lovers worthy of the name—yes, cursed, cursed, and damned!—unless you permit the fervent curiosity of some discreet accomplice, who will take on all the damnation for you, to separate, not too closely, at the most mysterious hour, the white curtains, O young girls, of the alcovean lily, or the petals, O young women, of your bed blooming like a white rose.

The Flower Who Was Cold

Nothing was more extraordinary or more charming than that flower in the field of snow. She was a very small rose on a very small rose-bush. She was so frail, with pale red tints, and the bush was so thin, that someone passing by would have been unable to explain how she had resisted the chill of the rude north wind. The custom of eglantines is not to survive the warm season.

However, informed of matters as I was, I was not unduly surprised by that flower in the snow. The previous April, a fay with butterfly wings had traversed the plain when it was verdant, had brushed the field at a single point with the tip of a light toe, and had left spring there. And the flower had been born, had blossomed and had not faded.

But she was very cold; she was reminiscent, with her slightly pink, shivering whiteness, of the nudity of a child in a cradle of frost.

As I was considering her, the little eglantine said: "Monsieur, there is no fate more miserable than mine, and it's very annoying not to be able to shed my petals and die like the other little flowers; for winter, impotent to wither me, is freezing me; I feel a thousand cold pins that have points of ice penetrating my delicate pulp. If you don't have an inexorable heart, take pity on me, I beg you. Do something, so that there is a little warmth over and around me, if only for a moment. All that I have of beauty and perfume I would gladly give for a ray of summer sun."

You can divine that I was very moved by such a speech. But how can one come to the aid of a rose shivering in the cruel air? There could not be any question of begging the clouds to open in order to let a few beams of warm light pass through; there was no warmth behind the bleak white masses. I had the idea of going into the nearby wood to collect branches in order to build a fire around the thin stem, but the guts of the north wind would soon have extinguished the flame and dispersed the embers.

What then? Would I be obliged to let the pretty supplicant suffer in the long winter, without relief? Fortunately, I am not one to fail to be sufficiently fecund in ingenious imaginations. I ran to the lodgings where the friend with the golden hair was waiting for me faithfully. I told her about the adventure and told her my plan. She did not hesitate to go with me, having dressed in haste, wrapped up in furs.

We soon arrived in the field of snow, and my friend leaned over the flower and let down her hair.

"Oh, how sweet it is to blossom in the sunlight!" said the little rose in the field of snow.

The Wishes of an Eglantine

As the smallest of fays—there are fays so small that they could nestle in the dimple next to my friend's mouth—emerged when the dawn began to redden from the eglantine where she had found refuge the previous evening from a cruel enchanter mutated into a scarab beetle, she said:

"My dear eglantine, pretty flower of the bush, scarcely opened, I want to show my gratitude for the service that you rendered me in according my hospitality in the narrow calyx of your rosy innocence. Since I am omnipotent in spite of my stature, smaller than the blades of grass on the edge of the wood, I shall not fail to accomplish the wish that it pleases you to form.

"Come on: reflect, choose, and request. What would it please you to have? What would it please you to be? Would you like the breeze of an ever-perfumed spring to caress you eternally, and never to shed your petals? That a luminous stream made of molten diamonds should flow past your stem and offer you a fleeting transparency in which to mirror yourself delicately?

"Perhaps, enclosed between the leaves that are like the bars of a jail, you envy the flight of the butterflies dispersed among the corollas and the skylarks that cleave the air? If such is your desire, you shall be the amaryllis smitten with carnations, the melicerta that climbs, fluttering, the twigs of lilies of the valley, the darkling beetle swooning with amour in the caress of sunbeams; or I can make you into a bird, which brings the awakening of heaven to salute to the still-somnolent earth with its bright call."

"Dear little fay," said the eglantine, "I thank you for your good wishes, but I have higher ambitions."

"What do you desire, then, my darling?"

"Learn, Madame. The other day, I saw Mademoiselle Mésange go along that path with her lover. The bushes of the pathways, which brush so many happy couples, had never admired a young person so perfect in her slender grace. For myself, I was utterly ecstatic in considering her, and I strove to lean over in order to take a little of the perfume sweeter than mine that she had in her dress. But what brought my enthusiasm to a peak is that, for an instant, in order to allow him to take a kiss, she tipped her head back, her mouth partly open, beneath her lover's lips, and I perceived between the nacre of vivid teeth, like an exquisite coralline wriggle, the tip of a pink tongue. Oh, good little fay, nothing is more charming or worthy of admiration than the pink tip of Mademoiselle Mésange's tongue; and that is what I would like to be."

"Damn!" exclaimed the fay. "One can't say that you're a flower limited in your desires. You wouldn't have shown more pride if you had wished to be changed into the most beautiful ruby in the nocturnal tiara, of which the star Aldebaran is made. But since I engaged my word, I ought not to take it back, and your wish, little flower of the road, will be granted immediately. In any case, since you're so pink already, a part of the work is done."

It was thus that the hospitable eglantine became the exquisite tip of the little tongue that wriggled like living coral between Mademoiselle Mésange's teeth.

It would be difficult to express how happy she judged herself to be—and was, in fact—at first. In addition to the glory of being more illustrious than the ruby Aldebaran, she knew the pleasure—for Mademoiselle Mésange never wearied of being a little greedy—of insinuating herself into the perfumed creams of cakes and the very small Bohemian glasses into which Caribbean liqueurs are poured. But what delighted her a hundred times more was existing in the delightfully odorous moisture of a mouth more tender than the most amorous roses, and gliding between the pearls of the finest teeth in the world, and posing on lips so red and so delicately fleshy and one might have thought them a calyx made with the pulp of a scarlet fruit. She did not even experience any displeasure when moved by a strange instinct, she quivered and elongated, imbued with dew, under a very slow, very long kiss...

But there is no happiness that does not have its down side; it only requires a thread of spider-silk to put a shadow over a path. Only a few days had gone by when the eglantine lamented bitterly, appealing for help to the little fay.

"Uh oh! What's wrong, my dear eglantine, now the pretty tip of a little pink tongue

"Alas, dear fay, I'm as unhappy as possible, if not always, at least at times. For Mademoiselle Mésange's lover has the truly extravagant habit of not limiting his kisses to his friend's lips. Too often, he seizes me, as I flee vainly, won't let me go, and bites me between his ferocious teeth. That is a torment I did not expect, and which I can't endure any longer."

"What can I do to extract you from that torture? Would you like to become a little flower of the path again, far away from Mademoiselle Mésange?"

"Distance myself from her? Cease to be a part of her? Oh, no. But know, Madame, the wish that I have formed. I am aware that in the double widening of her corset, Mademoiselle Mange's young breasts swell delightfully, and their roundness is that of a great pearl, with an roseate orient like a woodland strawberry. I would like to be the reddening tip of one of the breasts that throb, like turtle-doves in a nest, in the double widening of slightly somber plush."

"Damn!" cried the fay. "One couldn't say of you that you're a fay limited in her desires. You wouldn't have shown more pride if you had wanted to be the drop of blood that a young angel who had pricked her finger while embroidering the veil for her celestial wedding sometimes allows to fall on the snowy lawns of the paradisal gardens. But since you've obliged me, I'll serve you again, and your wish will be granted immediately. In any case, since you're so pink already, a part of the work is done."

It is thus that the eglantine, after having been the tip of an exquisite little tongue, became one of the strawberries or embers that ripen or catch fire in the orient of Mademoiselle Mésange's breasts.

Oh, how armed and proud she was! How she stood up, triumphantly, like the blood-stained spearhead of a victorious young warrior. Certainly, no destiny was as enviable as hers. All the aromas of the most flourishing of cleavages rose toward her, and she had the glory of having an incomparable perfume herself. What appeared to her to be divine was to feel herself, under the tension of fabrics, slightly sunken into the warmth of firm plump flesh; but what was even mote ecstatic and prideful was, in the evening, when all clothing was removed, naked before the mirror, to be reflected, sovereignly roseate, amid all the whiteness of a body of living snow and palpitating alabaster. She did not even experience any displeasure when she felt herself brushed by the breath of Mademoiselle Mésange's friend, which wanted to be a kiss.

But since there is no perfect felicity down here, and a sensitive plant can suffer to the point of supreme anguish under the scarcely-posed wing of a butterfly, the eglantine, in her new condition, did not take long to lament, and to demand the help of the good little fay again.

"Uh oh! What's wrong, my darling eglantine, now a strawberry or an ember in the orient of a breast snowier than pearls!"

"Alas, dear fay, Mademoiselle de Mésange's lover is no less cruel in regard to what I am now than he showed himself to be ferocious in regard to what I was. If he bit his friend's delicate tongue with a frightful barbarity, he treats the ripening or flamboyant summit of a snowy breast no better. That is a torment I did not expect, and which I can't endure any longer."

"I think that this time, educated by experience, you'd like to become a little flower of the path again, far away from Mademoiselle Mésange?"

"Oh, no Madame. I've formed a new wish; without distancing myself from her, without ceasing to be a part of her, I shall escape from the peril of wicked bites. I shall flee, yes, I shall flee, but without quitting her. It's in the most delightful of shelters, in a retreat bushier and more odorous than the mosses of the woods, that I shall avoid the sharp outrage of overly amorous teeth."

"I don't quite understand," said the good little fay.

"Come closer," said the eglantine, "for it's appropriate to whisper."

It was in near silence, more perfumed than sound, that the conversation continued beneath the slightly-lifted batiste.

"Damn!" cried the fay. "That's the proudest desire that can be formed! You wouldn't have shown a more extraordinary ambition if you had wished to be the ineffable jewel by means of which all hoped-for joys are realized, and which was hidden by Viviane, in order that it would never be rediscovered, under the flowery brushwood of the forest of Broceliande. But since you received me, my darling eglantine, in your narrow calyx, I can oblige you one last time, and your wish will be granted immediately. In any case, since you're so pink already, a part of the work is done."

It was thus that the eglantine...

But as soon as the wish was accomplished, the good little fay leaned toward her and said to her, with a mocking laugh:

"Good, good! Here you are, where you wanted to flee, well hidden, very distant, my darling. No matter; in your place I wouldn't be tranquil; for, supreme and sacred as the mystery is, in which you've isolated yourself, so tiny, the cruel fervor of an excessively smitten lover is perhaps quite capable of surprising you there, redder and better perfumed, and not sparing you, alas!"

What Fays Cannot Do

You would try in vain to imagine anything more dismal and desolate than that land in the black mountains. The peaks were so high and so close together that the inhabitants of the valley had never seen the sun rise or set; only a few rays, at midday, caressed the aridity of the rocks and brushwood. There was not one floret, not one songbird; but between the fir trees and the thorn-bushes full of anger, long snakes slithered and savage foxes lurked; and owls hooted in the intervals of landslides reminiscent of ruins.

In consequence, little Jocelyn, the youngest son of a woodcutter who lived there, always had a soul full of an obscure melancholy. Once, overwhelmed by sadness and ennui, he let himself fall to the ground, weeping and uttering deep sighs, like someone who would have liked nothing better than to be dead.

But there was a fay who wished him well, because one day, as he passed by, she had seen him make a detour in order not to crush an ant wandering far from the nest. She emerged from between the two rocks, under the appearance of a very old woman, wrinkled, toothless and utterly ragged, her back bent and with both hands on a staff. In a hoarse voice she said to him:

"Well, little Jocelyn, you have the air, it seems, of a child who doesn't possess all that he desires. It isn't the time to weep so many tears or utter so many sighs when one is scarcely fifteen or sixteen years of age like you."

"Alas, good woman," he replied, "Who wouldn't be as desperate as me, if they were in my place? No destiny, I think, is more frightful than always to remain in this lugubrious country. I've heard my father say that lands of light and joy exist down here, but, captive in this valley, I shall never see them."

"Why not travel, little Jocelyn?"

"In this solitude walled in by mountains there is no road by which to flee; and I feel too weak, because of the chagrin that make me ill, to climb from one block of stone to another, all the way to the summits from which one can see all of the sky and all of the earth. It would require a great bird to fly away from here carrying me between its wings."

"That," said the fay, "is a wish that is soon granted; you couldn't ask for anything simpler and easier."

Having said that, with the end of her staff, she touched an owl that was watching them spitefully from a hole; the nasty creature, descending to the ground, suddenly became a enormous and magnificent eagle, which developed plumage the color of gold and snow. Without the need of any counsel, the child extended himself on the back of the splendid winged beast, and as soon as he had thanked the obliging fay with a gesture, he felt himself lifted far from the tenebrous depths of the valley.

No words can express Jocelyn's rapture when he admired the immense azure space, the vast daylight, and the whiteness, gilded at the edges, of clouds impelled by the wind. The earth enchanted him too, with its distant blue seas, its blond plains, its rivers, in which the reflection of the clouds passed by, and its cities of marble, glittering in the sunlight. But what completed a joy for which he had never hoped, was a delightful garden not far from a great palace with porphyry also incrusted with gems, in which there were so many roses with ardent colors that one might have thought one was seeing a blooming conflagration.

As soon as the eagle had flown away, after giving him a sign by a movement of its neck to get down, Jocelyn walked through the pathways, his eyes and soul dazzled. He could not weary of gazing, respiring and touching the open calices, which seemed to be smiling at him. He thought that their beauty and their perfumes were entering into him. He experienced the delight of sensing that he was full of roses.

In the rose-bushes a thousand little birds were singing: nightingales, warblers, wrens and robins; and between the florid bushes trees rose up from which a thousand fruits were suspended: cherries, oranges and peaches. It was only necessary to lend an ear to hear the most divine birdsong; it was only necessary to raise a hand to collect the most exquisite meal.

Another joy—incomparable, this one—was offered to him. The day after his arrival in that paradisal abode, as he opened his eyes under the branches that had sheltered his slumber, he saw a young woman at one of the windows of the palace who was more beautiful than all the roses, whose voice—for she sang intermittently, thinking that she was alone—resonated more sweetly than that of the nightingales, and whose lips, redder than the cherries, had to be more flavorsome to kiss than the finest peaches.

In her hair she was wearing a small crown of pearls, which revealed that she was the daughter of the king, but even without the crown one would have divined that she was royal, so radiant and pretty did she appear. Then little Jocelyn thought that he no longer had anything to desire down here, except to remain forever in this peerless place. Happier than one can say, he spent his days between the flowers and the fruits, amid the fluttering of singing wings, watching the young woman in the luminous diadem, and his nights dreaming about roses, red-tinted oranges, warblers and the princess at the window.

But one day, he sat down under a tree, weeping and uttering deep sighs.

The fay who wished him well did not fail to come to his aid; she emerged from between two clumps of blooms, under the appearance of a lively little bee, sparkling with gold, with her two wings beating. She said to him, in a buzzing voice:

"Well, little Jocelyn, you have the air, it seems, of a young man who doesn't possess all that he desires. It isn't the time to weep so many tears or utter so many sighs when one lives in such a beautiful garden, near to such a beautiful young woman."

"Alas, pretty bee, who wouldn't lament as I am if they were in my place. I've heard tell that many lovers on earth marry the women they love, but I shall never have for a wife the daughter of the king who sings at the window."

"Why don't you ask for her in marriage, little Jocelyn?"

"The son of a woodcutter, in these pauper's clothes, I dare not enter the palace. How they would laugh at me if I confessed that I aspired to the hand of such an illustrious damsel! In order to marry her, it would be necessary for me to be a prince dressed in satin and orphrey, and it would also be necessary for her to love me."

"Those," said the fay, "are wishes that are soon granted. You couldn't ask for anything simpler and easier."

Having said that, she brushed the hair of the sad lover with a light wing. Suddenly, he was dressed in the richest garments, feeling at his side a sword with a jeweled hilt, and coiffed in a cap with a diamond-encrusted plume.

He had not yet had time to admire his adornment when the king's daughter, followed by a long cortege of lords and ladies, approached him, saying: "Know, Prince, that from my window I recognized in you the nephew of the Emperor of Trebizond, and I love you with all my heart. Come into the palace, then, I beg you, in order that I can present you to my father and we can be married."

When he was the husband of the king's daughter, who was more beautiful than the roses and sang better than the birds, Jocelyn knew such intoxications that if an angel had said to him: "Come with me, Sire, and I'll cede to you my place on the highest step of the celestial Throne," he would have replied: "Thank you very much, good angel, but I have something better than that!"

And he was not only the husband of an adorable princess; he was also, after the death of his father-in-law, who had designated him as his successor—a very glorious monarch.

Thanks to the fay, he succeeded in all his enterprises. Whatever he wanted, she said: "That is a wish that is soon granted." He dispersed more than a hundred armies, conquered cities, reduced peoples to slavery, and imposed tributes on four emperors. After so many triumphs he wanted even more triumphs, and he filled the world with the sound of his trumpets, so that in the end, he was the most illustrious and the most fortunate of living men.

One evening, however, he let himself fall on to his throne, weeping and uttering deep sighs.

The fay who wished him well, showed herself without delay; she emerged from between the curtains if the dais under the appearance of a little alerion that was in the royal blazon,[4] and, devoid of feet or beak but speaking by means of the friction of its two wings, one *gules* the other *sinople*, she said:

"Well, little Jocelyn, you have the air of a monarch who is in great pain. It isn't the time to weep so many tears, or to utter such deep sighs when one is, like you, the greatest sovereign on earth."

"Alas, beautiful bird of my blazon," he replied, "who wouldn't experience an intense pain if he were in my place? I no longer have any reason to believe that the queen, my wife, is behaving as honestly as is appropriate. If she hasn't yet made the gift of herself to the prettiest of the pages who serve her, it won't be long, and, I think, it won't take very much."

"Why not imprison her in some tower, King Jocelyn?"

"Imprisoned, she would love the one she prefers to me all the more, and I feel no less jealous of the tenderness of her heart than the treasures of her person. It would be necessary,

---

[4] An alerion, or avalerion, is a mythical bird included in Medieval bestiaries, on the basis of a description given by Pliny, and integrated into many heraldic designs, often depicted, like this one, without a beak or legs. *Gules* is a heraldic red while *sinople*, which originally indicated a shade of red, was later used in the same context to refer to a green hue.

pretty alerion, for you to put into her the loyal desire and the virtue of not betraying me either in reality or in thought..."

This time, the fay did not reply as quickly as usual.

"Sire," she said, eventually, "Your Majesty would do well to limit his ambitions of happiness to the joy of holding a beautiful queen in his arms and the splendor of the throne and conquests. For I was able to have a child carried between the wings of an eagle from a sinister valley full of shadow to a garden of enchanted roses; I was able to make of a woodcutter's son into an imperial young man loved by a princess; to someone who perhaps did not see the blades of swords glittering without anxiety I was able to give the glory of victorious clarions; but know, King Jocelyn, that rendering a woman faithful is something impossible even for fays."

The Naked Princess

It is necessary to believe that the providences are not jealously inclined to dispose things for the perfect contentment of humankind, for if they were, they would not have failed to give all the modesty to the ugly, with the consequence that none would be left for the beautiful. Think of the enchantment of our eyes if nothing that could displease them was displayed, and nothing was hidden from them of that which might delight them.

Alas, that is not the way things are. It is usually the damsels and ladies least provided with charms who are the most inclined to swift unveilings, while one could cite a hundred cases, at least, in which exquisite, beloved, adored, beseeched individuals hesitate for a quarter of an hour before according a lover the sight of a snowy arm or a pale breast florid with a rose.

Now, Princess Azelie, whose beauty was famous in those days throughout the world, showed herself grimmer than the most modest. Her robes which descended all the way to the tips of her toes, were made of fabrics so heavy, golden satins or silver-striped velvets, that the amorous wind renounced trying to lift them up no matter how much desire it had to do so, and she had long sleeves that joined up with her gloves. She scarcely consented to allow her face to be seen by messengers followed by long corteges who came to ask for her hand on behalf of emperors or kings.

She showed herself to be even crueler with regard to a mage who lived on a nearby mountain. Although he was, it was said, the most knowledgeable of enchanters, he did not wear a long white beard, nor was hid cranium possessed of a shiny ivory roundness; no, he was as young as a page, with golden hair that curled over his shoulders. But, handsome as he was, and even though, in the depths of her heart she perhaps found a little tenderness for the pretty sorcerer, Princess Azelie, with all the signs of the most violent anger, expelled him from her presence because, one day, having encountered her in an avenue of acacias in flower, he had knelt before her, troubled by amour, his heart and his eyes crazed, and implored her not to hide the little finger from him, so slender and so delicate, with a pink nail, that she had beneath her glove.

To make a enemy of a mage is a perilous thing, as Princes Azelie learned subsequently, to her cost.

Once, it happened that, emerging from a slumber, she found herself stark naked on a lawn. In broad daylight! Stark naked! In light that enveloped her like the gaze of a million eyes! Full of horror, she was wondering how it could be that she was there, without garments, in that bright solitude, when she saw the young mage before her. He was laughing, with a mocking expression.

She understood that the evil came from him, that he was avenging himself, by means of his sorcery, for the great modesty with which she had offended him. She did not think of imploring him, having a haughty soul. She fled, running, always running, hoping for some shelter where she could hide the incomparable glory of her perfect beauty. The amorous breeze that had once been unable to lift her skirt, bewildered by joy, now had nothing more to desire.

Azelie uttered a cry of triumph. She had just perceived a cottage with the door open and the windows closed, which appeared to be abandoned. She hurtled into it, found herself in darkness, and thought that she was saved. But there was a terrible prodigy; the walls of the obscure dwelling gradually became less dark and less opaque, almost transparent, entirely diaphanous, ending up as walls of crystal. The nudity of the princess was no more veiled than the daylight. The young mage, not far away, was looking at her, laughing.

She opened a window, jumped out, escaped, and started running again, leaving behind her a wake of whiteness and perfume. She arrived in the vicinity of a large wood; she felt content, for in the density of the ferns and branches she could hide from all curiosities the frightful pinkness and the frissons of her wild young body.

Alas, she had scarcely plunged into the forest than all the trees—trunks, branches and leaves—slowly sank into the ground. The princess was stark naked in the middle of an immense luminous plain where there had once been a forest. The young mage seemed to be taking pleasure in considering the expression, simultaneously furious and crestfallen, that the young princess could not help manifesting.

She recommenced her flight. After many hours, avoiding towns and going round villages, so much did she fear being seen in the state in which she was, she reached the shore of the sea.

She did not hesitate. She dressed herself in the blue and black waves; she hid in the depth of the water. To die? She consented to that, provided that, when dead, she was dressed. So she threw herself into the tumultuous and mysterious ocean.

As soon as she had penetrated the waves, however, as soon as the indifference of the sea had formed again above her, Princess Azelie shivered, for the waters gradually lowered further and further, and disappeared, vanishing into the soft sand. She remained stark naked on the rocks and large algae of the dried-up ocean.

The young mage was writhing with laughter.

Then she understood that it was pointless to struggle against the power of the enchanter, and resolved to enter into composition with him.

"Sire," she said, "forgive me. It is certain that I gave evidence of a modesty that was perhaps excessive on the day when I refused to show you my little finger with the pink nail. But would you care to consider that you have punished me terribly for my surplus of modesty? Please enable me to resume the clothing appropriate to my sex and my rank. I swear to you that, as soon as I am dressed, I will not fail to offer my little finger to your gaze, and my entire hand."

He laughed even more loudly.

"That is a strange proposition," he said. "What desire could a man have to look at your hand who can admire your naked beauty in its splendid totality? However, it pleases me to show that I am merciful. You want to be dressed, young princess?"

"Alas! Yes, I want to be!"

"Be dressed, then."

He conducted her to a high reef, which dominated the swell of the sea even in the most violent tempests, pushed her toward a block of granite, which opened up and closed over her, and fled, laughing. And since then, Princess Azelie must be very satisfied, for no gaze, not even that of the irresistible sun, can see her through the vestment of stone that envelops her eternally.

That tale, I told this morning to Marion, in order to prove to her by means of a striking example how dangerous it is to refuse the exquisite vision of a little rosy skin to a poet who begs.

Poets, even the most humble, are mages of a sort. And Marion was doubtless very moved by the punishment that might be reserved for her, since I obtained without too much delay the intoxication of resembling the amorous breeze that, after having tried in vain to lift Azelie's skirt, finally embraced, desperately, the entire naked princess.

The Most Beautiful Memory

Scarcely had they entered the luminous hall with walls of roseate porphyry encrusted with amethysts than the three young princes, still almost children—for the eldest, Aymon, was seventeen, Colomban was sixteen and Roselin only fifteen—said, speaking in unison to the good enchanter sitting on a jade throne, with his feet in the mane of a tame dragon:

"Illustrious mage, who has acquired by means of so many prodigies and generous actions, an unparalleled renown in all the countries of the world, know that we are the sons of a king, who would like to be poets."

The good enchanter burst out laughing in his beautiful beard, the color of a white rose.

"Nothing but that?" he said. "Poets? You want to be poets? Which is to say that, simple heirs of a monarch, you intend to become similar to triumphant gods? To be a poet, children, is no longer to be ignorant of anything, is no longer to have anything to desire, since one possesses everything, and yet to find in its possession the unlimited delights of desire. The man who has been granted the gift of poetry lives in the eternal enchantment of rhythms that rock him, and he treads on carpets of crimson and flowers, and his head is in the stars. The birds love him, the roses love him, and women die of love for him.

"You want to be poets! I believe it. You don't have bad taste. Do you know that, justly shocked by your impertinence, I ought to have you thrown out of my palace by those giant negroes clad in red satin, who are my servants? But I remember having seen, a long time ago, the young archduchess destined to become your mother picking poppies in a field of golden wheat; and she had the prettiest grace in the world in picking those flowers; and besides, you were recommended to me by a nightingale, one of my friends, who has the custom of singing in the evening, in a large flowering tulip-tree, opposite the window where you come to dream. I want to do something for you, therefore. One of you shall be a poet; I consent to that. I order it! And I think, little princes, that you're going to thank me on your knees."

They fell to their knees, with expressions of the most sincere gratitude, but deep down, they were not as satisfied as they affected to appear.

"One of us, illustrious Mage? Which one?"

The enchanter replied: "The one that show himself to be the least unworthy of the glory to which you aspire. Listen to me carefully. For a year, you will travel the world, separately. You will gaze at people and things. Then you will come back to my palace of roseate porphyry encrusted with amethysts, and to the one who brings back the most beautiful memory, I will grant the gift of poetry.

The year having gone by, they reappeared in the dwelling of the illustrious mage whose beard was the color of white roses.

They bowed profoundly, for they had been very well brought up at their father's court, and they knew how it is appropriate to behave in the home of an enchanter.

"Well, little princes," he said, "what has happened to you in your travels? What has appeared to you, among all things, to merit admiration? Speak before your brothers, Aymon, since you are the eldest."

"What I have seen of the sublime," proclaimed Aymon, his eyes radiant with glory, "is a battle at sunset on a vast plain. The armor, when struck, rang and was resplendent. Standards, like great terrible birds, floated over the tumult with the flapping of torn wings. The cries of victory carried away in their whirlwind the death-rattles of the defeated, and the swords quivered in the air, luminous and clustered, like a million stems flowering with steel lightning. And when the vanquished fled toward the horizon, bloody and howling, the victorious young general appeared on a white horse on the summit of a hill, in the streams of celestial gold and crimson, his plume palpitating in the air."

The good enchanter said: "It's certain that it's a magnificent spectacle, when the weather is fine, to see heroes in shiny armor killing one another. I won't hide the fact, Aymon, that you have some chance of obtaining the gift of poetry."

But he turned to Colomban. "And what have you seen?" asked the mage.

"I've seen many things that didn't seem to me to merit the amazed attention that other people granted them. The royal parks in which so many beautiful princesses stroll, letting their satin robes trail, between the sumptuousness of starry peacocks; courtesans amusing themselves while men talk to them about amour, and the noise the rubies make falling one by one into a cup made of a single pearl; the power of kings, the opulence of misers, luxuries, triumphs and glories—what is all that, pray? Truly, I despaired of encountering anything of which the memory was worthy to live within me, when I encountered a town in which the plague was making great ravages. There was pity in seeing so many people dying and so many cadavers in the streets, on the thresholds, everywhere.

"The contagion was lurking in the air like an evil wind, and I was getting ready to leave that lugubrious place when I saw women appear who were going from one sick person to another, offering remedies and consolations. They were not afraid of contracting the horrible disease. In order that those wretches should suffer less, and be less abandoned, they braved disgust, peril and probable death! And I felt full of a fervent adoration for those merciful women, and I understood that I would not see anything more beautiful on earth."

The good enchanter said: "It's certain that it's a noble spectacle that is given to us by the devotions of charity. I won't hide the fact, Colomban, that, like your elder brother, you have some chance of obtaining the gift of poetry."

But Roselin, the youngest of the three sons of the king, as fresh and as frail as a flower on a long stem, had not yet spoken.

Interrogated, he replied: "I haven't paid any heed to battles on the plain, under the setting sun, nor to charitable women caring for the sick in cities where the plague is making great ravages, because, on the day of our departure, at the first step, I saw something after which I was no longer able to see anything else, and it certainly won't be me who will obtain the prize."

"What did you see, then child?" asked the mage

"This," said Roselin. "As I was entering the suburbs of a small city, there was a young woman at a window who was weeping. I approached her. Yes, she was weeping. Her eyes, the color of the sky, resembled cornflowers damp with rain. I thought that she was very pretty.

"'Oh, Mademoiselle,' I said to her, 'what is the cause of your chagrin?'

"'The cause of my chagrin,' she replied, 'is that my fiancé, the only living being who is dear to me, has left me in my house in order to follow, at all hazard, a passing gypsy girl.' And she sobbed into her pale hands.

"Then I wept too, and since then, in my travels, I haven't seen anything, my eyes were so delectably veiled by tears."

The good enchanter exclaimed, blooming with pleasure in his white beard: "The poet will be you, my son, for nothing is as noble or as sacred as the dolor of amorous virgins, and it's you who have brought back the most beautiful memory. Yes, I shall grant you the gift of sonorous rhymes, but know, child, you who weep with young women in tears, that you are already a poet!"

The Good Almanac

As I was thinking about a poem that, although it was only a dream, scarcely charmed me and will not please me at all when I have written it, the postman came into my room and handed me, with the usual compliments, next year's calendar. I gave him the customary tip, and when the man had left after the customary thanks I cast a glance over the little cardboard square with the red letters and the black letters, bordered with golden paper.

That new almanac differed little, alas, from the previous almanac. Saints of both sexes—whom we no longer employ—dates, days, festivals, and the phases of the moon. In duration, nothing changes, or scarcely changes; one time resembles another. I thought that the events of the twelve future months would be very similar to the events of the twelve past months: always the same return of vain hopes, false joys, true disappointments; always the banal recommencement of living. It's truly not worth the trouble of inhaling and exhaling the air.

With my hand, I pushed away that fragment of icy cardboard, where nothing desirable was promised to me. In the melancholy of a function already fulfilled many times over. I began to write the new poem that would be no better than my old verses; and when I occasionally raised my head toward the mirror, I saw in my eyes the dry gaze that is sadder than tears.

In the cool radiance of winter sunlight that was traversing the glasswork of the Japanese blind and tinting it with a thousand colors, however, a light form, slightly white, slightly pink, slightly blue and also a little golden, was sketched out; it became animated, and grew, and a little woman was quivering and standing on a beam of light, all gauze and gleam, part-ballerina and part-dragonfly.

It would have been necessary never to have gone to sleep in the eternal forest of Broceliande not to divine that it was a fay; she had beneath her eyelids all the bright azure of primal hopes, and the rose of her smile was made of all the eglantines of youth.

"Bonjour, fay Illusion," I said.

"Well, my comrade, you're not as old as one might think, since you still recognize me," she said, shaking her hair, from which so many little white stars spilled over the parquet that they seemed like snowy daisies: stars or daisies that went out or melted very rapidly.

She leapt on to the sheet of paper on which I was writing, and balancing on a toe so light that that it did not blue the ink of the final rhyme, she said with a laugh that twittered like a nest full of waxwings: "You did well to push away the calendar that the postman gave you in exchange for a little money. Does it exist, everything that is true? You would have to be very stupid to care about months, weeks and days. Thanks to my advice, you're someone who has no clock on his mantelpiece, for fear of knowing what time it is! Personally, I'm bringing you the only almanac that is worth worrying about, the adorable almanac that pleases the dreams of young women and poets. Come on, comrade, take it and look!"

What she showed me was a leaf from a rose-bush, which ought to have been withered, since it was winter, but which seemed green, since it was offered to me by the fay Illusion. And on that leaf, between the fibrils, there were no names of saints of either sex, no Mondays or Tuesdays, no festivals, no phases of the moon, but these adorable words could be read, which might have been traced by the feet of a beetle dipped in a dewdrop:

Innocence, tenderness, first rendezvous, confessions, departures, returns, kisses on the eyelids, kisses on the lips, faithful amours, happy marriages, laughter of enchantment and tears of delight...

And other words even more delightful.

But I shook my head and I said: "I don't want your almanac any more than the real one, exquisite and cruel fay! I've known for a long time, alas, the lies of your joys and the

100

bitterness of your sweetness. Go away, go and deceive some young heart that you haven't disappointed yet; and I scarcely envy him, for I know that by means of tomorrow's delights you will render him more sensible to despair."

She was no longer there; a cloud had passed before the winter sun, behind the Japanese blind with the extinct glasswork.

I had resumed writing, since it was, after all, necessary to do something, when there was a loud noise of breaking glass nearby, and having turned round, I saw, half-emerged from my bookcase, haughty and magnificent, her head crowned with laurels and her breast clad in the gold and parchment of fine bindings, a tall virgin reminiscent of a virile Muse.

Although I had never considered her at such close range, I nevertheless recognized her as the most illustrious fay of all; she had a radiance beneath her eyelids that put splendor into the daylight, and the royalty of her face was made of all triumphs. Sublime as she was, though, she nevertheless resembled somewhat—being another illusion—the dainty ballerina-dragonfly who had just flown away.

"I salute you, fay named Glory!" I said to her.

"You aren't as humble as you'd like to make people think, since you dare to look me in the face," she said, shaking her crown of laurels, from which luminous leaves scattered, as dazzling as a spray of stars.

She approached me and, placing one if her hands on my forehead—it was as if she had crowned my head with flames—she said, in a voice as resonant as a clarion call and the tumult of a crowd: "You did well to reject the calendar of the little fay who insinuated herself all the way to you by gliding on a sunbeam. What do happy marriages matter, faithful amours, tears of delight and the laughter of enchantment? That's hardly worth occupying the mind of a man given to august ambitions! Personally, I've brought the only almanac that pleases the dreams of warriors and poets. Come on, take it, dreamer, and look!"

What she showed me as a golden tablet, and on that tablet were not traced the hypocritical words: *Innocence, tenderness, first rendezvous, confessions, departures, returns, kisses on the eyelids, kisses on the lips*, but engraved there, in accordance with the days of the month, were these promises: *Talent, genius, success, honors, acclamations of peoples, flag-decked windows, floating banners, and slumber beneath the flagstones of a temple shared with the gods.*

I shook my head, and I said:

"I don't want your almanac any more than the charming calendar, magnanimous and redoubtable fay. I have not known myself the disillusionments of your intoxication, not being one of those who were elected to be illustrious martyrs, but I have seen the greatest suffer, I have heard the groans of the thinkers who give souls the alms of the aurora and paradise, more desperate than those of the obscure beggars of the roads,.."

She was no longer there. She had slipped away behind the Shakespeare or the Hugo of the bookcase; a few sad things remained on the parquet, which were still gleaming: scattered fragments of glass, luminous and broken.

Devoid of joy and hope, I had recommenced writing. Those verses, that poem, what was the point of them? Occasionally, lifting my eyes toward the mirror I saw the gaze that is sadder than tears; it seemed to me that a form was very vaguely sketched in the mirror: a reflection, not of my face, but of my thought: the thought issued from the tenebrous depths of my soul, which had become my gaze. That form became animate and grew; it was like a sad young woman, all crepe and shadow, reminiscent of a bride in mourning; and I recognized her.

"It's you, fay Melancholy!" I said to her.

She spoke, languidly, with the sad smile of asphodels; her voice had the inflection of all beloved voices that one will never hear again.

"You did well to disdain the banal calendar that the postman brought you, with which other men are content; you did well, too, not to welcome the one that promises enchantments and youthful tenderness, and the one that promises grandiose tumults and triumphs. Alas, among the trees, it isn't the flowery rose-bush or the glorious oak that is right; it's the willow, because it weeps. Here, take this, friend, look!"

"What she showed me was a page without red letters and without black letters, without the names of saints of either sex, on which no dates were marked; but nor was it decorated with tender chimeras that lie or sublime chimeras that deceive; it was a blank page, entirely blank, on which absolutely nothing was written.

And I said, then: "What a pity, fay Melancholy, that you too are a vanity, like the other two fays. Illusion-Amour and Illusion-Glory! With what an infinite delight I would have accepted your calendar for next year, for no almanac is worth as much as this one, devoid of months and weeks, dates and days, and with no vain promises, of a year in which nothing will happen, in which nothing will deceive: a year in which one will not live!"

The Sweetest Urgency[5]

By the will of a cruel fay—it was, I think, Alcine, if not Melandre—a little princess named Argentine had been transported, in her earliest years, to a desert island. What the reason was that had determined the fay to such a malevolent action I shall not waste time telling you, because it scarcely matters and is of no relevance to my story. Only know that the exiled child had much to lament in that uninhabited country.

Not that it was bleak or sinister; to the contrary, all the most beautiful flowers of the earth were abundant there under a pale azure sky in which white and pink clouds passed like flocks of angels; birds clad in a hundred agreeable colors sang in the evergreen bushes, stirred by a breeze so perfumed that you might have taken it for the breath of carnations and roses, everywhere in bloom; and the sea, which came, murmuring delightfully, to swoon upon the shore, brought, instead of seashells, pearls, diamonds, rubies and topazes in thousands, with the result that the sand seemed to be made of precious stones.

When Argentine, for the pleasure of seeing herself well dressed in the mirror of steams, had adorned herself with large leaves or flowers, held together by thorns, she put a few of those radiant gems into her hair, and she laughed, although she was so sad, on finding herself so pretty.

It was no longer the solitude that made her unhappy; abducted while very small from her father's palace, and no longer knowing that there were other living beings than herself down here, she could not suffer from being alone, since she

---

[5] A revised version of this story, in which the princess is named Eudorine and the fays named as perhaps responsible for her sad fate are Urgèle and Oriane, was reprinted in *Le Carnaval fleuri* as "Faim plus forte que la faim" [Hunger stronger than hunger].

did not know that one could be otherwise. No, what was terrible for the young princess was that there was nothing on the island that one could eat. Nothing at all! In all directions, there were branches with red and white closed buds, but not one fruit, even very small; not one strawberry, not one mulberry; and when Argentine, whom hunger was pressing cruelly wanted to put flowers of grass into her mouth for want of more serious nourishment the grass or flowers, by virtue of a malevolent miracle, became little birds or insects which flew away very rapidly.

You will doubtless be astonished that the poor princess had not died after very little time. That is because you cannot imagine how powerful and cunning the fay was. Thanks to her, Argentine, who suffered cruelly from being deprived of nourishment, did not waste away, and when she was sixteen years old, she had been dying of hunger for fourteen without over having died of it. To tell the truth, her pangs were indescribable. Nothing could distract her from them except, rarely, the very brief pleasure of looking at herself, well adorned, in the water that slept or flowed under the trees. All day long, and by night too, she went back and forth, running and stopping, putting her hands to her breast. Sometimes she licked the rocks, filled her mouth with sea water, and tried to walk on the hard gemstones; alas, nothing appeased and nothing deceived the hunger.

It is very singular that, in the evenings, the little stars in the sky, which are charitable, did not weep to see her so unhappy; doubtless the fay had rendered them as malevolent as her. And often, having no other desire than to satisfy her incessant appetite, having never known, even though she was of an age to love and be loved, the dreams the trouble the damsels most ignorant of tender things, Argentine, her arms raised in the nocturnal air, screamed at the moon, which might perhaps be good to eat, and which she would have liked to bite.

It was too much. In the end, the fay Alcine, or Melandre, experienced remorse for the barbarity in which she had been obstinate for so long—even the most evil people have merciful moments—and resolved finally to free her victim from such a frightful torture. She ordered someone in her retinue to descend to the island with a large basket full of the most beautiful fruits in the world.

As the princess was wandering, famished, along the shore, she saw a well-dressed page coming toward her, carrying the gilded basket of peaches, apricots, plums, grapes, figs and red cherries. At that very moment, she divined that they were exquisite under the teeth, all those pretty things, and she ran, avid, delighted and almost terrible, ready to seize, to tear and to swallow.

But when she came close, the bearer of the fruits—what he might be, she could not imagine, not remembering any other human being—appeared so delightfully pretty with his curly blond hair, his tender blue eyes, his fresh pink cheeks and his lips redder than the cherries, that she stopped, ecstatically.

Was he good to eat too like the things in the basket?

Perhaps...not in the same fashion, she thought; and she looked at him, and found herself glad, although devoured by hunger.

Finally, she leapt forward—but before biting into the fruit, she kissed him on the lips.

The Wish Granted, Alas[6]

Any delay was henceforth impossible for me. It was with the most ardent prayers and the most decisive gestures that I threw myself at the knees of that exquisite and cruel socialite. Doubtless touched, finally, by my long suffering, and convinced by the recklessness of the assault of the valor of the assailant, was she not about to forsake her barbarity?

How mistaken I was. She rejected all my hopes with a glance, and said with a little laugh: "With regard to loving a poet, that's a stupidity that I shall surely never commit."

"Eh!" I cried. "By virtue of what crime have poets merited losing the esteem of young women? Are they not able to love as well as other men, and do they not have as well the pleasant privilege of immortalizing in enthusiastic praises the beauty of their beloveds?"

"Their mania for praises, Monsieur, abundant in figures of rhetoric, is precisely what I fear. No, I would not want what had happened to my friend Lise de Belvelize to happen to me."

What had happened to Lise de Belvelize, then?

The cruel woman told me.

"Once, when my fried was getting ready for a ball in front of the mirror, and the chambermaid had just left, a Chinese vase on the mantelpiece shattered into twenty pieces, and from the debris emerged, no larger than a bee, clad in four or five pearls and coiffed with a eglantine petal in which diamonds represented dewdrops, a dainty individual whom one could only recognize as a fay—and, indeed, she was one.

---

[6] A revised version of this story, to, appeared in *Le Carnaval fleuri*, entitled "Inconvénient des métaphores" [The Inconvenience of Metaphors], in which the friend who endures the unfortunate adventure is named Rose Laurier.

"'Lise,' she said, 'my sisters shelter in the evening in the calices of carnations and roses, where they are entirely at ease. It is also in flowers that I make my bed, but in the flowers of plush and malines lace that blossom in the curtains of your alcove. You can imagine that I hardly sleep, attentive to the tender words and delicate caresses with which you enchant the fortunate insomnia of your lover, and I have conceived a great amity for you because of the pretty words you are able to say, and the even prettier gestures in which you excel. I have therefore resolved to render you some good office. Make a wish! Faith of a little fay, it will be granted.'

What can a woman, even very beautiful, desire?

To be even more beautiful.

Lise remembered—it was an assembler of rhymes that she loved, the unfortunate woman!—sonnets, rondeaux and ballads that celebrated, with so many metaphors and not without some exaggeration, the attractions with which she was provided, and asked to become as miraculously charming as she was in her friend's verses.

"'Excellent!' said the fay, bursting into laughter. 'Finish dressing; as soon as you're at the ball, your wish will be granted.' Then she disappeared, the debris of the Chinese vase having come together around her as a flowers closes again.

"Lise hastened to go to the fête, where so much astonishment and admiration saluted her. But things were far from passing in accordance with her hopes. Scarcely had she entered the hall ablaze with candlelight than there were mocking whispers around her, laughter, *uh oh*s and *aha*s, and a hundred fingers pointing at her.

"What had happened? Full of anxiety, she ran to a mirror. The heart of a tiger would have been softened by the plaintive cry that she uttered. She saw herself, in fact, similar to the beauty created by her lover's reverie. Her blonde hair was no longer gait, but golden clusters of wheat; instead of her eyes, two sapphires shone blue; her mouth, which had ceased to be a mouth, was a rose. She really did have the neck of a swan; angelic wings quivered on her shoulders; and her breasts—previously warm and palpitating flesh—were marble!

"She shuddered on thinking about what might have become of so many other treasures veiled by lace and silk, and fled, pursued by the irony of woman and the pity of men.

"Poor friend! It required no less than eight or ten flirtations pushed to the extreme, with engineers, bankers and blacksmiths, to undo all that poetry. And you can well imagine, Monsieur, that, suspicious of the traps that imagist rhymers and little individuals emerging from Chinese vases might set for us, that I shall refrain carefully from risking the misadventure of being beautiful to the point of no longer being a woman at all."

Thus the exquisite and barbaric socialite excused herself for not loving me—but she did not make me believe it, even though the apparition of a fay rendered the tale so plausible; and I knew full well that if she rejected my ardent pleas and my vainly decisive gestures, it was because on Sunday, in the plaza, her heart had been won by the banderilla of a supple and muscular bullfighter with a bronzed face, as closely shaven as a provincial actor.

The Little Fays in the Air

Not far from the forest of Broceliande there was a field of wheat and poppies, which, no matter whether it was spring, summer, autumn or winter, never ceased to be golden and crimson; if there were terrible storms, that did not prevent the poppies and the wheat from undulating as slowly and delightfully as they did under a breeze that scarcely brushed them. For that field did not belong to any lord or rich peasant; a dependency of the forest, it was the property of the fays.

Many singular stories were told about it: that amorous couples who bowed their heads there to unite their lips there at nightfall suddenly felt themselves seized by crazy laughter, which was ill-suited to the kiss; that if they went on—which is to say, if they contained the laughter within kisses—little sprites did not take long to appear, who made a game, not of taking them away from you, which might have been very useful, but of putting back, all the way to the neck, the garments you were in the process of removing. Worse still, young persons were seen who went into the field of wheat and poppies when August was burning the sky and the earth, with the blushing resolution not even to keep on the stockings that grandmother knitted, came out again clad up to the ears and higher, even with furs, which the sprits had added.

It is a strange pretention to want to prevent people from stripping naked when they want to do so, and without a doubt that field, although magical, would have been avoided carefully by all lovers endowed with any common sense, if the renown had not spread throughout the land of the prettier games, more amusing than anything that can be imagined, to which the fays delivered themselves when the lovers had departed, weary of being teased and dressed again.

What were those games? No one knew, but everyone agreed in saying that they were the most charming in the world; throughout the land it was a commonly said of a man full of wine: "Of course he's content—but he's not as content as the fays of the field of Broceliande." What could they do to amuse themselves, then, the Ladies of the poppies and the wheat, that was worth more than the dream of a drunkard beating the walls under a black and rainy sky and believing that there are no more stars in the night because he had drunk them all? What had they invented, Abonde, Oriane, Meliandre, Fenilyce, Revelyne and Nigrane, and you too, Alaleine, the favorite of my rhymes, who, in the refrain of a popular song, blends with the name of the daughter of the Swan?[7]

Now, no one wanted to surprise the fays' secret more than little Vivonne.

It was not that she was without joy herself. Oh, no! It happened that she did not refuse her mouth to her friend-fiancé, whom she loved with all her heart. Oh, how whole-heartedly she loved him! And the young woman who gives her lips to a mouth that she loves has nothing whatsoever about which to complain. Soon, he would marry her. In the meantime, he kissed her lips, and also her teeth. Good. She had a heart full of a sweetness she could not have described. Yes, truly, her heart was so full of delight that it weighed heavily within her breast. And she thought that the fays were certainly not as happy as her. Even so, it was her desire to surprise their secret; and one evening, the moon being propitious—so a knowledgeable witch had told her—she slipped along the wall, leapt over a ditch and found herself before the field of wheat and poppies haunted by the fays...

Oh, how charming it was!

---

[7] i.e, Hélène [Helen of Troy], the daughter of Leda, seduced by Zeus in the guise of a swan. The names Fenilyce, Revelyne, Nigrane and Alaleine all appear to be improvised, and the popular song cited is untraceable. I have reproduced the name Fenilyce as it appears in the book, but cannot help suspecting, given that it surely ought to rhyme with Revelyne, that it is a misprint for Fenilyne.

What she saw right away, over the entire field, in the moonlight, was muslin and gold, but it was quite possible that the muslin, instead of being fabric, and the gold, instead of being metal, were made of clouds and radiance, and that the radiance and the clouds, with their resemblance to muslin and gold, were little fays wandering in the air was also very probable. With the consequence that Vivonne, her head between the branches of a bush that, out of pity, had no thorns, watched the diversions that the ladies of the forest of Broceliande gave themselves in the field of poppies and wheat.

And you could not have imagined anything more exquisite than the fays' games.

Some of them, in long trailing robes of yellow satin, were strolling through the wheat two by two, holding hands. Sometimes they stopped in order to salute one another ceremoniously, saying things to one another that seemed to be complimentary and entirely agreeable. Others, sitting on carpets extended by servants with butterfly wings, were playing chess, or knucklebones, or spillikins, and appeared to be taking an extreme pleasure therein. And what precious stones all of them had on their fingers, around their wrists and in their hair! There was not one who did not make, as she moved, a sound of rattling jewelry.

Seeing and hearing so many things, it was as if little Vivonne were mad with pleasure, with her head between the branches of the bush, which, although it had no thorns, nevertheless tickled her under her ears.

But what completed her surprise, admiration and envy was a troupe of little fays—they were blue, and as transparent as moonbeams in the form of women clad in gauze—who were leaping from poppy to poppy all over the field, above the wheat. Yes, from flower to flower, on the tips of miraculous toes, they were running, flying, returning, running again, flying again, but coming back, resembling women more beautiful than women, who might have had butterflies for feet. They were so light that not one stem bent and not one flower even trembled under the passage of the ardent dancers!

From time to time they paused, and then smiled, and laughed; and it was evident that they were taking an infinite pleasure in running from flower to flower. They imagined wagers as to which of them, leaping from poppy to poppy—without breaking a single one, it goes without saying—could arrive most rapidly at the ditch of the field. And there were a thousand giggles at every victory and every defeat.

Heavens, how agreeable it would have been for Vivonne to join in with such pretty games! She could not hold still any longer; she emerged from behind the bush and, showing herself, she said: "Oh, Mesdames the fays, teach me, please, how you dance like that on the tips of poppies! It must be infinitely agreeable, I think, and I'd dearly like to do as much!"

Abruptly, all the dances were interrupted, and almost all the fays cried: "Ah! Little girl, little girl, come here! How pretty you are! Come here, I beg you. You're utterly pretty! Oh, truly, you'd like to dance like us on the extreme summits of the flowers? It's very amusing, in fact, and not difficult. It's sufficient to be light."

"Oh," said Vivonne, "light I believe I am. No boy has ever complained, while dancing, of my heaviness in his arms, and once, when a thorn had stuck in my heel, my friend-fiancé, without flinching—it's true the he's very strong—carried me from the edge of the wood to the farm. But as scantly heavy as I am, I couldn't, I imagine, walk on flowers without breaking a single stem. You must have a secret that I'd very much like to know, for it would please me so much to flutter from calyx to calyx like the bees and the dragonflies."

The fays, having paused momentarily, seemed to consult one another, and one of them, descending from a poppy, said to Vivonne: "What will you do with your heart?"

"With my heart?"

"Yes. It's the heart that is heavy, because it is full of pities, ardors, amours and melancholies. It's the weight of your heart that prevents you from walking, without bending them, from pistil to pistil. We have no hearts ourselves, because we're fays. And we can walk, with gliding feet, over the col-

113

ors and the perfumes of the meadows. Come on, little girl, be like us. Renounce having a heart! If you consent to that, a sprite very expert in operations of that sort will withdraw the heart from your breast; and, lightened, you can flutter with us between the corollas and the breeze. Come on, come on, decide quickly—is it necessary to call the surgeon sprite?"

But Vivonne burst out laughing.

"Fays," she said, "you can walk without me in the fields of Broceliande over the poppies and the what. To be sure, it's a pretty dance, your fluttering dance, but I intend to remain as heavy as I am, weighed down by a heart by means of which I love, and am worthy of being loved..."

Then, carelessly, she returned to the village where, by virtue of the pleasure she had in feeling her heart beat faster when her friend-fiancé appeared, she recognized that she had had done very well not to throw her heart to the poppies. And in the meantime, the poor little fays recommenced playing at the summits of the flowers, and pretending to take pleasure in being so light—oh, too light.

The Fay Liar

In those days there was a fay who had never told the truth. Many people were inclined to believe that she had once been a sibyl in Cumae, a pythoness in Delphi, or the branch of an oak tree in the forest of Dodona. What is certain is that in the clearings of Broceliande and the isles of Avalon, and even in the rest of the world, she was known as Liar, and no living person, woman or fay, had ever merited her name more.

To tell the truth was as impossible for her as it is for the night to be day. As soon as she perceived snow, she could not help crying: "There's a land in which there are enormous crows! But why, instead of flying through the air, are they all settling in the fields or in the trees?" When someone showed her a forget-me-not she said: "Bah!" and if she had been offered, in a cup of silver jade, a filthy slug, she would have said: "Oh, the delightful turquoise and enamel butterfly! But why has it been put on such an ugly black stone?"

One day—the event has been related to me and affirmed by Puck, otherwise known as Robin Goodfellow, who is more up-to-date than anyone else with the little adventures of Faerie—when she was following a path through the forest that was blocked by an elephant, she turned round and said: "Oh, let's change paths, I beg you, for I can't bear to crush an ant."

It goes without saying that I am not talking about little lies, in which she took pleasure all day long, such as assuring someone that she had flown to the Sabbat when she had not flown, or swearing that she had been there on a night when no one had seen her there, or shouting: "That's the grotto where I spent my wedding night with the Emperor of Trebizond"— who, in any case, having a great many beds at his disposal, would have refrained carefully from getting married in grottoes. No, I am only relating some of the truly extraordinary lies of the fay Liar.

What ancient malediction or what bilious genius had imposed upon her the need to be so prodigiously false? I have no idea, but its function was to make her say, on seeing a negro: "Hey, Pierrot!" and, on seeing Pierrot: "Look, a charcoal statue!" and to a feather: "You're heavy!" and to a lily: "You're dirty!" and to a rose: "You're ugly!" and to a woman: "You're flawless!" Even in the midst of the worst tortures, she would not have consented to tell the truth.

Once, full of rancor because of fables by which she had duped them, sprites and sylphs, aided by gnomes, carried her far away from the edge of the wood into a solitude where no one could come along to thwart their designs, and they undressed her—(Oh, how pretty she was when undressed, although deceitful, as has since been observed in many young women who are not fays)—and beat her with thorny branches, and scratched her with brambles and thistles. But she never ceased smiling, and said: "Yes, yes, they're very soft, those smooth leaves and silky frills with which you're all tickling me, but can't you lay on a little harder? For, in truth, I can hardly feel it."

Now, in those days, I was already, even though I was not yet the lover of Mademoiselle Mésange, the most fortunate and most unfortunate of living men—the most fortunate because the woman with whom I was smitten had all the charms of a little Eve whom God had made, not for man, but for himself; and the most unfortunate because my darling was deceiving me with an obstinacy and a frequency of which nothing can give any idea.

Oh, how she deceived me! It goes without saying that she would not have refused her lips to any of the baritones or tenors which then, alas, as in our days, infested like pirates the land of Tendre; and that, many a time, she was smitten with a gymnast leaping, as if flying, from one fixed bar to another. That I could, if not admit, at least understand. I could explain, by considering the jewelers' shops forbidden to my Bohemian poverty, why she did not reject the caresses of financiers with frightful hands ablaze with gems. But sometimes she betrayed me, without any plausible reason, with the old, the ugly and the infirm—with the poor, in a word—solely for the pleasure of treason!

Now that I can think of those things with a certain calm—for a thousand years have gone by—I am led to believe that my unfaithful mistress was unfaithful as the fay Liar was a liar, by virtue of an invincible law. And what added to my despair is that her deceits did not remain secret; on the contrary, everyone knew about them, recounted them, proclaimed them and discussed them.

I couldn't go out without a friend sniggering: "By the way, Jocelyne"—that was the execrable and adored name of the traitress—"was walking in the wheat-field a little while ago with a very handsome young man; at first, one could see their heads but soon, one couldn't see them any longer." Or someone else might say to me: "If you had spent yesterday evening outside certain windows, which aren't those of your house, you would have been able to admire, through the charity of the curtains, a young woman in a chemise who resembled Jocelyne strangely." And another: "No, no, don't take another step; in the next alleyway you'll encounter Jocelyne with her head on the shoulder of the new lover that she has!"

Others knew other stories—true, alas—and it wasn't only men and women who denounced the perfidies of my mistress. I couldn't go into a wood without hearing the violets whispering in the moss: "You see that poet passing by? That's the one whose friend, yesterday, pressed to remember you in an excessively brutal embrace, nearly crushed us all, greenery and florets alike!" What the finches sang, on seeing me, with their little bell-like voices, wasn't their customary song but the legend of my darling's treasons, and the cooing of all the turtle-doves imitated, in order to mock me, the infidel sighs of Jocelyne. With the consequence that a rage, at the same time as a bitter sadness, took hold of me and tortured me.

That the perjurer would cease to deceive me, I knew to be impossible; but at least I could have been spared the horror of always hearing, perpetually, the recitation of her treacheries. I would have given the most precious things on earth, if I had possessed them, for someone, no matter who, just once, to tell me that my mistress only loved me.

I thought about the fay Liar.

It was not an easy adventure to penetrate all the way to the grim solitudes where, because of the universal hatred, the fay had been obliged to take refuge. I traversed many a forest white with snow, many a sea mountainous with icebergs, and scaled many an icy torrent before arriving at her boreal domain. But great as the annoyances and perils of the voyage were, I supported them without complaint, so much did the fortunate hope comfort me of finally knowing someone who would say to me: "Your mistress isn't deceiving you!" That affirmation—never heard, alas—which would be to my ears what honey is to the mouth, what the aurora is to the eyes, I would finally hear!

I went on with such persistence, falling, getting up, and falling again—it did not matter—until I finally perceived Liar, in all the splendor, snow and ice of her palace near the Pole, and I saluted her, my teeth chattering and my fingers frostbitten.

"Good day, you who hate me," she said. "Isn't this an abode very close to great cities, and wouldn't it be very comfortable if it weren't little too hot?"

Those words filled me with ease. Oh, how she knew how to lie!

"Great fay," I said to her, "It isn't the temperature that's at issue for the moment. I'd like to interrogate you about a matter that interests me very much."

"Oh, what's that? Explain yourself."

"Do you believe," I asked, "that Jocelyne is faithful to me?"

She stood up, as if in a surge of enthusiasm.

"Yes! Yes! Certainly, she..."

I palpitated with joy. What I had never heard, I was finally about to hear! I listened...I listened..."

But the fay did not finish her speech. She went pale; she shivered. One might have thought that a combat was taking place within her, the combat of two equally powerful wills. And she was still silent while I implored her, my hands extended.

Then, suddenly, she cried: "She deceives you! Morning, noon, evening and night, always, always, she deceives you, she deceives you!"

"What! You too!" I sighed. "You speak thus, false fay?"

She seemed desperate. She added: "Oh, what it costs me to tell the truth for once! But there are evidences to which one cannot object, and the lie for which you were hoping, poor man, is impossible, even for the fay Liar!"

LUSCIGNOLE

PART ONE

I

My mind looking into the past, into the furthest distance of childhood, so far away, in a foggy, damp climate, under a gray sky veiled as if by tears, I see a city, long straight streets devoid of pedestrians, and in the middle, isolated by its height, a very ancient cathedral, a heavy round dome with a triple elongation, slender in the air, and a cross on which the opaque white fog, breaking up, puts the tatters of a martyr's robe.

Almost all day long the city remains silent and solitary; rarely, down below, an officer's saber clinks on the paving stones of the sidewalk alongside the small houses, or the sound of drinkers at table emerges through the half-closed door of a tavern. More often, toward the new suburbs, the tall chimneys of which pierce the thick fog blackened by soot, the gasp of a machine shakes walls, a shrill, acerbic whistle that lacerates. Then silence returns, and solitude; one might think that each house with bright windows without passing forms is occupied by the void of a diaphanous, deserted coffin.

Shortly before evening, however, after the muffled closures of doors, which succeed one another from echo to echo, long convoys of women, in ranks of three, descend from the outlying districts toward the habitations. They are factory workers. Tall, wan, exsanguinated and ragged, they wear straw hats with strings knitted under the chin, narrow shawls of yellow or maroon wool with faded floral patterns, grossed over the flat chest and which taper to a fringed point behind toward the worn heels of masculine shoes, too large for them, which click at every step of the bare feet. Each one similar to the others, and all of them resembling living poverty, they proceed, without laughter, without gestures, at the even march of soldiers, passive and ultimately resigned to the discipline of eternal labor and despair.

Sometimes, one of the women breaks ranks, without an adieu to her companions, turns into a side-street, draws away and disappears; her place is immediately filled by the first in the following rank, replaced in her turn; there is a prompt evolution in the entire file, regimented, without disorder. Others separate, more frequently, as the convoy moves further forward into the quarters where the wretched reside; but, decreasing in length, it continues marching in the darkening dusk, in lines of three. Reduced to a few ranks, it does not cease advancing, diminishing continuously.

Finally, there are no more than three women, then two, and then no more than one alone. She keeps going, between the closely-packed houses, unhurriedly, at the even pace of a soldier, her straw hat and woolen shawl gradually plunging into the shadows.

The cathedral is also bleak, in its grandiose perenniality; an age-old august melancholy amid the ennui or the anguish of the moment, an austere and bleak reproach of the antique faith renounced by the inert satisfaction of the fortunate and the rancor of the poor.

Even pious individuals scarcely frequent it, sensing their pusillanimous fervor taking fright before the gigantic portal of bronze cleft by a thrust of the claw of the colossal black Satan of legend; their hearts would be oppressed by an excessively solemn religion at the sight of the vast altars with noble colonnades, the pulpit toward which a broad spiral stairway rises, and from which, when the quadruple screen is folded, darts the blaze of a enormous mosaic of rubies and chrysoliths.

Humble adherents, bourgeois men and women, employees of the state and small businessmen, are ill-at-ease saying prayers devoid of confused amour, offering paltry contrition at confession—fulfilling, in brief, all the mediocre duties of current devotion—near the throne of worn marble where the great Emperor sat, and the stone that covers his giant dust, between the sepulchral blades of so many warrior bishops and the grille—redder with blood than rust, it is said—of the frightful reliquary where the innumerable bones are heaped up of martyrs who proclaimed faith in God in the ecstatic spasms of torture. They prefer the small new church, the familiar sister of the houses, pretty and amiable, which one can enter without emotion, smiling, as if one were visiting a neighbor; where one kneels beneath a sky blue ceiling starred with gold—one could have a similar one painted in the hall of some château, if one were rich enough—and one sits on mahogany chairs like those in the dining room.

There, the Lord is only the good God, and, in the great tableau of the master altar, the work of an artist that one encounters in the homes of common friends, he has an expression so benign, with his long unshaggy beard, that one really could mistake him, if it were not for the azure drapery and the armed archangels, for the portrait of a grandfather one had, an excellent fellow who never scolded and always had, in the days when one was small, toys and pockets full of sweets.

The consequence is that the ancient cathedral in the middle of the sad city is deserted more often than not. It scarcely opens, except for rare visitors, artists and tourists, guided by the beadle or the sacristan, and it soon reenters into its peace, isolated from all vibrant life. But what was in it in the days when processions knelt down under the crosiers of bishops and the scepters of emperors, still occupies it, and magnifies it with majesty and sacred terror.

The silence fills it with unheard voices, the solitude populates it with impalpable re-existences; the august past blossoms there in the void. Empty, with its cold stones painted with a fresco of phantoms by the reflections of stained glass, and its staircases, some of which rise up without windows all the way to the platform where the sky is, while others descend without the memory of daylight toward the crypts, where the whiteness of tombstones imitates shrouds standing upright, with altars of pale marble haunted by the kneeling absences of penitents deceased for a thousand years. Its corridors are traveled by an effacement of footsteps, and its sepulchers, from which chimerical survivors rise up, and the choir, where innumerable arms in sacerdotal sleeves that no eye will ever see, are posed in canticles that no echo will ever repeat.

It is full of nothing, but in that void ten centuries of pride and faith reside, mysteriously eternalized. Whoever enters suddenly recoils, alarmed without any cause for that alarm. But who knows whether, by night—for night gives what is not the fluid reality of shadow— the dead of yesteryear are not, in fact, alive, and whether the tombstones like upright shrouds might not climb the stairways of the crypts again, spectral or resuscitated? Who knows whether the man who watches over the platform might not descend, as was his custom, to light the candles, and whether the Emperor, skeletal flesh clad in iron, with his tombal blade lifted, does not kneel down sonorously on the flagstones while, their bones having been recovered and put in place, the martyrs break the trellis and the grilles, and, sliding sinuously between the pillars, form a glorious procession, bleeding from the wounds of their blissful tortures, renewing antique rites in the terrible cathedral?

But in the time of the story that I am going to tell, the old church had for a familiar inhabitant and a little friend, a girl nine years old, very lively, very thin and very dainty, who was the niece of the beadle. Marthe was her baptismal name but she was nicknamed Luscignole by a priest of the parish, because she whistled and sang like a nightingale.

II

Luscignole, therefore, as soon as she could walk, took her first steps on the stone where the name of the Emperor, king of the Romans, was engraved, and it was one of her first games to climb up the pillar of the font and dip her fingers in the holy water, in order to such it greedily afterwards; she found a taste of salt therein that amused her tongue.

When her mother, the widow for two years of a merchant of images of sanctity and the sister of Alas Schlemp, the beadle, died—of destitution, needless to say, for she earned hardly anything hiring chairs and selling candles in that church devoid of a congregation—nothing changed for the child except that she was deprived of a few scoldings a few rare kisses from a slightly peevish mother. She slept, as before, in one of the three rooms that Alas Schlemp had obtained to house them on the first floor of the tower, and idled after school hours in the solitude of the antique edifice.

That she would have preferred, in her early years, to play in the streets with other children, let out in bands, is probable, but her uncle demanded that she absent herself for as long as possible, in order that, if any strangers presented themselves to visit the cathedral, he would be alerted immediately, either in a little room in the tower, full of caged nightingales, where he spent a good part of the day, being very fond of bird-keeping, or in the neighboring tavern, where he spent the rest of his time drinking brown beer and Schiedam until his was stupidly drunk.

Gradually, isolation between the old walls became a habitude devoid of chagrin for the little girl. Not that, as she grew up, she became morose, following the example of the Elect of stone, who dreamed with bleak white eyes and a finger over the lips, or the motionless figures extended on the sepulchers, but, on the contrary, because she rediscovered in the lugubrious forms, in religious or funeral things, the vivid joy that her childhood had put into them by smiling around them.

The immemorial church did not age her; she made it puerile. Cheerful and frivolous, sometimes uttering mad cries like rockets of sound, she was the bright tumult victorious over obscure silences; and, slightly hoarse with the memory of *Pie Jesu*s and *Dies Irae*s, the echoes tried to laugh with her, and succeeded, not without a residue of a growl, to which she paid no heed. She laughed in the surliest corners, and mocked the frowns of the tumulary icons. One day when, by chance, she gleaned a long garland of roses left trailing over the flagstones after the funeral of a rich man—a converted Jewish banker who had had the supreme whim of having his mortuary office celebrated in the Carlovingian basilica—she used it as a skipping rope, and made double unders between the recent silence of the organ and the scarcely-extinct candles.

She had no need, however, for a little of external life—a funeral procession—to penetrate into the cathedral in order to smile and find pleasure there. She had invented games in which the august antiquity of the marbles and bronzes were obliged to join. Coming and going, never still, she played shuttlecock with an Our Lady whose motionless hand, lifted like a racket, sent back the feathered cork.

If a little sunlight cared to traverse the stained glass window to the bronze Saint Synesius and the fourth station of the cross, she wagered—not without cheating a little, for she stretched her head slyly—that the sunbeam would gild the tip of her nose before alighting, a butterfly of daylight, on the venerable nose.

To the cherubim with inflated cheeks, the absence of bodies veiled by tufted golden wings, crowded in the haut-reliefs of painted stone, she said: "What if we were to play hide-and-seek, eh? Would you like that?"—and she went to huddle, watching out to see if anyone was peeping, either in the sarcophagus of Augustus, or behind a screen of the trip-tych on which the eleven thousand virgins were painted, or under the copper lid of the enormous baptistery decorated by the granite robes of the foolish virgins weeping over their ex-tinct lamps; and she shouted "Ready!" waited, laughed, shout-ed "Ready!" again, and because no one had found her, re-turned to the chapel of the cherubim and thumbed her nose at them triumphantly, perhaps persuaded that they had followed her and searched in vain, and that they had returned to their places in chagrin.

She hoisted herself up on to the pedestals of kneeling knights, hoisted herself further and tried to see what they were hiding behind the partly-raised visors of their helmets, and said: "Pfui! Nasty man!" at their dusty breath.

She had a yen to play with the infant Jesuses in the arms of the holy Virgins, but dared not ask them, less familiar with them than with the cherubim—who, after all, were only the winged scamps of Heaven—and fearing the reproach of the maternal Marys.

She picked quarrels with the zigzags of daylight over the tiles of the parvis, between the grooves of the pillars and over the gilded flowers of the candlesticks, becoming annoyed because, out of malice, they did not want to allow themselves to be picked up.

Once, having spotted a nest that swallows had made under the advancement of the exterior portal in the neck of headless saint, she went to take it, carried it away with all the chicks chirping, and placed it near the master altar in the broadly twisted mouth of the dragon defeated by the Angel; and it was an amusement for her to watch the father bird and the mother bird—for she had not closed the bronze shutter—carry food all day long to the little swallows in the devil's mouth.

But did she not have little friends to play in the cathedral? Yes, indeed. Who were they? The mice of the reliquary. They were very thin, grayish white, like the bones of martyrs; they sometimes stuck anxious inquisitive heads slyly through the trellis of the railings, withdrawing them at the slightest sound.

Luscignole's first thought, on the day when she saw them for the first time, was to go and tell her uncle; for, after all, it was not appropriate that there should be mice among the sacred bones. Could it be admitted that the skull of Saint Catulla or the tibia of Saint Hersilien might be reduced to dust by vile sacrilegious teeth? But Luscignole also thought that harm might come to the little creatures, that traps might be set for them or cats would be shut up in the reliquary. They were so dainty, with their malicious little pink eyes and their brief lively lips.

The child thought of a way of arranging everything; she would safeguard the relics while sparing the mice. What means? She bought cakes with a little small change stolen from her uncle's pocket—for she was so ingenuous that she had no honesty—and crumbled them near the grille of the ossuary; it was certain that intelligent animals, as these appeared to be, would not fail to prefer fresh flour, recently cooked and well folded, to humeri, ankle-bones and ribs so long stripped of flesh, to which sanctity could not be sufficient to give any considerable succulence.

She was not mistaken in her anticipations. The mice risked leaping through the mesh of the trellis in order to nibbles the delicacies, taking pleasure in those new meals; grateful, they even became familiar with the person who offered them. They lost their fear of being approached by her, allowing themselves to be caressed, eventually becoming accustomed, when she knelt down, laughing, and distributed crumbs prodigally, to climbing along her hands, along her arms and around her neck. There developed, on either side, such an amity that Luscignole—unless someone arrived to alarm the little girl and the little animals—no longer wandered around the cathedral, laughing in the faces of the ancestral figures and playing hide and seek with the golden cherubim without being followed by the tumultuous trot of twenty little gray mice.

In addition, Luscignole had other pleasures, more serious and more worthy of the nine-year-old girl that she was about to be. The august relics contained in the Emperor's chapel, to which many pilgrims came from all over Christendom to worship for three days every seven years, did not only consist of a few pale bones. In a smaller reliquary, a mysterious chamber of which Luscignole stole the key, there was a little of Jesus's crib, a splinter of a cedar plank once planed by the good carpenter Joseph; one of the nails of the cross; a thorn, still pink with a drop of the divine blood; and, more precious than all the other relics, one of Our Lady's chemises, a pale rag hanging on the wall.

Very pious, in spite of the bad examples that had been given to her by her friends the mice, Luscignole lingered gladly among those sanctities in the high-ceiling chamber forbidden to everyone, almost dark and darkened further by old, sweet, spare odors, the incense of a invisible odor.

One thing annoyed her, which was that the underwear that had once brushed the divine Mother was in such a poor state, yellow here and holed there; the long time that had passed since it had been tailored and sewed was no excuse for such dilapidation. So, one evening when Alas Schlemp—who had been calling and searching for his niece all over the church for a hour—finally found her, she was squatting, very busy making a repair, by the light of the first star, to the Virgin's chemise.

It would, however, be an exaggeration to say that Luscignole spent every hour, before and after school in the cathedral. Often, and more often as she grew older, she went into the tower to keep Alas Schlemp's nightingales company, eventually almost forgetting the gray mice of the reliquary.

III

The city counted Alas Schlemp's nightingales among its finest glories. There were forty of them, in cages hanging from the wall of a small room in the tower. Mute by day, they sang in the evening with violently sonorous throats, an indication of perfect health, and their song, never interrupted before its completion, was astonishing in its splendid clarity.

It was a habit dear to the citizens who lingered in grave conversation around tables laden with foaming pitchers to go to the Cathedral Square before going back to the lodgings where their wives and daughters had been asleep for a long time, to listen to Alas Schlemp's nightingales, which, one after another, sometimes two by two and sometimes all together, filled the nocturnal silence with their beautiful pure voices. The heavy beer-drinkers, attentive, standing in a circle, did not speak, their hands on their bellies, nodding their heads in approval.

The keeping of songbirds was in great honor in the city where this story is unfolding; it was not to shoemakers curbed over their knees in the workshop or to girls in mansards that the pleasure of twittering cages was left; the most considerable individuals, by virtue of age, fortune and social status, did not disdain to devote their leisure to taking care of warblers, sky-larks and bullfinches. The prosecutor in the criminal court was no less proud than he would have been of an oratory triumph of having obtained first prize for the beautiful cooing of turtle-doves in the last regional competition. In fact, they had cooed as remarkably as possible. The rector of the Faculty of Theology was justly proud of his scarlet-breasted finches, which, in whistling contests, had finally constrained to silence—which is to say, to death—four enraged canaries; and the professor of Roman Law was infatuated with his robins.

But for nightingales Alas Schlemp, was triumphant.

The beadle did not inspire much sympathy. His body of a thin dwarf, with an enormous round head set directly on his shoulders—it might have thought that it had sprung from the body a minute before, in an explosion of anger—gave the impression, less of a man than one of the gnomes, grinders of hops or rollers of barrels, that are seen in the frescoes of taverns. And while the pink roundness of his tiny eyes lurked maliciously beneath think eyebrows, he had very unpleasant lips; one of them, the upper, was so thin and retracted that one thought one was looking at the lip of a hyena; the other was so thickly heavy and sweating that it resembled the lower half of the mouth of a gorilla. In addition, his feet, under the tottering, sometimes forwards and sometimes backwards, of his thin body, overloaded by the head, were always moving very rapidly, like the paws of a dog pushing away its ordure.

And he was a very redoubtable drunkard.

When, after a dozen tankards of beer, he had emptied a dozen glasses of Schiedam, if someone seemed to be looking at him without politeness, he would gladly attack the drinkers sitting facing him, and between the overturned tables and stools he had the furious dislocations of a writhing and drooling epileptic. A few extra glasses of Schiedam rendered him utterly extravagant. He raced out of the tavern like an escaping beast, ran through the streets, falling over, getting up again, beating the walls with his arms, hammering his head against doors, until, finally, opened by a projection of stone or the corner of a shutter, his head fell, and, after having caused the light body to pass over it thanks to its thrown weight, was immobilized, as if dead, with the nape of his neck in the gutter.

Then he stood up again, calmly. One might have thought that he was no longer drunk. He was even more so after that overturning crises. Without a tremor, with all the appearances of perfect health and perfect reason, he was formidably drunk. The more placid he seemed, the more terrible he was. He accomplished sagely the most frightful follies. It was something like a lucid blindness.

If he encountered in the black city a furtive, uncertain cat that was about to cross the street toward the ventilation shaft of a cellar, he lay in wait for it, slightly to one side, very subtle and very sly, calculating his strategic advantages; and when the beast took the risk, he extended himself heavily over it with a teeth-grinding laugh, like the lid of trap, took hold of it unhurriedly and methodically, and strangled it with one hand, his head turned to see whether anyone was coming. Then, taking a knife from his pocket, he skinned the corpse at his leisure, adroitly, as a taxidermist would do, and took pleasure in looking at the smooth pinkness of the little naked cadaver.

It was even said that someone had surprised Alas Schlemp one rainy evening, with his backside on the sidewalk, butchering on his knee—where he had placed a handkerchief by way of a tablecloth—the bloody corpse of a sewer rat, which he then commenced to eat raw, choosing the best morsels as a delicate diner reserves for himself the wings of a served chicken; and, pausing momentarily in the hideous repast, under the flickering street-lamp, he advanced his heavy head with his pink blinking eyes, listening, apprehensive of being surprised, like an alarmed and observant monkey clutching something half-eaten in its thin paw.

That there was some exaggeration in the stories that were told about Alas Schlemp is probable; he was doubtless only a drunkard who became rather violent after drinking, of whom there are many. At any rate, he would have been greatly scorned, and might even have lost his position as beadle, on which he lived and enabled his niece to live, if he had not been forgiven many things because of his artistry in making nightingales sing.

And that was only right, for it is a difficult art.

IV

Nightingales are wild.

It goes without saying that we are not talking about those nightingales taken from the nest as chicks, which, not having known the primitive charms of the free forest, are rapidly domesticated. Those never sing with the voice that makes distant echoes swoon in the moonlight. They do not receive lessons from the father and the grandfather, torn by amour on the conjugal branch.[8] They are agreeable twitterers and that is all, the equal of the warbler or the loquacious hedge-sparrow, not masculine and proud lyrical birds, Pindars with brown wings. We are talking about nightingales caught as adults in spring, in the young woods going green again.

Those are the only ones whose voices can, in cities, evoke the lunar solitude and the immense azure. One of those, when captive, does not want to sing, does not want to love and does not want to live. For a long time, he huddles in the dark depths of the cage, between the green cloth with which the cunning of the bird-keeper offers him the resemblance of the lost foliage; he does not get carried away by tumultuous anger, his bristling wings colliding with the bars, nor bloody himself between the steel, the skull or the beak, as some mediocre

---

[8] Most literary nightingales, following mythological precedents, are female, but Mendès' natural history is accurate, for once (he routinely makes grotesque mistakes with regard to the natural history of insects); it is, in fact, only the male birds that sing.

house-sparrow might, the excessive dolor of which will be rapidly consoled. No, he, the somber guest of the trees, in whom a great soul loves and weeps, isolates himself in his despair, refuses the most enticing nourishments, solemnly obstinate in his refusal of slavery.

And if one puts a female beside him, even the one for regret of which he is dying of a infinite and grave melancholy, he will kill her, in order not to be tempted to debase in the cage the illusion of the free nest; or, at least, austere, without a twitter, he will keep apart from her, nobler than the lion, of which, similarly wild, he is the winged brother. The lion does not hesitate to accept servitude, to the extent of coupling behind the grille of a menagerie, but the nightingale does not want to engender winged slaves.

Unless one is a practicing bird-fancier, as the writer of this story is, one cannot imagine how much care, science, cunning, strategy and patient love—yes, love!—is necessary to persuade nightingales to tolerate imprisonment, to live in it and to sing in it. It is by dint of loving them that one reconciles those melancholy lovers to existence; if Alas Schlemp was able to flaunt the glory of having forty—forty!—nightingales in the room in the tower which sang as well as their brothers, it was because he cherished them madly.

Madly.

That paltry and vile creature, whose mind, like his body, was dwarfish, stupid when he was not drunk and ferocious when he was, melted entirely into tenderness at the thought of his dear birds. He invented, dim-wittedly, exquisite delicacies in order not to frighten them when he took the floor-plate from the cage in order to clean it, when he refilled with fresh water the porcelain mug beside the trough over the maize pulp of which he had spaced symmetrically the stumps of mealworms, still wriggling, which he had just cut up, with such minute zeal, with a slender knife.

And from the very first whistle, the precursor of the song, that came from afar, close as the bird was, in which the immemorial silence of forests seems to order the sudden silence of all human noises, Alas Schlemp was ecstatic! Agape toward the voice, he had within him the religious delight, the promise of paradise, that the already-melting host puts into a Christian's heart. Then, as the august ode was affirmed in clear repetitions, the trills like thin swirling eddies breaking the long sheet of sound and redoubling the frenetic final modulations, imitating the delirious hiccups of a soul succumbing to an excess of mortal joy, he swooned, veritably, with drool on his lips; and, base opacity traversed by light, deafness full of music, crawling toward the wings, he resembled some gnome, hideous and rapturous, who, from Nibelheim, was rising up toward the auroral bird of Siegfried.

Even the heavy drunkenness of beer or the frantic follies of Schiedam did not render him insensible to the mysterious charm of the singing speech. The day after an evening when, in the finally frightened tavern, his throat inflated by alcoholic furies, he had nearly strangled two or three peaceful drinkers, he could have been discovered in the room in the tower, sitting in a low chair, weeping like a little child because the last plaint of his birds, the delectable voice of the shadow, had just dispersed in the first glimmer of dawn.

V

Loving them to such a point, Alas Schlemp was jealous of them. It was not without anger that he thought, on listening to them by night, that other people, grouped in the Cathedral Square, could also hear them. For a long time, like a miser who does not want anyone prowling around his strong-box, he forbade Luscignole to enter the room with the forty cages.

However, an ardent and tender curiosity attracted the child toward the captives, whose song, issued as if from far away, sometimes traversed the penumbra of the cathedral, mingled with the crepuscular gleams that traversed the silence from the stained glass windows. By dint of patience, and dainty fashions of bringing her uncle his pipe and saying to him: "The people are stupid who say that you cut your face yesterday on the paving stones of the street; no, no, you've never looked better!" and by means of caressant puerilities, she contrived to be admitted to the presence of the birds.

Then, the mice forgotten—she was ten years old now—she neglected the bronze Synesius and the Our Lady who played shuttlecock with her motionless raised hand. An instinct and the unconscious hope of some fraternal return ordered her to love the nightingales

She took pleasure in the narrow square room with the white walls, where the cages were spaced out at equal intervals on high. They were like little wooden jails with thin steel bars; and, drawn all the way to the middle of the cages, a green lustrine sheet added a backcloth of shadow and mystery to them.

Luscignole, who was not tall enough, could not see the prisoners, even if she climbed on a chair or on to the table. But, crouched in a dark corner like them in the midnight of their prison, she divined them, knew that they were there, shivered with tender emotion at the sound, so slight, of a slender foot leaping from one perch to another, or an abrupt rustle of shaken feathers. And if, even though it was daylight, they almost hazarded, in a voice that they could hardly hear themselves, a twitter in which the future nocturnal hymn was sketched, she was content to the point that she laughed in a whisper.

In the evenings, when Alas Schlemp was lingering in the tavern, she emerged from her little bed, in her chemise—it did not matter—barefoot on the tiles, in order to hear the singers at closer range, and then she felt infinitely, delectably troubled; it would not have taken much to make her weep.

Once, she was overtaken by a sudden sob because one of the birds, after the exasperated frenzy of singing, had fallen silent so abruptly that it might perhaps have died. Her arms extended, she cried: "Oh, I beg you, sing, keep singing! Sing, then! You aren't dead; sing you, who aren't dead!" And, tottering, she would have fainted in anguish if, resurgent from

134

the cage, the august voice had not spread forth, aristocratically, in the night.

Futile as her age was, she did not always have those fervors; sometimes she sniggered with laughter because a nightingale had sung in a excessively melancholy fashion.

Soon, however, she became less frivolous, finally acquiring gravitas because of the austere old church in which she lived. What made her love the nightingales was that she bore within her, while still a little girl, the reverie and the solitude of the cathedral, just as they had, in their little sonorous hearts, all the distance of the forest.

Physically, too, she resembled them.

Once, hanging on to the metalwork of the window, with the tips of her toes on the edge of a frame, she succeeded in seeing one of the birds, pensive, with one foot in the air, separate, its eyes dull, fixed and strange, almost terrible; she was astonished, so little did it seem to her that she differed from the winged prisoners.

And she ran to a mirror.

It was true; she resembled them. She had tresses similar to little brown wings and a thin mouth that advanced, almost pointed, in the form of a beak; and, even though her eyes had more light and life within them than there were in theirs, she saw there, in the similar roundness, a widened fixity that she had would never believed that they had in the days of the pink-eyed mice..

And in thinking that she was like their big sister, she loved the nightingales even more. She no longer limited herself to taking pleasure in them; it was a tender need, a cherished duty, for her to watch over them, to protect them. It seemed to her that she was responsible, like an elder sibling, for those little captive souls.

More than once she deliberated as to whether she ought not to open the cages and the window, in order that the nightingales could fly away to the woods that they doubtless regretted so much; but she was restrained by the dread of her uncle, the redoubtable drunkard, who would have killed her if she had taken it into her head to render liberty to his birds. She resigned herself to caring for them and defending them.

Finally softened by the tenderness that she testified toward them, Alas Schlemp initiated her into the minor tasks of bird care. She acquitted them marvelously, with a methodical gravity that one would not have expected in a little person who was very stupid by nature. Wherever she was, whatever she was doing, even in the middle of plating hide-and-seek with the cherubim of the haut-reliefs, she became serious immediately if the idea crossed her mind of a danger threatening the dear little wild beasts, and she ran to the tower, ready for any devotion, any audacity.

Thus, although she had a great fear of cats—perhaps because of her firmer amity for the little mice of the reliquary—and even though a frisson ran through her merely at the sight of one of the treacherous beasts that extend and suddenly plunge their claws, the beadle surprised her one evening standing in front of the door to the chamber of the birds, violent and terrible, lifting up a stool, menacing a thin prowler of the gutters, truly frightening, with famished eyes, which was about to pounce.

Sometime after that, the idea occurred to her that she ought to be able to sing like the nightingales, since she resembled them. Yes, why should she not sing like them, being their sister? It was evident that there was something absurd about that, which could not endure.

She tried to imitate the beautiful nocturnal songs.

Now, every evening, for long hours, before her uncle returned, she listened to them not only for the delight of hearing them, but in order to discover the secret. Elongating her lips, inflating her throat with little spasms, she made herself a beak and a throat full of mute twitterings.

Why did she not proffer a sound, a silent imitator? Because she feared that her voice was to different from the one she dreamed of having because it would be terrible if the nightingales fell silent, indignant at an insulting parody. It was far away from them, in the depths of the cathedral—and then only after many hesitations—that she risked singing, a little, in a low voice, ready to interrupt herself immediately if the illusion were impossible.

Well, from the first trial, she was not very discontented with herself. Undoubtedly, she did not have the mysterious eruption of the first note, in which it seems that a soul is approaching, the slow pure whistle that enchants the night with such melancholy; but the rapidity of the trills was nevertheless possessed of a sufficient resemblance.

And it appeared to the child that, from day to day, she made great progress. She almost began to take pleasure in her own singing. One evening, almost sure of herself, she had a great temerity: she dared to confront her voice with that of the nightingales!

Very close to them, she whistled, from the most distant depths of her soul; she twittered with all the volubility of which she was capable; she gasped the supreme modulations frenetically; and the birds did not fall silent; they even responded to the chirping, mistakenly!

A great joy filled her. So, veritably, she had succeeded in conquering the song of the nightingales; was she finally their sister entirely, even in the voice?

She received a great blow of a fist in her back.

Alas Schlemp had just come in, and was annoyed. What! That child had imagined that she could succeed in equaling the sublime birds? Truly, that was pitiful; she could boast of being very impertinent and mad. And he struck her furiously, swinging his arms, writhing with laughter, while she wept all the tears in her body, not because she experienced a great deal of chagrin in being beaten—oh, my God, no, a few punches were not serious—but because she told herself that Alas Schlemp was right, that she knew better than her, and that she would never be able to sing like the nightingales, without a miracle.

It arrived, that miracle.

Once, as she went into the room in the tower, she re-coiled in fear, Alas Schlemp was so livid, backed up against the wall, his eyes staring,

"Uncle!"

"Here," he said, "look!"

What he showed her in his open hand was the cadaver of a bird. The most beloved, the most admirable, of the nightin-gales was dead. A little while ago, on opening the cage to fill the trough, the beadle had found him amid the sand of the floor-plate, lifeless, bristling and horrible. And it was an irrep-arable loss. Other nightingales had succumbed before; they were sorrows quickly forgotten; they would easily be replaced the following spring. But that one was not one of those that can be replaced. He was the honor and the example of the aviary in the tower. Old and resigned to slavery, but retaining the majesty of the ancient and free solitude, singing as the likes of Dante sing in exile and the likes of Tasso in prison, he was superb and incomparable. It was his voice, above all, that, rising into the narrow night of the city, gave the illusion of lunar distances and limitless spaces.

The child had taken it from her uncle's hand; she kissed it, desperately, poor defunct creature, and wept into its plum-age.

Alas Schlemp disappeared, sobbing; doubtless he was going to the tavern; he would drown his pain in the furious folly of Schiedam.

But the child resolved to give the bird a worthy funeral. She remembered that in the side of the layer of stone that cov-ered the dust of the great Emperor, a corner of the slab had once been broken under some heel, which shifted every time one set foot on it.

She went down into the cathedral; she lifted the fragment of stone, and made a little grave beneath it, in the friable ce-ment, with her fingernails.

The cadaver of the bird was there, close by. She took it, put it in the grave, and replaced the stone. The nightingale and the Emperor were interred next to one another.

She went to an altar to the Virgin and took a bouquet of flowers, which she shredded over the sepulcher.

She went to the font to moisten one of her fingers, and sprinkled holy water over the sepulcher.

Then, on her knees, Luscignole thought, tearfully, that there are no beautiful obsequies without music, and she lamented; she lamented melodiously and harmoniously, her voice exactly similar, this time, to that of the nightingales, because the soul of the dead bird was singing in her.

PART TWO

I

Now they were entirely happy, Luscignole and Alas Schlemp, she because she was so well able to sing like a nightingale, and he because she did it so well. He was in such haste to return to the tower every evening in order to hear his niece and his birds that he did not always give himself time to get furiously drunk; as he went up the staircase he only stumbled two or three times, so scantly was he drunk.

In truth, no enchantment was worth as much as that of hearing the child sing. She threaded the sounds, formed the trills, prolonged the plaintive notes, which alternately put the soul into joy and delectable melancholy. Although he was not sentimental by nature, Alas Schlemp could not help becoming fond of the little girl who caused him such pleasures, and eventually he came to love her, sometimes caressing the tresses of her brown hair, which resembled wings, just as he had loved the noble nightingale—dead, alas, and lying under the stone next to the Emperor.

He was not alone in listening to the little virtuoso; the bird-lovers rarely failed, on summer nights, after the tavern closed, to come to the Cathedral Square; and with a great deal of joy they experienced a great deal of surprise, for they knew that the beadle had lost the best of his singers, and did not know yet that he had been replaced by Luscignole.

It appeared to them, in sum, quite extraordinary, and even insulting to them, that that good-for-nothing, a beadle with a face horrible to behold and a repulsive drunk, had such birds, while they, professors, judges and rich bourgeois—men, in a word, of decent society—had to limit themselves to screeching finches and stammering warblers. Their former admiration had definitively mutated into envy, and that, as is

140

customary, did not take long to invent nasty suspicions and spread malicious gossip.

Some time thereafter a rumor ran around everywhere in the city that, in order to charm his wild captives to that degree, Alas Schlemp had recourse to reprehensible practices, perhaps to the practice of sorcery. No one went as far as to allege that the beadle had made a pact with some Belphegor specially charged with tempting bird-fanciers, but even people who did not believe in God or the Devil did not fail to recall, slyly the ancient legends in which domesticators of hawks, cormorants and storks sold their souls in return for precious secrets.

People who would have laughed at such rumors were the great ornithophiles of Amsterdam, Rotterdam or The Hague; they would have guessed quickly what means, perhaps reprehensible but not supernatural, Alas employed to render the voice of his nightingales clearer, more persistent and more magnificent. The petty local people did not have as much science, or as much perspicacity. On the faith of serious individuals, they did not hesitate to believe that the beadle lived in good intelligence with Hell.

Such superstitions, in spite of the incredulity of modern souls, were less implausible than they might seem in the city in question; in spite of the factories whose chimneys lacerated the air with acerbic whistle-blasts, and the bleak female workers in whom the complaining rancor of hunger and the anger of deprivation were brooding, it was still full of the illusions of the past. It had not forgotten the story of the Empress who kept under her dead tongue the inestimable pearl brought by the Serpent, nor that of the pool where the pearl disappeared, nor that of the basket full of marine sand that Satan had on his back and which, falling from the diabolical shoulder, finally discouraged because of the clever words of an old man, put a hill into the country.

An old city, in the provincialism of its antique reverie, is inclined to admit the strange, and even the impossible. Those envious of Alas Schlemp would not have taken long to attain their objective if, as is probable, their goal was to raise a scan-

141

dal that would attract the attention of the clergy of the cathedral to the beadle and finally free them of the nasty gnome and his nightingales.

He continued to go, scarcely sobered up by music and slumber, from the tower to the tavern and, dead drunk, from the tavern to the tower, unaware of the plots and the peril that was increasing every day.

Once, a soon-to-be-centenarian mendicant, who was obstinate, in spite of the rarity of visitors, in remaining outside the bronze portal cleft by a thrust of the Satanic claw, her head wobbling and a copper coin always ringing in the pewter goblet that served her as a begging-bowl, made a sign to Luscignole and whispered to her: "Truly, a little damsel as sage and pious as you, always buried in the church, ought not to stay with a man who is in society with the Devil."

"Eh? What man are you talking about, pray?" said Luscignole.

"Alas Schlemp, the beadle."

"It's my uncle, good woman, who is in society with the Devil?"

"No one doubts it in the city. What's astonishing is that in going up the staircase you've never seen the tip of his tail or scented an odor of scorching."

At first, the little girl roared with laughter, but the old woman went on: "It won't do you any good not to believe me. What's true is true. You can ask anyone whether it isn't certain that Alas Schlemp has consented to be taken to Hell within ten years, on condition that he obtained the secrets that make caged birds sing better than they sing in the woods. Anyway, you only have to watch him when he's alone with his nightingales! You'll see that he isn't with them as other people would be; for myself, I wouldn't be astonished if they aren't devils from Hell themselves disguised as birds."

Luscignole drew way pensively. It was true, though, that it was extraordinary that such admirable voices emerged from Alas Schlemp's cages. It was extraordinary, also, that she sang herself like the voices of profound forests. It might be that there was some magic in all that.

She was a little soul whom the chimeras of fear sometimes haunted, as they did the distances of the colonnades, the vicinity of the baptistery at dusk, and the tombstones. Having hidden in the sarcophagus of Augustus or behind the mortuary stones did not prevent her from dreading the possibility of a whiteness perhaps phantasmal, gliding between the sepulchers. Her mother had told her a hundred times over that the Devil had once lent large sums of money to a convent of discalced Carmelites who were not rich enough to finish building a cathedral; full of rancor, perhaps he did indeed return to the temple where, thanks to a very cunning monk, he only obtained in exchange for his good offices the heart of a she-wolf instead of the soul of a Christian.

Luscignole's uncle had very often frightened her with his drunken anger and the ferocious mobile wrinkles that sometimes shook all the skin of his face; she also knew that he had been surprised in the streets by night eating sewer rats raw. But now he frightened her even more, in another fashion; she imagined that a singular odor emerged from Alas Schlemp's hands and garments, of sulfur and soot.

Finally, one night, she had a dream in which the nightingale that she had laid to rest next to the Emperor under a corner of the slab appeared to her, a thin specter with vague wings.

He spoke, or, at least, he sang, saying troubling things in halting modulations—for dead birds stammer slightly: that Alas Schlemp was not good for nightingales, that he loved them, but that he loved them badly, and that she would do well, she who was so good, who had never had any malevolence for the captive singers, who was like their big sister, to...

He fell silent, and vanished.

She woke up sweating, her first upon her temples, and she thought for many days about the dream she had had...

II

After that she spied on the disquieting bird-lover.

More often than not, having closed the door of the aviary-room behind him, sitting on the low chair looking up at the cages, he did not turn round because of a noise so slight that he had mistaken it for the leap of a nightingale from one perch to another, or a rustle of plumage. But at other times, because of the fall of the latch or a clumsiness on the part of the child, bumping into some woodwork, he stood up furiously, as if someone had indeed been on the point of surprising him in some sin, and, throwing himself toward Luscignole, he threatened her with a raised fist, or even beat her, while the poor child was crying and weeping. The sole means she had of not being labored by blows until she was seriously wounded was to be a nightingale; immediately rapturous, he spared as a bird the person he might have killed as a little girl.

In any case, neither threats nor beatings turned her away from her plan. Whatever might happen she would follow the unfinished advice of the phantom nightingale.

What was it, then, that she hoped to discover? She did not know, exactly, so desirous was she, and so frightened too, of the possible discovery. Oh, what if it happened to her one morning, suddenly, as her head passed between the door and the wall, to perceive some hideous form, black or red, with a blue and green phosphorescence here and there—as images of Beelzebub or Lucifer represent them—horned on the forehead and cloven-footed, leaning toward Alas Schlemp as he was filling his feeling-troughs, giving him in a whisper, its lips hardly moving, the counsel of an infernal mixture appropriate to exasperate the singing soul of little creatures? Or what if, in the evening when he came back from the tavern, after drinking in the Schiedam the intrepidity to confront demonic presences, she saw him attentive to the information of a goblin or a kobold, which, with a flute devoid of music at its lips, was teaching the birds the trills by means of the mute precipitation of its fingers?

144

At these ideas, frissons ran through her from head to toe; almost a bird, she seemed to sense all over her the bristling of fearful plumage.

But no, she did not surprise anything veritably abnormal in the attitude of the bird-lover, or in his fashions of acting. He got abominably drunk, as he had always done, and treated her rather brutally, only becoming tender, with rapturous ecstasies in his atrocious pink eyes, if, in order to give him joy, she became a nightingale with the nightingales.

It truly had not been worth the trouble of drilling a hole in the door large enough to peep through, since, even unperceived, she had not discovered anything.

She came to think that the centenarian mendicant had been mad for a long time, that she did not know what she was talking about, and that little birds sleeping beside emperors do not, in fact, rise from their tombs in order to give advice to little girls who whistle and twitter as they did when they were alive.

But Alas Schlemp, when all was said and done, seemed strange to her.

It was toward the beginning of April. Then, in the gray atmosphere of the city, which mingled the mists of its sky with the vapor of its factories, there were furtive glimmers of sunlight. Breezes with an odor of distant woods traversed the air, putting slight gaieties even into the sad tresses of the workers under the straw hats that seemed less frayed; and from the almost green shoots of bindweed rising to the windows of the tower, little budding points surged, the timid promises of flowers. A swallow started weaving in the mouth of a gargoyle; it was after the first cry of that small creature that the changes that arrived in the behavior of Alas Schlemp became truly evident.

Far from sleeping late in the morning, as was his inveterate habit, he got up early. From the next room, through the thickness of the wall, Luscignole heard the sound of clogs on the bare tiles. She got up in her turn, very quickly, and went to put her eye to the crack of the door. She saw singular things, not frightening in themselves, but frightening because of the fear she had in seeing them as such. The bird-lover was bending iron wires, rounding them into a semicircle, and connecting them two by two by linking the four ends with other wires, densely packed. Or, near the window, with a cord knotted to the catch, he was passing silk threads sliding from a shuttle back and forth and winding them around a short ivory stick, which was extended when he made a movement of his little finger; and mesh formed, becoming a net.

At the same time, Luscignole saw on the table round tubes of tin-plate, sheaths of some sort; they were only about fifteen or twenty centimeters long.

What was the purpose of all those devices? With the aid of reminiscences, she had a presentiment of the employment for which they were destined, but she could not take full account of many things.

Then, two or three times, she noticed that he was shaking large earthenware pots in which he kept mealworms, which he picked up with handfuls of bran, and inspected attentively. "Good, good!" he said, because a big black fly crawled along his thumb. Luscignole knew the metamorphoses to which mealworms were subject; the fly did not astonish her. But why had Alas Schlemp said "Good, good"? She fled quickly, because her uncle was heading toward the door.

The next morning, she had a greater surprise. With her eye to the hole in the wood, she did not see the bird-lover. She ran to the next room, where he slept; that room was empty too, with the bed unmade. Alas Schlemp was not in the tower, and he was not in the cathedral, where the child searched for him for an hour. Such an infraction of the beadle's habits was absolutely extraordinary.

But what was even stranger was his appearance when he returned.

At about midday, Luscignole, who was keeping watch in a corner of the great bronze portal, saw Alas Schlemp arrive at a run, without a hat, with twigs in his hair, grass in his beard, his pockets swollen with she knew not what, and his coat inflated over his chest to the right and the left, as if by stolen goods. And, although that hour he could not be drunk yet, like a man who has just carried out some evil coup, his face was distraught and very pale, like that of a wounded murderer who has lost blood in his criminal struggle.

Rapidly, he entered through the narrow postern of the tower, went up the spiral stone steps three by three—so quickly that he bumped his head on the walls repeatedly—opened the door and closed it again brutally.

Then, there was the sound of a key turning.

When Luscignole arrived on the landing she found the door shut; and, singularly, when she tried to look through the hole, she saw nothing but darkness. By chance or precaution, something opaque, a sheet of cloth or a coat, was intercepting the light. All that Luscignole could perceive were comings and goings in the room, the displacement of cages, and the very small sounds of pouring water and the frightened cry of a bird that has hurt itself, or which someone is hurting.

She returned to the cathedral, weary of futile spying.

What had happened, then? What had her uncle done that morning, away from home? What was he doing now in the aviary-room? She decided to be patient. In a few hours, she would know everything. After dinner, Alas Schlemp would go to the tavern, as was his habit; she would go into the room, of which he never took away the key.

A disappointed expectation. When the meal was over— the twilight of the April evening was giving a melancholy tint to the stained glass—the beadle did not quit the tower. His lips quickly wiped, he returned to the aviary and shut himself in again, and Luscignole, who had followed him, had her head bumped by the closure of the door.

What? She was not to know anything? Whatever was happening, she would not ever know it, in spite of the duty to which the phantom nightingale had counseled her?

Instinctively, she lowered her eye to the hole in the door. She saw a little vesperal light. Doubtless the cloth, or the coat hanging from some nail, or from the key, had fallen off in the shock of the closing door. Luscignole could see! She looked fixedly and ardently, her eye obstinate. She had so much desire to know that she was no longer afraid; it was necessary that she learn the truth, no matter how horrible that truth might be.

In the somber twilight she saw Alas Schlemp go from one wall to the other, stopping by the table with the curt gestures of someone arranging objects.

Oh my God! What if the night became entirely dark before the accomplishment of the event?

But there was the sound of a striking match; Alas Schlemp, with his back to the door, had the light round him, a kind of aureole enveloping him entirely. Doubtless he had lit a lamp placed on the table.

No; when he turned round slightly, the match extinct, he only had shadow over his face; it was only a few moments later that a glimmer—a singular glimmer, certainly not that of a lamp—licked his face, his neck, his shirt and his hands with a pink flicker.

Luscignole could not be mistaken about that: charcoal was beginning to burn in the furnace on which she, as a little housekeeper, warmed irons to pass over the linen. Why had Alas Schlemp lit that fire? In the flame that it dispersed, she distinguished on the table three or four of the tin-plate sheaths that she had noticed before; then—unexpected utensils perhaps of some frightful task—there were long pipe-stems with a bowl for tobacco; and, not far away, very similar to knitting-needles, very slender, pointed shiny lances. The more widespread redness of the heater tinted things cruelly, including Alas Schlemp's face, which was leaning forward, sinister.

Because of a movement on the part of the beadle—more reminiscent of a demon than a man at that moment—Luscignole's gut was squeezed by a twinge of anguish.

After having stretched out one of his hands, Alas took one of the slender lances delicately between two fingers, and, holding one end, he put the other end into the burning charcoal.

Oh! Why was he doing that?

She trembled, and stopped herself trembling, fearing that her presence might be revealed by a knee bumping into the wood of the door.

He was no longer moving.

Two or three times, however, he lifted the lance, the point of which was already pink, put it back into the flamboyant embers, and waited.

He took it out again; the tip was no longer pink but blanched. Then, holding the little lance reminiscent of a knitting needle between the thumb and index finger of his tight hand, he picked up one of the long slender tubes, resembling a pipe-stem without a bowl, and, thus armed—armed, yes, but against whom?—he used the nail of his ring finger to slide off the lid, in which little holes were visible, of one of the tinplate sheaths.

What appeared was the little brown bristling head, with round eyes, of a nightingale.

Luscignole thought fearfully, that she was about to lose her mind. What was that bird—one of the dear birds whose sister she was—doing there? What was about to be done to it? She foresaw, she divined, that something terrible was about to happen. She wanted to cry out, but dared not, still watching, bewildered.

Tightly held in one of those round tubes into which one puts wild birds recently captured in order that, immobilized, they cannot break their pinions or fray their down, the nightingale remained motionless, its head caught between the tight uplift of its wings. Only its eyes were alive: haggard, profound, wild, nostalgic eyes that no longer saw the vast mysterious forest.

By those eyes, Luscignole was astonished. The eyes of the singers in cages, she remembered, did not seem to be made of such somber lightning; they would have seemed dead eyes by comparison with these. Oh, how the grandiose plaint of the exile lived in these, and the refusal of servitude, and the defiance of the night of prisons!

149

Meanwhile, Alas Schlemp...

"No! No!" she screamed.

But her scream—a gasp, rather—died in her constricted throat.

Alas Schlemp had not heard anything. His face all bloodied now by the scarlet charcoal, he continued his work.

To one of the eyes of the nightingale he applied, very precisely, without the slightest deviation, the white tube. With the scrupulous circumspection of a mother who, in order to part the lace of a new-born's cradle in order to kiss him without waking him up, he had blown away the smoke of the furnace here and there, and now, so adroitly, with a hand that was simultaneously light and sure, he insinuated the white-hot needle into it, toward the eye.

She howled, Luscignole!

Perhaps she only thought she could hear herself howl, or perhaps, entirely focused on his frightful duty, the gnome-executioner could no longer hear anything. He finished it; he finished the task while, terrified, and also menacing, her fingernails plunged into the door like the talons of a bird into the bark of a tree, she was still gazing, in a vertigo of horror.

The point reached the eye; for there was, with a slight sizzling sound that she doubtless imagined, a stiffening of all the feathers on the proud martyrized head, and a quiver of the entire tightly-gripped body, so violent that it made the heavy tin-plate sheath roll twice.

Then, the tube and the needle having been removed, Luscignole saw a little round eye, in which there was no longer the nostalgia of profound forests, which was null, which was dead, poor little eye where an infinite starry reverie was reflected.

Placidly, Alas Schlemp had replaced the needle to heat up, because, in order to dry the other eye, it was no longer sufficiently hot. Two or three times he withdrew it from the embers in order to see whether it was pink, in order to see whether it was white; he waited, patiently.

The child, behind the door, went mad. Once, while playing in the apse, she had heard a deacon say, speaking to an archpriest, that the cathedral was under threat from the bad people of the city; that the unfortunate factory workers of both sexes, weary of what they dared to claim was the deafness of God, the avarice of the rich and the cruelty of employers, had often premeditated setting fire to the church, an ancient symbol of servitudes still continued. The deacon's words, scarcely understood, forgotten, she suddenly remembered. And she admitted, forgetting the games of hide-and-seek with the cherubim and the five-fingered racket of the Holy Virgin that blessed and played, almost approving of the little mice for having wanted to gnaw the bones of the reliquary, she admitted—she regretted having made a repair to Our Lady's chemise—that one could set fire to a old building where such abominations occurred. She would have set fire to it herself had she been able to do so.

At the same time, she understood why people hated the beadle, why the centenarian at the portal had reproached her for living with someone who kept society with the Devil. Well, the Devil had nothing to do with it. But Alas Schlemp was far worse than he would have been if he had sold his soul for some secret of bird-handling. The truth was that the monster did not limit himself to imprisoning the nightingales, something already cruel; scarcely had he captured them than he blinded them, in order to isolate them more from everything, in order that, no light awakening in them the unquiet reminiscence of the dear natal forests, green gold or moonlit, they would sing more assiduously, more perfectly.

She also understood why the bird buried next to the Emperor had appeared to her. He had come to lament, the poor winged revenant, the torture to which he had been subjected while alive, to which others, his peers, would be subjected, and to ask her, a little girl who was not wicked, to defend and save the wretched and dear captives, to spare them the eternal night beneath burned eyelids.

And thinking about that, it seemed to her, almost a little bird, that the frightful torture would be inflicted on her one day, that she would have a red dot in her irises, and that she would no longer be able to see.

What could she do, though? How could she oppose the sins of Alas Schlemp?

While she hesitated, also in torment, the torturer, very adroitly, insinuated the white-hot needle into the tube, toward the nightingale's other eye.

This time, she uttered a cry of horror and rage that was repeated by all the silence of the cathedral; and, running down the staircases, pushing doors, raising her arms in the open air, she fled.

III

She ran through the streets rendered nocturnal by silence, silenced by the night. She did not know where she was going, or where she could go. She continued fleeing.

For an instant, the idea of taking refuge in the cathedral, of requesting shelter from the profound crypts, and protection from the holy images of angels that had been sheer little friends for such a long time; of demanding pity for the nightingales from what remained of celestial mercy in the tunic that she had repaired and under which the heat of Madame Mary had beaten. And perhaps, beside the heavy sheet of granite weighing over the bones of the Emperor, the bird-revenant would have risen up, clad in a tiny white shroud holed by the bone of a wing, and would have told her what it was appropriate to do.

But she was afraid of everything that was close to Alas Schlemp.

Wherever she hid in the church she would have rediscovered the face reddened by the crackling furnace and the point of the needle reddening or whitening outside the long pale tube, and in spite of the darkness of the sacred cellars and the motionless aid of the mages, she would be unable to avoid the frightful approach and the hand on her shoulder of the burner of eyes.

She was still fleeing. No passers-by. Extinct windows, as dead as the eyes of blinded birds. For greater sadness, there were stars, here and there, in the blue-black. Why were those stars still shining, when the eyes that mirrored them were closed forever? And then, truly, what were the people asleep behind those placid walls thinking in their dreams? Should they not have got up, gone out, armed themselves and run to the tower, and punished with insults and blows the execrable executioner of frail singers? Oh, my God, the poor little things, they were blind, all of them, all, alas; some only recently, others for such a long time.

Luscignole finally knew those things. She remembered the strange eyes, so dull, so fixed, in the depths of the cages, and, maddened, she reproached herself. She had profited herself from the crimes of Alas Schlemp. It was because he was horrible that she had had so much joy in hearing the nocturnal birds; and since, on hearing them sing so well, the idea had come to her of singing like them, she even owed to those abominable practices the nightingale voice of which she was so proud.

She was still running, her arms thrown backwards, with an instinct to repel pursuits; her undone hair, which was followed, pale gold mingled with pale gold, by the radiance of the stars, made a blonde wake in the nocturnal streets. It was like the tail of a tiny comet traveling very rapidly and very far.

Luscignole traversed the mute obscure city, traversed the bleak outlying districts and, seeing beyond them the red blaze of nocturnal factories and forges, she had the thought, magnifying things by means of fear, of a hundred Alas Schlemp, enormous before enormous furnaces, heating iron bars in prodigious forges in order to burn the eyes of giant nightingales. Her panic redoubled, she launched herself more rapidly into the distance, into the unknown, toward the blackness brighter with stars. For there are more stars over the plains than over the cities: the modesty of stars that do not want to be seen.

Out of breath, sometimes staggering, she ran and ran. She climbed a hill—it was the slope of the hill fallen from the Devil's basket—thought that she could not go any higher, climbed further, and, having hastened so much that she no longer knew whether it was her hands or her feet with which she was touching the ground, let herself roll down the other side. Finally, dying but ready to revive to flee again if the menace of Alas Schlemp and his needles appeared, she found herself sitting on the edge of a wood, where the moonlight allowed her to see that there were violets in the thickness of the grass.

Then, alone, having quit everything, orphaned of everything, what did she do, poor fugitive child?

She sang.

Yes, as the wildest nightingales, on the very day when they are caught, sometimes modulate their most beautiful odes in their first despair, still neighboring hop—soon they will fall silent, and will only sing again when finally vanquished and blind—she sang, the bird-girl. And her song was a nightingale song so melancholy and so delectable that all the nightingales of the woods, here, there, elsewhere and everywhere, awoke under the branches and leaving the surveillance of the nest to the silent female, and ecstasized the immense night with their melodious plaint, to which a poet without shelter passing along the road on the far side of the hill might have listened, and retained it in his heart and his soul, in order to make the melody and the rhythm of some noble elegy.

Exhausted by aguish, and also by joy, she fell silent when they fell silent—there was a pink line at the point where dawn was nascent—and she went to sleep in the heather that made her a kind of great nest.

When she awoke, the wood was charming...but she recognized it. She remembered having come, when very young, with her mother, to this tiny forest, where the people of the city had picnics on Sundays; for Luscignole's mother sometimes tried to sell flowers in order to earn the few liards that she did not earn selling candles And in spite of the pink of the dawn at the tips of the quivering plants, in spite of the whiteness left on the grass at the edge of the forest by the round-dances of the fays, in spite of the twittering of the hedge-sparrows and the light gliding buzz of dragonflies, in spite of all the fresh clarity that turned the unstable undersides of the branches green and stirred there, Luscignole wept, because she was so close to the city.

She had thought she was liberated forever from the evil Alas Schlemp; alas, her poor little legs had covered too little ground in an entire night of escape. What could she attempt now? Which way should she go? The horror of roads where one begs appeared to her, immeasurable. And if she tried to continue fleeing, she would be found. People would say that, mischievously, she had gone all alone to walk in the woods, and everything would finish thus, and she would be taken back to the tower where birds were blinded. What made her even sadder was that, at present, in the daylight, the nightingales were no longer singing.

In the distance of the road there was a sound of little bells, pretty, amusing and multiple, as if Oberon were coming from that direction.

It was not a dwarf, capricious and jingling, that appeared, but a horse with bells on its harness—a very old piebald horse, paltry, coughing, limping, wheezing and gasping, but cheerful in spite of everything—making something like the sound of a Chinese hat in the glad puerility of the early morning.

Behind the horse, at the bend in the road, a vehicle appeared—a cart or a carriage, it makes no difference, four planks underneath, four to the right and fur to the left, between the rotation of the wheels, beneath the roundness, embodied by rushes or a tent arched like a tunnel, from which emerged, with oaths and laughter, and all the noise of a wandering household, an advancement of alert infantile heads.

Luscignole was astounded.

She was astonished, above all, by one of the infantile heads, a floury muzzle surmounted by a wig, from which a point of pale flax emerged, grotesquely.

"Clown," cried a coarse voice in the early-morning cough of inveterate drunkards, "tell Polyphemus to stop."

The clown was the little infantile face bewigged with flax. Polyphemus was the horse. They chatted to one another; the young boy, perhaps a dwarf, climbed on to the nag and spoke into its ear. The nag approved with a nod of the head. And the vehicle stopped moving.

An exceedingly obese man clad in a crimson robe, on which golden storks deployed their wings, got down, the toe of his shoe not lingering on the footstep, and leapt rapidly on to the road. He was followed by a very old damsel, not pretty, with make-up crumbling over her cheekbones, who was thin, emaciated, slightly green and sizzling with crimpled gauze, reminiscent of a centenarian dragonfly; a very tall, very spare, similarly emaciated clown resembling an immeasurable water-snake, so shiny was his clinging part-yellow and part-blue coat; three wolves, perhaps dogs, but wild; and an enormous polar bear, its head nodding.

The bear, however, removed his head and showed the ruddy young face of a cheerful gamin, saying: "What's good about this bear costume is that it stays warm in the chilly hours of the morning."

Then three little girls clad in spangles tumbled down.

As for the first clown, he continued chatting to Polyphemus—but he was obliged to hold on him, sometimes by the right ear, sometimes by the left ear, because he had set himself definitively astride the animal's neck.

The man clad in crimson and storks, who was the chief, grumbled: "Rotten   night! There's no worse sleeper than Cunegonde. She isn't content unless she sticks her legs out of the caravan."

The name Cunegonde was that of the centenarian drag-onfly; she replied peevishly: "No means of stretching! Japhet was wedged against me."

"No?" said Japhet, the polar bear with the human head. "I ought to have let myself be stifled by the human serpent, who repeats his exercises in his dreams?"

The human serpent, the tall thin clown glinting like a snake, objected: "It's the fault of the dogs, truly. while dreaming, they were biting my calves."

"You're bragging!" said the old dragonfly.

In the end, it was recognized generally that the dogs had been the sole cause of the bad night; they did not protest, letting people say what they wished, barely growling

Meanwhile, the obese man said: "The most urgent thing is breakfast."

"Yes."

Who had said yes? Everybody, except for the clown, child or dwarf; he interrupted his chatter into the left ear of Polyphemus.

"Good! Breakfast, with what?"

"There are the provisions!" cried the dragonfly, alarmed.

"There were. We ate them last night: me, the kids and the dogs."

There was an explosion of anger. But the dwarf was exaggerating. Under the tent they found half a loaf of coarse brown bread, a few bones from an old stew and even a basket of mulberries bought from a little beggar in yesterday's village for the sake of charity.

A few minutes later, all those people, a company of performers traveling to a nearby fair, sat down in the grass by the edge of the wood and ate, greedily and cheerfully, without desiring a better meal. The dogs that resembled wolves, sitting in the violets, awaited the remains, while Polyphemus, the cart behind him lighter, browsed the grass, along with little flowers and the trail left behind by the dancing fays.

Luscignole, half-hidden behind the trunk of a larch, watched those strange individuals, frightened by them, but only a little, and then looked at them again, with a surprise in which there was always less alarm. She realized that they were traveling players eating their meal on the grass after a night jolting in the cart, and knew that they were not wicked, since they were laughing together. Perhaps those vagabonds would not be scorned by serious people, and would not put out the eyes of poor birds.

What inspired confidence in them most of all was the presence of the little girls clad in spangles, whom she thought very beautiful; and the wolves did not seem vicious. She was more and more emboldened; finally, she approached them

"Good day," she said, with a pretty curtsey.

"Hey, where has the kid come from?" asked the minimal clown, with an astonishment in which there was benevolence. A dwarf, he thought he was a giant, and was gladly protective, with indulgence.

She had courage, especially because the dogs had not growled, considering her without anger. "I came out of the wood," she replied.

"And where were you before?"

"In the cathedral," she said.

To have come from a wood and a cathedral must have been a sufficient explanation for those individuals accustomed to all shelters; they did not ask any more. Only Japhet, the ruddy-faced youth who was displaying his head outside the bearskin interrogated further: "And what do you want, child?"

"I would like to go with you," she said, "to act in the comedy."

"Well," said the man clad in crimson and golden storks, the leader of the company, "that's difficult. Firstly, the troupe is complete. It's certain that the human serpent, who is very thin, will die in two or three months unless he fattens up by drinking, but in the meantime, there's no employment to take. Anyway, you're too small and not supple enough to imitate boa constrictors sliding through the bars of chairs."

"And then," said the dragonfly, who was cantankerous because she was old, "one doesn't pick up children on the road like that. The girl might be a thief."

"There are no thieves," said the clown. "Rich people pretend that people steal their money in order to dispense with giving it to those who never had any. Look, two men enter a tribunal. The millionaire says: 'This ragamuffin stole my watch,' The ragamuffin is convicted. All right—but wrong."

"Yes," said Japhet.

"Why?" asked Cunegonde.

"Because, if millionaires have watches, it's because they stole them from the ragamuffins six thousand years ago."

"Where?"

"In the earthly paradise."

"Stupid," said the dragonfly. "Anyway, people can't take children with them without knowing who they are—afterwards, we'd be accused of stealing the children..."

"If people steal them," said the clown, "it's the fault of those who leave them on the road."

"...And without knowing," she continued, "what they can do."

"That's true," said the chief. "What can you do, kid?"

"Me?" said Luscignole.

"Yes, you."

"I don't know," she said.

"What? You don't know what you can do?"

"No."

"And you want to come with us?"

"Yes."

"Let's see. Can you even dance on a tightrope?"

"No."

"Can you jump from one trapeze to another?"

"No."

"Can you ride a horse bareback?"

"No."

"Can you eat fire, swallow swords or throw daggers into a wooden board around a lady holding out her arms?"

"Oh! No, no."

"Well then, what is it you want us to make of you?"

"You're right," said Luscignole, turning away.

"Good!" said the dragonfly. "Let her go! Let her go back home to her parents, if she has any. There are quite enough

159

mouths to nourish in the troupe without taking charge of all the vagabonds we encounter. Besides which, this one isn't pretty."

"Because she's too young," said the clown, laughing. "At fifteen she'll be fine."

Luscignole drew away; they finished their meal. Then they lay down in the now-flattened grass on the edge of the wood, drowsily. That idleness in the early morning air, among real trees, under the real sky, seemed pleasant to them, habituated to Argand lamps, sweat, and smoky parades. They filled themselves with healthy life.

Somnolence, aggravated by digestion, plunged them into the thickness of the grass, lying next to one another. Satisfied, the spangle-clad girls slept with their heads on the les hollow bellies of the dogs.

But then:

"Sapristi!" said Japhet.

"What?" said the crimson man, with a start.

And the others also shook themselves.

"Nothing, nothing," said Japhet. "But it's extraordinary, all the same. Nightingales don't usually sing after daybreak, and I never heard a nightingale sing like that one...listen! Listen!"

They listened, even the least awake and those most weighed down by fatigue. For under the branches, doubtless nearby, perhaps far away, there was the most admirable birdsong that the echo of the solitudes can hear. The precursor whistle astonished the silence and the trills spilled forth hectically, and the gasp of the supreme sobs finished in a furious explosion that died away.

"He certainly sings well, that bird," said Cunegonde, charmed herself.

Luscignole emerged from between the trees. She approached, and said: "The bird is me."

"You're hired!" said the man in the robe decorated with storks.

And they took her with them. The clown, child or dwarf, said in the left ear of Polyphemus: "Gee up, gee up! With a virtuoso like that, you'll be eating nice fresh Lucerne from solid silver mangers!"

IV

I do not believe that there is any town in the world more ancient than the one in which, because of the fair held there every year for two weeks in April the troupe of traveling players arrived with Luscignole.

Scattered over the ruddy vine-clad hill between two crumbled ruins, one of which had been an altar of Bacchus and the other a temple of Minerva—because drunkenness is the backside from which wisdom depends—it tumbles down in old houses with cracks everywhere, in the stumps of collapsed towers, toward the great peaceful river of monotonous waters. For a distance, one might think it a large flock of black rams, horned and hairy, suddenly petrified in mid-fall. It is not very vast, but still too large, so sparse are the inhabitants, and if they sometimes venture outside their homes—they rarely go out perhaps fearing that a chimney might fall on them, or an entire facade that can no longer hold together, as soon as they cross the threshold—they make as little noise as possible with their footfalls, gliding through the eternal dusk of buildings on the brink of falling on top of one another, with the air of specters passing through a phantom city.

Everything is silent in the town. The barking of a dog, or the cry of a child behind the vacuity of windows, are almost forgotten sounds. Only the wind circulates, plaintive and obscure, between the prolongation of houses. And the hours are not chimed there; except for the Post Office, where, at the back of the ground floor room, a pendulum tick-tocks in a tall black case, there is no clock in the entire empty silence. But at night—not a single window illuminated!—people here and there hear, but do not see, rare travelers, who might be ancient night-watchmen dead for many years whose ghosts are mak-

ing their customary round belatedly, crying the hours in a ancient language made of strange croaks, which no one under-
stands any longer.

In any case, there is no need of darkness for the town to
be somber; even in the bright days of summer it is isolated
obscurely beneath the immemorial melancholy of motionless
clouds.

Then abruptly—as if the black flock of rams petrified on
the hill were waking up and gamboling—it starts, becomes
animated, launches forth and amuses itself, chiming the hour
on a hundred clocks, bell towers full of clanging bells, taverns
and theaters, vivified by footfalls, laughter and songs; and in
the evening, fireworks light up between the ruins of the altar
of Bacchus and those of the temple of Minerva, beneath the
frightened dispersion of the ancient clouds. The monotonous
river, languidly astonished, carries away crazy words and lively music and the hops and skips of dances, in a gliding elegy
to the waters in which Lorelei sang.

That awakening is the annual fair: a fair celebrated
throughout the world because of one peculiarity that is envied
by those of Leipzig, Dresden, Nizhny Novgorod, Srinagar and
Neuilly, famous as they are.

It is to the fair in question that all the animal tamers in
the world come to make a provision of ferocious beasts. The
likes of Bidel do not capture lions themselves in pitfall taps in
the Saharan sands; the likes of Pezon would jib if the obliga-
tion were imposed on them to trap tigers in nets in dense jungles.[9] Even the beautiful and brave charmer of wild beasts

---

[9] François Bidel and Jean-Baptiste Pezon were animal tamers
who became famous when such acts were very much in vogue
in France during the 1880s. The unnamed female lion-tamer
that the author cites is fictitious, but might be one that he had
featured in two previous stories, "L'Homme à la voiture verte"
(1863; tr. in *The Exigent Shadow and Other Strange Obsessions* as "The Man in the Green Caravan") and "L'Ours blanc"

whose breasts were lacerated by a sweep of the claw of a jealous panther would have recoiled before the necessity of going
herself into distant solitudes in search of cheetahs and ounces
that are trained to leap through blazing hoops. Thus, there is a
market of wild beasts, and it is in the sparse town on a ruddy,
vine-clad hill that it is held.

No one knows the reason why, for such transactions, that
place was chosen rather than another. It does not offer any of
the conveniences that the advent of beasts rather rebellious to
transport would seem to require. No railway line ends here; no
diligences arrive that are finally irreparable after so many ac-
cidents. No matter; it is here to which, from the luminous pro-
fundities of India, the black undergrowth of the Congo, the dry
sands of Egypt and the marshes of Florida where triple-
tongued coral snakes go to demand venom from the poisonous
hearts of orchids, all the monsters, all the biting, tearing, killing animals, flood on long, flat barges similar to rafts, along
with the sliding tangle of reptiles whose idleness still remem-
bers being coiled around bamboos broken beneath their
smooth weight.

So, arriving in that town, the beasts are new. A prodigious thing: dealers in wild beasts—heroic merchants!—bring
lions here that were still drinking from the crushed teats of
camels a month earlier; tigers that have spent so little time
enclosed behind odious bars that they still have the illusion of
being able to rush them between their beautiful teeth free of
caries. And those animals, eaters of raw meat, which only
know of humans, very rarely, the taste of their flesh, and also
monkeys—for there are monkeys frolicking amid the ferocity—similar by virtue of the candor of their instinct to the innocent companions who follow the army of Rama, and parrots
so ingenuous that no vanity troubles them as yet in imitating
human language, bring the town to life, the night-watchmen

---

in *Pour les belles personnes* (1886); in both cases she is
named Cunegonde.

falling silent, with all the howls and all the chatter by which the mysterious solitudes were once amused.

The fair is not only terrible, however, with so many savage gratings at grilles and fuming mouths from which long pink tongues protrude. The hunger of jungles, the thirst of sands and the rage of violated deserts are sold by auction there, along with the beautiful white teeth and the yawns and the hectic manes and the bloodshot eyes of sovereign beasts, now merchandise, but traveling performers, taking advantage of a celebrated occasion, also come to amuse the people flooding from all the neighboring regions.

The April when the wandering company that brought Luscignole went there, the fair had a particular splendor; the amusements that it offered were remembered for a long time in the vicinity. There were circuses with vast tents stirred by the wind. There were heavy horses saddled with satin platforms braided with silver and gold, circling beneath flights of starry muslin in which the pink of a leotard stood out. There was a giant so enormous that, hung from a stake, his trousers, with immeasurable legs, prolonged their double shadow from the other side of the street to the highest story of a very tall house, and a dwarf so small that his little habitation of painted wood, with twenty tricolor windows—sometimes he stuck his head out of one of the window sometime the skylight in the roof—would not have sufficed to shelter a nest of little squirrels.

Trombones sounded the glory of a female colossus, whose prodigious calves, in pink cotton stockings, were made to vibrate by an electric floor. Monkeys and dogs performed a pantomime in which a marmoset, a refractory conscript condemned to death, fell before a firing squad, retaining in one of its hind paws, tremulously, a half-eaten sugar-lump. Conjurors with fingers so quick that the eye was alarmed by them caused little balls to circulate from one cup to another and disappear as if beneath the invisible paw of a cat. A ballerina, gliding over an iron wire, tickled with the toe of a pink shoe the dangling black tongue of a macaw perched on the cord of a trapeze, under the braying of a brass band.

Negroes ate raw rabbits, almas raised and lowered their bellies impudently, wrestlers threw yellow gauntlets with red leather backs at apprentice butchers in blue blouses, and the enraged music of three balls danced between the tents, inflated by the warmth of odors and breath, and rifle shots sounded curtly, and swings moved furiously or were abandoned, wearily, in dying curves, while, as soon as dusk fell, amid an atmosphere reeking of Argand lamps and the air splashed by rockets, hyenas laughed, jackals yapped, panthers mewled and lions roared, rearing up with their claws on the bars.

As soon as the stall was pitched—four stakes stuck in the ground and connected by gray canvas—in which the glorious company appeared of the chief clad in storks, the old dancing dragonfly, the human serpent, Japhet, the bear who admitted to being a man and the clown, child or dwarf, a peerless acrobat, along with the three little spangle-clad girls astride the three wolves, the other fairground performers observed a singular drop in their receipts. Even the masters of menageries who had come to buy an orangutan, an elephant or a royal tiger drew away from the auctions in order to go to the little stall, which was incessantly full, all day and all night; and that was because of Luscignole, for never had such a perfect whistler been heard.

Undoubtedly, undoubtedly, come from distant lands, from America or Spain, in theaters, in concert halls, some accompanying themselves on the xylophone, others accompanying the birdsong with the adroit cooing of flutes, damsels in white robes had been heard, who, inflating a cheek with a finger over a nostril, proffered sounds almost similar to birdsong. But people quickly recognized, even with eyes closed, that they were only mediocre imitators; in addition, without mentioning their trickery in underlining their voice with a xylophone or a flute, it did not take long to learn that they were making use, hypocritically, of small gold or silver whistles hidden between the teeth and the lip, or an apricot kernel honed against a whetstone and pierced all the way through.

But Luscignole really was a nightingale. Even the most degraded souls were sometimes filled with melancholy, sometimes with serenity, on hearing her whistle so naturally, so miraculously. One was tempted to believe that she had a bird beneath the edge of her dress, near the throat. No one could know that she carried within her the soul of the nightingale asleep in the cathedral beside the Emperor.

Her success was such that the director of a spectacle that barely belonged to the fairground, where the benches and chairs had elegance and comfort akin to a city theater, offered large sums to have Luscignole in his troupe.

"Five thousand florins!"

"A pittance!" said the chief clad in crimson and golden storks.

"Six thousand!"

"Pooh!"

"Seven thousand!"

"Bah!"

"Eight thousand!"

"Fie!"

"What do you want, then?"

"To keep Luscignole."

Nevertheless, as life was no longer tenable in the stall or in the cart because of the rages of the dragonfly, the disdainful dancer, who could not tolerate the triumphs of the whistler; and as the bear Japhet, the clown and the human serpent, artistes humiliated by the dazzling success of a comrade, and even the three little girls and the wolf-dog, growling with jealousy, we looking at the girl with nasty expressions, the chief of the troupe ended up showing himself less intractable, and consented to surrender his star attraction for ten thousand florins, an appreciable sum. Luscignole was informed that, after the fair, she would leave with the director of the great theater.

Leave? The idea caused her chagrin at first, because she had acquired the habit, in the early morning, when she was not whistling, of going to the cages of the wild beasts.

That was singular; she, so dainty and so frail, was interested in the enormous monsters; she had an amity with them, like a fraternity of savagery, she singing and they roaring. And when there was no one in the menagerie-bazaars, she sang, as a kindness, for the ferocious beasts, which lay down then, their heads on their paws, and did not howl any longer, and gazed at her for a long time, with the profound reverie of the desert and the night in their eyes.

But she thought that it would be necessary anyway, when the fair finished, for her to be separated from the wild beasts, which would be sold and dispersed, and she did not see any inconvenience in going with another master. On the contrary, she came to rejoice in that change, thanks to which she would go further away, even further from Alas Schlemp. She would be content, provided that she was not forbidden to sing and that she always drew further away from the horrible man who burned the eyes of birds.

And soon she knew glory: true glory.

After having charmed the humble people, peasants or bourgeois, from village to village and town to town, she conquered the great mercantile cities and capitals where there are gentlemen and princes. For, certain of success, the director of the vagabond spectacle now dared to confront true connoisseurs. The relative luxury of the theater-stall had become sumptuousness.

A famous painter depicted on canvases with golden fames adventures in which, around the nightingale Luscignole, a hundred humiliated nightingales were seen falling, vanquished, from the branches, or in which ambassadors red, green and yellow plumage, some similar to pompous macaws and others to rutilant birds of paradise, prostrated themselves before the little girl, for they had come to ask for her hand on behalf of the king of the land of birds, the august Lyre-Bird, whose portrait was carried by four blackbirds, beaks in the air.

In the morning, gaudily clad valets went on horseback along the boulevards and the streets sounding trumpets, who announced the imminent performance and proclaimed the glory of Luscignole. And in the evening, in order to enter the theater, the public—not the mob of mediocre people, but the sumptuous affluence of great lords and haughty ladies—thronged the Oriental carpets between crimson velvet drapes.

The auditorium, especially, was resplendent with satin, gold and furious spangles, triumphant rivals of precious stones. Beneath a ceiling, which was a silken sky starry with adamantine scintillations, the chairs of the boxes, the armchairs and eve the stalls for the floor or the paradis had covers of rare fabrics. The chandeliers of imperial theaters, whether in Vienna or in Saint Petersburg, are not resplendent with more magnificent opulence; in brief, the hall was worthy of the people who came to be seated there.

But for what spectacle? None, except that of Luscignole, who advanced alone as soon as the curtain was raised, in a décor of branches; and as soon as she was seen, people were astonished, delectably.

Very slender, although she wore the garish costume of a traveling player, her resemblance to the birds struck the most distracted eyes. Her brown tresses were the wings of a nightingale; that little protruding mouth, less pink, would have been a nightingale's beak. There was even a commencement of flight in every step the child took.

Then she began to sing; there was universal enthusiasm.

Since she had quit the tower of the cathedral she had made further great progress. She no longer limited herself to the ordinary twitter of nightingales perched, with one foot in their plumage and ruffled with effort, in the profoundest mystery of the trees. No, she began by scarcely chirping, like a tiny bird hatched an hour before in the nest, almost inaudible, faint murmurs in which the promises of the glorious future hymn were barely revealed. One might have thought it a vague rustle of two smooth young leaves rather than the voice of a bird.

Soon, however, the song was affirmed; it imitated that of a young nightingale already hoping from branch to branch, but who is not yet in love, for whom the nest is still the cradle. Already, listening to the sonorous lesson of the father, who laments melodiously on the branch, he attempts long whistles, trills and the gasps that are reminiscent of the amorous agony of a soul No matter! He scarcely succeeds in equaling the stammering loquacity of black-headed warblers.

It is necessary, in order for him truly to sing in accordance with his race, that he be reinforced, that when autumn arrives, he has traversed the skies, crossed the seas, and that from distant countries he brings back to ours, when spring returns, the simultaneously profound and bright immensity of unshadowed skies, and the sonorous silence of ruined temples, and all the virgin unknown of august forests. Then, truly, alongside the female brooding eggs, who is listening to him, he is grave, tender, powerful and sublime.

And Luscignole became, at that moment of the concert, entirely that miraculous voice; from that little mouth in the form of a beak—she dislocated her arms slightly in the effort, like a bird, writhing all the way to pain—infinities emerged, modulated furiously or with melancholy, of light, of darkness and of solitude.

And finally, she fainted, drained of strength, drained of life, drained of soul, one might that thought. Sometimes, one finds the cadaver in the heather, its plumage still ruffled, of a nightingale that has died of having sun too much. It could be feared the Luscignole, her eyes wide, her throat inflating and collapsing, had also succumbed to the fury of her song.

After the final sob, however, she suddenly smiled, prettily; then the furious enthusiasm of the crowd, uttering cries and throwing flowers, enveloped the triumphant virtuoso.

Her renown was such that it reached all the way to the German court. For the day of a grand gala at the palace for the opening of a Great Exhibition, the dowager empress sum-

169

moned Luscignole at the same time as singers illustrious for a long time in Paris and Munich.[10]

That was a great honor for a child who was, after all, a fairground whistler, to be associated with such famous artistes. But the strangest thing was that, in spite of princely courtesy, Mallinger, Niemann, Madame Krauss and Schnorr himself, the irreproachable Tristan,[11] were hardly complimented—they remembered the humiliation they suffered that evening for a long time—for all the admiration went to Luscignole alone. When that child had played the nightingale for a moment, people forgot that Siegfried had just hear the solar cry of Brünnhilde, finally awake, and it was for the bird-child that the audience went mad.

The next day, the Empress mother send Luscignole, in an enormous coffer of tropical hardwood, so many puppets and dolls that twenty toyshops could have been stocked therefrom; there were also innumerable lead soldiers from Nuremburg, for the Empress, very Christian, was something of a warrior. The Grand Duke of Weimar[12] sent the little girl via a chamberlain who bowed to her as one bows to a Royal Highness, the

---

[10] The dowager empress of Prussia when the present story was published was the eldest daughter of Queen Victoria, also called Victoria (1849-1901). Her husband, Frederick III, had died in 1888, succeeded by Wilhelm II. The great exhibition that the author has in mind was presumably the one held in Bremen in 1890.

[11] Mathilde Mallinger (1847-1920), Albert Niemann (1831-1917) and Ludwig Schnorr von Carolsfeld (1836-1865) all became famous in association with Richard Wagner's operas, among whose first performers they were. Gabrielle Krauss (1842-1906) was not associated with Wagner, but she was the leading soprano of the Paris Opéra in the late 1870s and early 1880s.

[12] Charles Alexander, Grand Duke of Saxe-Weimar (1818-1901) was an important protector of Richard Wagner, and also befriended Hans Christian Andersen.

most exquisite bonbons that can be found in the most renowned confectioneries; he had them distributed in twenty
boxes, the least precious of which was a marvel of sculpted
tortoiseshell and gold. And a few days later the Princess of
Wales,[13] having returned to England, sent Luscignole a box,
not of wood but of silver, of grapes ripened in the royal green-
house. Oh, how many other presents: toys, bonbons, necklaces, bracelets, rings—for courtiers followed the example of
their masters—honored the girl who had been a nightingale in
a tower, in fairgrounds and at court!

So famous, was she happy?

Yes, happy, doubtless. It was such an astonishing fortune, all that triumph, for her, so humble, whose mother had
hired out chairs in a church. Then, in sum, one is content,
when one has sung, to be applauded; and it is amusing to play
with golden dolls and to crunch perfect bonbons, and to orna-
ment oneself with jewels, when one has earned all that, and
earned it well, by whistling.

Not entirely happy, however.

As a little girl, she was rather frightened by so much society, by so much acclamation, by so many people compli-
menting her who were princes and queens. She remembered
the silent cathedral, the sarcophagus of Augustus, where she
had hidden in order not to be found by the cherubim of the
haut-relief, the games of shuttlecock with the holy Virgin with
five raised fingers, blessing and playing—all her childhood in
the intimacy of an immense solitude; and it embarrassed her,
very often, to be seen, to be heeded, to be admired by too
many tumultuous persons. She would have regretted the evenings when she had sung for Alas Schlemp if she had not remembered the frightful white-hot needle going through the
pale tube toward the eyes of nightingales.

---

[13] Alexandra of Denmark (1844-1925), the wife of the future
King Edward VII and sister-in-law of the Russian Tsar Alexander III.

Then, as a little bird, she felt ill-at-ease on stages on in halls, amid sets and between walls. Her true life would have been to live in the woods, because the free air passes between the branches there. She had been wrong to ask the nomad troupe to take her away; she should have remained on the edge of the wood; doubtless she would have succeeded in evading the pursuit of Alas Schlemp, and, gradually accustoming herself only to drinking the troubled water of ponds and only eating prowling golden flies or flying ants, she would have become a veritable nightingale.

At the same time, another muted desire was mysteriously secret within her: that of living in a cage.

Nothing was so strange, since she was the sister of free wings, but nothing was more natural since, very young, she bore within her the soul of an old bird who had finally become resigned to captivity And in the evening, before going to sleep, in the lassitude of the admirations of the enthusiastic city and the applauding court, the vision haunted her henceforth, tenaciously, of a green solitude in which she would be simultaneously a nightingale in prison and a nightingale in the forest.

She would have liked to live in a cage hanging from a branch

However, her glory amused her. One is a bird, but one is a virtuoso, and one does not always disdain acclamations. She gladly accepted an invitation to go, the following spring, to Saint Petersburg, where the Tsar had said to Prince Fédro-Schemyl[14] that he would gladly see her at court. But what

_____

[14] I have left this name as it appears in the original, although it is presumably a misprint, referring to a character in Mendès' novel, _Le Roi vierge_ (1881). Prince Fledro-Schemyl, based on a real individual, similarly transfigured in a story by Auguste Villiers de l'Isle-Adam, who went with Mendès to see the première of _Die Walküre_ in Munich in 1870, when they must have seen the King and his entourage, even if they were too humble to be introduced by their friend Richard Wagner.

charmed her above all was to earn that a young king, the King of Thuringia,[15] very famous in those days because of his liking for music, had testified his desire to hear her.

V

Although he scarcely worried about matters of government, and rarely failed, in the hours when he ought to have been working with his ministers, to go and crumble brioches for the swans in the pond in the garden of the Residence; although he was not occupied in any fashion with the wellbeing of his people, his dreams—his dreams, not his sleep, for he slept so little!—having rarely been troubled by the famines that desolated the countryside and the people who were dying of starvation in the city streets; although, in order to marvel for an hour at a new palace or to have some work by Hans Hammer performed worthily, he had stolen with his own hands from the public treasury the sums destined to arm fortresses and maintain the army. Although he was, it is averred, brutal to his servants, savage to his friends, ingrate to his relatives, unforgiving of the slightest irreverence and cruel to the extent of giving his hawks living mice to eat that he had divested of their skin personally, it did not matter: no king had a popularity equal to that one, because he looked so handsome, like the young Duke Theseus of a ideal Athens, when he passed by at the head of his troops in his silver uniform, like a suit of armor, aid of cloud of scattered snow that the mane of his prancing horse gave him.

---

[15] The German region of Thuringia had no king in 1890, but the central character of *Le Roi vierge* is Friedrich of Thuringia, clearly a transfiguration, like the present character, of Wagner' great champion, Ludwig II of Bavaria (1845-1886), who spent all his royal revenues of ambitious artistic projects and was sometimes known as *der Märchenkönig* [the fairy-tale king, or, in French, *le roi fée*], who owed his initial popularity to his good looks but never married.

For there is, in the heart of peoples, a sacred instinct, which they cannot disobey; the simple conceive obscurely that Beauty is the sublime redeemer of sins and crimes.

Then again, one thing recommended Friedrich to the amour of all the women of Thuringia: prettier than the most charming young men, powerful among the most powerful monarchs, no princess and no archduchess would have refused to become the wife of such a king; as in tales of Faerie, ambassadors arrived in Nonnenburg followed by magnificent corteges, carrying in golden coffers the portraits of royal young women, but, instead of sitting on his throne to welcome the noble emissaries, he slipped away to the mountains, where he went to eat brown bread dipped in milk in the home of his old nurse; even little Lisi, an archduchess who had a hint of the peasant girl about her, whom he almost loved, he did not marry. At least he had had some tenderness, or only brief a caprice, for some lady of the court, or for one of the beautiful courtesans that the eternal tempted sends to kings, and to who he confides, under their red lips, the ruination of empires and the despair of peoples, or for one of the divas burned by art and amour in whom the devouring soul of Hans Hammer was incarnate?

Not at all.

Now, having never loved, and not being in love, perhaps he would love in future; with the result that every woman in the realm could hope to be the elected wife or lover one day; and although it was probable, as the illustrious damsels of the court thought, that that he would one day be smitten with the heiress of some famous name, it was possible, thought young marriageable bourgeois women, that, prowling incognito, as he was accustomed to do, in the streets of his capital, he might become enamored with a young person embroidering plumes behind a window, and it was scarcely implausible, thought shepherdesses and goose-girls, that next spring, while visiting his nurse in the mountains, he would fall for some poor girl, previously wild and rustic, of whom he would make a favorite or a queen in the palace of Nonnenburg.

And all the young women's hearts in the country turned, tenderly or recklessly, and incessantly as Clytia turned toward Apollo, toward the mysterious royal adolescent who, from so far away and so high, from higher still, dazzled them delectably.

Once, a despair nearly gripped them. The rumor had run around that during his sojourn in a distant capital, Friedrich had felt his heart finally softened for the Empress of that Empire; in fact, as soon as he returned, he had a pink marble chapel built in one of his gardens, where he prayed for two hours every evening. To what elect or to what saint was that chapel devoted? Neither to a saint nor an elect. On the guipure of the altar-cloth, between the golden vases and candlesticks in which the white stems of candles raised star-flowers, instead of a sacred icon, there was a relic; and that relic was, in a narrow coffin of glass, a white rose, still fresh, as if scarcely blossomed by the science of some marvelous chemist or magician: a strange floral mummy; a rose that he was said to have plucked one day from the corsage of the Empress of the distant land.

Thus, the king was in love, veritably, and he would never have eyes or a heart for his tender subjects.

But a few months passed; the forgetful individual ceased to come and pray in the chapel in the garden; the candles were no longer lit; the golden vases were extinguished; there were climbing ivy-stems, as on the stones of a ruin, over the saddened pink of the marble; and the increasing wildness of vegetation closed with a door or leaves and branches the chapel where the mummy of the flower finally faded in its obscure coffin.

And all the great ladies, all the bourgeois women and all the peasant women recovered their hope in regard to the young monarch, who was dreaming, still insensible but perhaps soon to be sensible, amid the radiance and the music, in the enchantments of some castle in the mountains where swans that were not birds, but machines clad in cotton wool and snowy satin, floated and sang on the crystalline blue of lakes in which the azure of a malachite ceiling encrusted with rubies and pearls imitated the astral sky, where all the deception of charming beings and exquisite things, were all the irreality of nature delighted, and perhaps desolated, the soul of the young king fatally smitten with an artificial Ideal.

The day when Friedrich summoned her, Luscignole was introduced with an abrupt impulsion into a very strange garden.

"Fräulein," said a youth, almost a child, clad in leather and iron, who was one of the king's young equerries, "you cannot see His Majesty but he can see you and hear you. Sing, then, if you please."

With that, he disappeared.

Nonplussed, Luscignole gazed at the garden.

It appeared to be very large, almost immense, with distant skies in the depths of long vaults of branches; however, once could not respire there as in an open space traversed by the wind; it was as if, by some miracle, one were a figure, really existing, in a painted landscape; alive, one felt that one were the captive of lifeless things; the breadth, the height and the entire space enclosed like a jail.

To tell the truth, Luscignole, a child who was more nearly a bird, trembling instinct posed on a vacillating branch, could not be impressed so subtly, but her unconscious mind experienced it, and in that vast garden, as in a narrow chamber closed everywhere, she was panting slightly.

The light, too, did not seem to her to be similar to daylight. Oh, she could certainly see, higher than the tops of the tall trees—magnolias, cedars, eucalypti—a radiant yellow roundness floating, which was the sun, but she did not recognize the solar splendor, and there were no true sunbeams in the daylight.

She began to feel afraid. Stepping back, she encountered plants, thought she was about to fall, retained herself, with her arms flung backwards, on branches that did not bend; and it seemed to her that the leaves she was touching with her fingers were not leaves. She turned round, touched again, looked at closer range, and saw the fine cuttings of silk that put the verdure in the trees...

Suddenly, birdsong! She raised her head, and perceived a reed-warbler, a svelte and russet bird, the fallen sister of the race of nightingales, hoping from branch to branch and twittering recklessly. That reassured her; it was as if an exile in a very distant country were encountering a compatriot. She ran toward the warbler as if toward a comrade...

She stopped. What was fluttering was not a little living body clad in veritable plumage but one of those small automata that one sees in the window displays of toyshops, and which, being serinettes impelled by the spasms of little springs, only sing if one turns the key. And the deceptive warbler, as soon as Luscignole approached, disappeared behind a raised floret, which fell back like the lid of a rat-trap.

Luscignole was completely terrified. She only had only one idea: to flee. She threw herself into one of the long avenues, a kind of leafy tunnel. She did not run far; her forehead soon bumped into a wall painted blue, which was the celestial distance.

Then she burst out laughing. She understood. She had been taken into a garden similar to the stage-sets in which she was a nightingale every evening; and, something of a ham— since she was not whistling for herself!—she had the pride of wanting to show that she was not a dupe. His Majesty, she had been old, could see her and hear her? Good. Doubtless the king was hidden behind some window painted with a flowery trellis, as people are in the depths of grilled lodges. It was a matter of being worthy of her reputation!

She struck a pose, her elbow on the bark of a tree, stamping her feet in the sand—not sand, but perhaps the friable and mobile dust of fine stones—and, after having smoothed her tresses, which she knew to be similar to the wings of nightingales, the bird-girl began to sing. Truly, she sang very well. One can assume that, if it had been a matter of entering into competition with her brothers in the woods, she would have whistled more simply and with a soul more replete with reveries of infinity, but at least, being an artist before an audience, everything that she had acquired of adroit method substituting for naïve inspiration, she employed it marvelously. One can make some effort for king who knows music.

In any case, it was in vain that she strove only to have talent; she bore a little sincere soul, indocile to yesterday's success, and she quickly became the puerile and honest poet— a poet of the woods and cages—who sang for pleasure and always thought she was hearing herself for the first time.

As she fainted with delight in the supreme swoon of the birdsong, a voice very close at hand said in a tone that was simultaneously supplicant and commanding: "Oh, again! Again!"

The person who had spoken was doubtless the king, the king of beautiful enchantments, the young fay-king, hidden behind the lie of some tree or some corner of sky made of a blue-tinted mirror.

She was a nightingale again, more delectably, more dolorously. She ran out of breath, and strength, and soul; exquisitely tortured, she fell silent.

But the voice of the invisible king, both more brutally and more tenderly, said: "Again! Again!"

She straightened up; she mastered herself; she sang again, in a more melancholy and more mysterious fashion at first, and then carried away in gasping melodies, to such an extent that finally, as if dead, she fell on to the grass made of gold wire mingled with threads of green silk.

She remained prostrate for a long time, in the simultaneous ecstasy and anguish of an inspired artiste who has done her duty in delivering her entire being.

A word extracted her from the cruel enchantment that would soon be forgotten, as a delight too formidable for consciousness to have retained the memory of it.

"Fräulein?"

She got up; she shook the frills of her fairground dress, as a bird shakes its plumage, rubbed her eyes, with the air of a child walking up, turned round, and saw, clad entirely in white, so tall and so pretty, in a coat made of silver, snow and stones the color of lilies, someone who was more charming than all the Prince Charmings of tales.

At first, in her alarm and her pleasure, she did not think that he could be the king—did she even remember that there were kings on earth?—but she thought that she had woken up in a world where angels took pleasure in listening to the song of nightingales and coming to compliment them after having heard them. Or rather, she did not imagine anything, except that she was happy beyond the possible because of that apparition, so white, so pretty, and also so arrogant.

She did not reply; she was still contemplating him, in a charmed alarm. She noticed—for ecstasy, sometimes, without losing anything of its immensity, attaches itself to details, in which it is reinforced—that the vision had eyes similar to little corners of sky in which a thousand stars are crowded, and that it bore, descending from the neck on to the breast, a necklace made of constellations.

Luscignole extended her arms, suppliant, as if to implore pity for so much joy.

Again, the voice of the adorable stranger said; "Fräulein?"

Then polite in her rapture, she replied: "Meinherr..."

But he stamped his foot angrily. "Say: Sire!" he cried.

She bowed her head. It was the king. She was simultaneously delighted and a little disillusioned, for he was very handsome, as the king was, but perhaps she had hoped that he would be better than a king."

In any case, habituated to the ceremonious fashions of courts, she murmured: "Sire!" after having inclined three times.

Calmer, Friedrich said: "In truth, you sing very well."

She bowed again.

"Are you very determined to follow the showmen who take you from city to city?"

"Oh! No, Sire."

"Would it please you to live with me, and to sing alone?"

"Indeed, that would please me!" she said. And she dared to raise her head.

She looked at the king; the king looked at her. There was, the eyes of each of them, a kind of confrontation of souls that were perhaps—who knows?—equally pure, equally sad equally puerile and also equally cruel, for nightingales are as ferocious as innocent young Neros. And they did not cease, the master of a great kingdom and the fairground whistler, to look at one another as if looking in a mirror.

Finally, after a start he said: "Stay in this garden momentarily, then, Mademoiselle and await my orders."

"Yes, Sire," she said.

And he disappeared behind a curtain of moss and roses, lifted and falling back; it was like the flight, a little while before, of the mechanical bird to the other side of the flower, which fell with the rapidity of the lid of a rat-trap.

With Friedrich gone, Luscignole's ecstasy vanished, but not entirely, leaving her a mildness and a languor, and that which remains of extinct splendor in a crystal where a star has been reflected.

She sat down at the foot of a very well-imitated cedar, in moss of silk and gold, and, perplexed. She wondered: *What's going to happen to me? Am I going to be a princess or is the king going to make me sing in the operas of Hans Hammer, of which there is so much talk?*

She waited.

The equerry clad in leather and iron reappeared, and bowed with the marks of the most profound respect.

"Deign to follow me, Fräulein," he said.

"Oh, gladly," she said.

He went ahead, parting the branches of the strange garden. She found herself in a hall in which golden columns were spaced out beneath a ceiling panted with obsolete mythologies. At a sign from her guide she marched between a double line of gaudily-bedecked servants, perhaps chamberlains, emerged from the hall, went up a narrow spiral staircase similar to those in the towers of cathedrals, went into a vast room with very ancient furniture, such as she had never seen before; and, the equerry having retired, three old ladies with white tresses beneath long veils of black crepe, in trailing somber dresses, like ill-tempered nuns in a very funeral cloister, got up from antique chairs and, after bowing three times, said in unison: "Fräulein, it's here that you'll lodge until the abode that His Majesty destines for you is ready."

VI

She became very bored in the severe apartment.

In the evening, the old ladies put her to bed in a great ebony bed, between tapestries in which a king was seen, here at the head of his red-clad musketeers, there receiving kneeling ambassadors, further away, dancing majestically amid dancers whom respect moved aside and ecstasized, elsewhere on horseback on the back of a river that an army was swimming across: a king who was handsome, no doubt, but too imposing, and coifed with an enormous wig so yellow that one might have thought it made of sunbeams rolled in curlers the night before.

Oh, how pretty he was, young King Friedrich, in his white garments embroidered with snow, lilies and pearls, who had, under short curly hair, sky in his eyes!

In the morning, the old ladies—always, for she did not see anyone but them, like lugubrious nuns guardians of a young novice—brought her chocolate and twenty delicacies; but, greedy as she was, she ate them without pleasure, with sighs of ennui that would have moved the most insensible individuals; the old ladies were not moved.

And the entire day was morose; for Luscignole was not permitted to approach the windows, veiled in any case by thick curtains that the daylight scarcely penetrated, and the noise of the city did not penetrate at all.

She had no other distraction than considering, in a long and narrow gallery neighboring her chamber, illuminated from above, portraits of women hanging from the walls. There were doll-like faces, too pink under powder, whose painters had imitated the make-up very well: noble pale faces helmed in black torsades, the faces of queens or empresses; and, upper bodies clad in strange frippery, women of all nations: Russians with pearly bosoms like those of Circassian Panagias, whose whiteness faded away insolently between splendid proliferations of silks; negresses with breasts similar, according to the brutal and just expression of a poet, to two halves of a cannonball; and beautiful Parisiennes, mouths red from recent kisses, who would dance in Porcherons and breakfast at the Rapée; not neglecting favorites of the previous century, powdered, musked and exquisite, a rose between two fingers, and ancient queens, Doves with Iron Beaks or Serpents of the Nile,[16] some bright golden blondes, others dark golden brunettes.

For a few hours, Luscignole amused herself with those portraits; there were forty of them, and her adroit curiosity ended up obtaining from the three old nuns the confession that it was the collection of the most beautiful women in the world once assembled by Friedrich I, a poet king, a tender and extravagant king, who was the grandfather of Friedrich II, the fay king.[17] But she wearied very quickly, pretty as they were and so amusing in their various costumes, of the sole company of those paintings; if, in order to divert herself from her morose life, she had not had the hope of glories that the king undoubtedly reserved for her, she would have died of chagrin.

But what if some other girl had been brought to him who was a better nightingale than her?

---

[16] i.e. analogues of Semiramis and Cleopatra.

[17] Ludwig II's grandfather, Ludwig I of Bavaria was celebrated for assembling a *Schönheilegengalerie* [Gallery of Beauties] in his Nymphenberg Palace, containing 36 portraits, mostly by Joseph Karl Stieler; the story presumably adjusts the number upwards to echo the number of nightingales contained in Alas Schlemp's tower.

From her guardians she only obtained the response: "Wait!" or "It is necessary to give His Majesty the time to prepare what he desires."

She thought that she had been waiting too long, and one evening, while she was being undressed in order to be put in the large four-poster bed, she decided privately that the next day, if nothing new happened, she would get annoyed and would say that she wanted to leave, that she wanted to go and sing in forests or in fairgrounds, as she was accustomed to do.

That evening, as soon as the old ladies had withdrawn, after having offered her to drink, in a Bohemian cup incrusted with rubies, a rosé wine that would assure her, they said, a long and good sleep, she felt so weary as soon as her head was on the pillow that she no longer had the leisure to think, and suddenly fell asleep, profoundly.

Asleep as she was, however, she was not entirely absent from life. Things happened around her that she perceived, chimera or reality, as vaguely as in the mist of a dream.

It seemed to her that she was slid out of the bed, that she was dressed in strange garments, garments that she had never worn before. Then she was lifted up and taken away. By whom? Confused forms, which had gold on their sleeves, richly-clad phantoms. Great care was taken not to do her any harm; she was touched by hands that barely brushed her. She was, however, taken away very rapidly.

Then, after stairways descended in opaque darkness, reddened here and there by torches, and more stairways, which spiraled—she would not have been able to make a movement or open her eyes, but she sensed that she was being moved and she saw the darkness reddening—a bright freshness caressed her face and, without waking her up, charmed her. It was like a breath of dawn in a very somber night.

Soon she imagined that she was laid down in a carriage; there were the whinnies of horses, the cracking of whips and the curses of a postillion. But she was quite sure that all of that was only a dream; she promised herself to remember it in order to recount it to herself when she woke up. There was a grating noise of horses pulling away. The carriage, with a surge that Luscignole sensed within her, traveled so rapidly, so very rapidly, that in the vagueness of the dream it was like an arrow carrying the archer away.

Stars posed in the windows like golden flies; then they ran away with the fleeing black glass, like the glimmers that roll in storm-clouds.

And Luscignole, motionless, as if she had been placed in a coffin before being hoisted into the vehicle, heard an immense and sonorous friction. Undoubtedly she was traversing a forest or traveling along the sea shore. How she would have liked to see, entirely! How she would have liked to hear, entirely! But an effort that she made to lift her eyelids, to concentrate her hearing, vanquished and sterile, plunged her further into darkness and silence; she was like a corpse.

A pink light of dawn—after how long?—traversed her eyelids, lifted her up slowly, gently, like the little finger of an early-rising fay, diaphanous and so light than it could scarcely be felt. She was astonished not to wake up in the former chamber with the imposing drapes.

Was everything that she had believed she had dreamed not a dream, then?

She rubbed her eyes, propped herself up on her elbow, and looked around.

She was utterly amazed, but not frightened. She was not extended on a bed but along an enormous wooden beam, like a tree trunk, horizontal in mid-air, leaning rather than lying; and coming to her from below were the fresh scents of a clearing alt=ready mist with dew, and coming from above, the blue tints, still nocturnal but already brighter, of a morning sky. Something tremulous brushed her forehead: a branch; a real branch. The cold breath of an entire forest, slowly stirred, passed over her delectably.

She did not budge. She did not know where she was; she was content to be there. She experienced the ease of someone who, after a long exile, wakes up in his homeland, or in a place similar to his homeland, in a house long desired. She felt at home; and she breathed in, with the charm of a convalescent drinking for the first time after a long fever, the air of the great wood and the vast sky and the quivering silence in which the last songs of the nightingales were fading away.

And the daylight gradually increased.

Little by little, Luscignole saw forms sketched out, lines affirming. While the azure above her was illuminated, the grass of the clearing below her was gilded here and tinted pink there. But it seemed to her that above, below, to the right and to the left, she perceived the sky, the grass and the forest as if through a trellis.

Then the thought occurred to her to consider herself.

It was in a costume made of dark brown feathers in which she appeared to be dressed, and—the sunlight tearing through all of the penumbra—she knew that she was a night-ingale in an enormous cage, with widely-spaced bars, hanging between the master branches of a gigantic oak, in the middle of a forest.

PART THREE

I

She was in a cage, in a cage in the middle of woods. Around her were the noises of the wild and charming infinity of a forest traversed by sunlight, from all directions came the freshness of verdure, the twittering of nests, the chatter of distant streams, and the odors of moist grass, which were vaporizing. She really was surrounded by the immense icy mildness if trees, and the severities of solitude.

The cage was very large. Made of bars that were the trunks of young ash trees, on which the bark had been left, it was broad, much broader than the chambers in which the idleness of city-dwellers becomes bored, wedged between two parted branches. It allowed the wind, and scents of green vegetal life, to enter from all directions.

A few hours after waking up, Luscignole, alarmed at first, then glad, understood that, by an incomprehensible magic, her double dream had finally been realized, of being simultaneously a nightingale in a cage and a nightingale in the forest.

Several days went by. Habitude rendered the solitude sweeter, the sunlight and the moonlight dearer. However, she did not sing, opposing silence to the songs of the nightingales that lamented, as soon as dusk fell, in the profound mystery— to the song of one, in particular, her neighbor in the same tree.

Where did she sleep? On one of the horizontal beams, hollowed out like a pirogue; furs had been put into it so that she would not be cold.

Where did she eat? In the large mangers in which, while she was sleep, invisible hands served a meal composed of delicacies agreeable to a little girl, and which, at the same time, would have pleased the appetite of a bird.

Every morning, when she opened her eyes, she perceived that the cage had been cleaned, the bars dusted, the water in the porcelain bowls renewed. People were occupied with her, taking care of her; she was proud, because she, a wild girl, was being treated as a recently-captured nightingale would have been.

How did she pass the time? Sitting on one of the beams, the one that was in the darkest shade, she watched the green flies that passed by, amused herself with the quivering of flying ants, took an interest in the rustle of leaves, was alarmed by the footfalls of a woodcutter over the grass. Sometimes she retreated into a corner of her dear prison, one leg in the air in the ruffling of her feathers, staring fixedly in front of her with round, wide open eyes; and she did not imagine that anyone could be happier than she was.

But what of the king?

On the third day after her imprisonment in the delightful solitude, in the evening, when the first starlight pierced the thickness of the leaves like vacillating silver arrows, she heard the sound of someone approaching. She divined that His Majesty was listening, and since she was the king's nightingale, she started to sing, rapturously.

She had never sung so admirably, for now she knew all the melodies of the forest, all the rhythms of the moon's rays gliding from branch to branch, and the harmonies of the infinite silence. In her voice, the mysterious soul of the forest swooned, and the nightingales listened silently.

Then she fell silent in her turn, having divined, because of a rustle of leaves and pated branches, that the king had drawn away. It was for him alone that she wanted to sing.

It was for him alone that she sang every evening, for the moment when the sound of footsteps denounced Friedrich's presence to the one when the rustle of foliage informed her of his departure. Oh, what pride, what delight there was for her in knowing that such a pretty prince, who knew music so well, was listening to her. It even pleased her that he remained invisible, because, unconsciously, she liked the memory of him better than the prospect of seeing him again. And truly, there is no happiness down here for which Luscignole would have traded her joy in a cage in the forest.

But one night, lying on the beam, she awoke abruptly with a start. Why? She could not have said. Her plumage bristling, she had the instinctive fear of a bird that senses the advent, without seeing it, of the soaring hawk or vulture that is about to swoop.

There was a sound of branches opened by a heavy pressure. Had the king returned? No, he did not have that heavy approach, furtive but heavy, and his invisible arrival parted the leaves with the abrupt surge, suddenly arrested of a wild and bold chamois. The ever-closer noise, as if it were prowling around her, that the frightened, terrified Luscignole heard, seemed to be that of a prudent malefactor, animal or human, redoubtable but fearful.

Who was coming, then? What did he want of her, that unknown individual?

Instinctively, she was certain that she had never been in greater danger. But she dared not look through the trellis of the cage toward the being that was advancing.

Eventually, there was the sound of a heavy fall, as if the newcomer, after a false step, had sat down in the grass, and then, nothing more. Except that in the black silence the lament rose up of the nightingale that had its branch in the tree in which Luscignole's cage hung. And for that bird, her neighbor—they had ended up knowing one another and loving one another because of the songs exchanged—she was afraid as much as for herself. For she knew full well that the enemy, silent now, was still there; he was watching, immobile, lying in ambush, doubtless waiting for daylight to accomplish some criminal act. She sensed the menace of a malevolent breath running in the wind.

Although wearied by terror, she did not close her eyes, and in the tree nearby, the nightingale must also have been alarmed, because, no longer singing, it had not fallen asleep, its head under its wing, in the security of the night. Luscignole could hear it distinctly, hopping anxiously from branch the branch, like a bird coveted and attracted by the mouth of a reptile, open in the grass.

Hours passed; there was a rosy tremor on the smooth leaves; here, there, further away, everywhere, the first redness of dawn insinuated itself into the forest and rose from the heather, still scarcely-visible in the sway of the wind, and grassy ravines in which the fleeting silver of streams awoke, and the damp clearing, from the white opacities, soon to be less opaque, by which the entire forest was enveloped. Still in the shadow, with its beeches and its oaks, their trunks like vague pillars, their crowns curbed into vaults, it was like an enormous and mysterious church, full of a mist of incense.

Then, a little clarity penetrating the profundity, Luscignole acquired courage, turned her head and lowered it, seeking to discern in the obscurity of the undergrowth the individual of whose presence she was aware, whose menacing wait she divined.

For a long time, she could not make out anything alarming. She was on the point of believing that she had been frightened mistakenly, and that only some innocent beast had been prowling in the night. But, having descended from the beam, with her face stuck to the latticework floor of the cage, she suddenly saw, in the mist that was becoming diaphanous in the increasing daylight, not underneath the cage itself but a little further away, toward the tree, a low black form, curbed over the earth: the form of a man lying on his belly.

For a long time the man did not budge. But then, little by little, he advanced his arm, and with a hand that mingled its red fingers with the grass he tore up the grass in clumps, laying bare a square of black moist earth.

Luscignole lifted her head again, because she had heard a rustle of plumage; it was the nightingale in the neighboring tree, agitating, also taking an interest in the sly work; and she saw that, extending its neck between two leaves, it was observing the man with an oblique eye.

She trembled. She knew how curious nightingales are, and, instructed in the practices of bird-catching, knew that adroit hunters take advantage of that curiosity in order to make those wild birds fall into traps. The unknown man who had lain in wait all night must be an expert trapper of wings; doubtless he was preparing some ambush into which the singer in the tree would fall.

She had a desire to make a noise, in order that the bird would fly away. But it was habituated, since it had her for neighbor, to the comings and goings within the cage, to Luscignole's little leaps and laughter, and whatever she did, it would not be alarmed. Oh, how anxious she was!

A flight through the heather and the branches redoubled her alarm. Alas, she was not mistaken; the man was no longer there, but on the freshly moved earth he had laced, wide open, a double round net, the upper part of which was supported by a needle in a notch in a slender stick, at the end of which, temptingly, a mealworm was writhing.

Nightingales are no less greedy than they are curious; if the bird that was watching with its neck turned perceived the living prey, it would not fail to descend from the tree; it would seize the worm with its beak, and the lid would fall, and its wings would beat in vain between the mesh of the net; then the hunter, hidden not far away behind a tree trunk, would come running and seize the poor little creature.

Then, in fact, the nightingale descended from branch to branch, with little hesitant leaps, and, with its head in the air, as if to fly away—but it did not fly away—it drew nearer and nearer to the peril.

Oh my God, now it was walking in the grass, on the ground, advancing, still advancing; it straightened its neck repeatedly, with an air in which stupidity was reassured by pride, again with an intention to take flight; but its oblique gaze did not quit the mealworm, and it finally found itself, unstable but resolute, suspicious but hungry, at such a short distance from captivity that an abrupt elongation of the beak would have been sufficient to make it fall into the trap.

Luscignole's fear was indescribable, as was her pity for the poor bird that was about to be captured, and put in prison, and its eyes perhaps burned, as Alas Schlemp did, in order that it would sing better.

An idea occurred to her. She started to sing; but to the ordinary song she added, mingled with the trills, a little cry agreed between birds since the commencement of species, which warns of mortal danger.

The nightingale heard it, understood, and with a sudden flutter of wings it escaped, far from the trap, among the complicity of leaves quickly opened and closed again, toward the sure refuges of the forest.

Luscignole had never experienced a greater pleasure; she had saved her little brother of the woods. He would remain free; he would sing all through the spring to delight his amorous female. And she had so much joy that she began to sing again, recklessly.

But that joy was short lived.

The bird-catcher, having returned, looked up in the air, because of the song, toward the cage that he had not yet perceived, mingled with the foliage of the oak—and Luscignole, full of horror, recognized the hideous gnome Alas Schlemp, who recognized her.

Well, yes, it was entirely natural that he was spying on nightingales in the spring forest, that monster who took pleasure in imprisoning the wings and burning the eyes of the divine singers. Doubtless he had to fill some empty cage in the aviary-room, and he had set forth to hunt with his traps and his frightful tin-plate cylinders, in which even suicide was forbidden to the prisoners.

Meanwhile, he looked at her ardently.

In his flamboyant little eyes the triumph was laughing of having finally rediscovered his finest virtuoso; and in his momentary immobility there was the imminent surge of everything toward her, in order to seize her and carry her away.

Luscignole was seized by such fear that she started leaping like a mad bird from one side of the cage to the other, ruffling her feathers on the beams, bloodying her face on the bars. But Alas Schlemp, with frightful laughter on his lips, had embraced the trunk of the oak and was climbing.

She saw one of the man's hands penetrate into the cage. She understood that, hoisted up, he was about to lift the catch inside, that the door would open, and that the execrable burner of eyes would recapture her.

Then she screamed; she howled: "Help! Help!" and she called again, adding the name of the king.

But Alas Schlemp precipitated himself into the cage and grabbed the vainly resistant little girl.

"Let me go!"

"Come!"

"Go away!"

"Come!"

"You have no right to take me!"

"Come on!"

"I'm the king's nightingale!"

"I tell you to come!"

And, clasping her against him, forcing her to shut up with a hand over her mouth, he put her under his arm as he might have done with a doll—she was lighter, being a bird—hung on with one hand to the edge of the cage, let himself fall into the grass, and carried Luscignole away through the forest.

II

On the other side of the mountain, at the bottom of the slope, there is an inn on the edge of a little lake, round and very blue, between a circular inclination of fir-trees. It is more like a tavern, because hardly anyone lodges there. It is there that beggars, doubtless thieves, emaciated vagabonds and dis-quieting prowlers who succeed in escaping the kingdom of Thuringia pause momentarily in order to recover their breath.

At night, any infrequent tourist who has gone to sleep in the solitary hostel sometimes wakes up with a start because of a loud noise of stones collapsing amid muffled appeals and whispers. If he opens his window and looks outside it is possible that he will see, in the nocturnal obscurity, a long cadaver dragged by ropes, like a ruddy sack, by four or five men, bent over, shoulders forward, groaning with effort; on the stones of the road, puddles of blood remain, black in the darkness or red in the moonlight.

The cadaver is that of a deer, killed by poachers in the nearby forest, which they will butcher shortly in the cellar of the inn, in order to go and sell it at the market in the next town, in red and hairy quarters.

A few tables of unpolished stone, each one on a single foot of oak from which the bark has not been stripped are spaced out in the tiled ground-floor room with a ceiling of sagging beams and uneven walls daubed with whitewash.

It was on a bench in front of one of those tables, after the journey through the forest, that Alas Schlemp finally sat down. He put Luscignole down on the hard wood beside him, as one sets down a parcel. She did not move, unconscious or dead. He too remained motionless, resting heavily on his elbows, his fists under his jaw, and did not breathe a word. Only his hoarse breath, that of an inveterate drunkard, sounded, increasing to a growl in the empty silence of the room.

But when the waitress, mannish and moustached, with the air of a rough soldier dressed as a woman, had placed on the table, with pewter mugs, an enormous pitcher of beer from which foam was overflowing and a bottle of Schiedam, he thumped the table with his fist and turned to Luscignole.

"Let's go," he said. "Drink!"

Luscignole shivered, and lifted her head slightly, without opening her eyes. She was as pale as a dead jasmine; there was blood around her lips, slightly advanced in a beak, because she had collided with the bars, and the frayed feathers of her costume gave her the appearance of a poor beaten little bird.

"Drink, then!" she said.

"No," she sighed.

"Since I tell you to drink!"

193

He spoke in a voice so harsh that the little girl was afraid of being hit. She moved away instinctively, and opened her eyelids...

She uttered a scream, so frightful was her uncle to behold. Ugly before, he was now hideousness personified, so much did his enormous head, hairy everywhere, hang down lower over a neck perhaps broken behind the fat flaccid wrinkled, so much did the drool that foamed on his lips give the impression of a rabid beast, and so red were his haggard little round eyes with ferocity. And he was dressed in sordid rags from which the roundness of bones emerged like stumps.

He understood that he was frightening the child, and became angry. Furiously, he grabbed the bottle of Schiedam, poured about a quarter of it into the beer—for nowadays, in order to get drunk more rapidly, he mingled the alcohol and the beer—and drank in the same way, greedily, the skin of his neck agitated by spasmodic gurgles.

Then, with a thick snigger, he said: "Yes, this is what I've become since you left, little wretch!"

He drank again, and continued, between hiccups: "Oh, thunder, what a dog's life! First, the cathedral burned."

"The cathedral!" cried Luscignole

"I don't know how that happened. That sheds and houses catch fire, I understand, there are planks, furniture, and fabrics. But a church, all of stone, no other wood than in the canon stalls, what can a fire find to eat in that? It's been said, since, that the fire was set by the workers in the factories, by means of cartridges and bombs thrown under the benches of the nave and in the stairways. That doesn't explain how the marble and the granite burned like straw—and they burned all night!

"When I came out of the tavern, amid all the screams of the city mad with fear and astonishment, scarlet tongues of flame were winding round the gargoyles, and fiery explosions were staving in the stained glass windows, which melted or shattered in embers of all colors, and while the dome collapsed in falls that shook the whole quarter, the great bronze portal became as red as if it were the door of Hell, all flames within."

"Oh my God!" said Luscignole, sobbing. For she remembered the good Virgin with the raised fingers, with whom she played games of shuttlecock, and the cherubim of the haut-relief, who were her little friends. Above all she remembered the dear nightingale buried next to the Emperor, whose sepulcher must have been smashed by some falling stone, crushing the thin bones. Alas, poor little skeleton!

Then, her voice tearful, she said: "But at least the tower didn't burn?"

"It burned like all the rest. Red fumes came out of all the windows."

"Then...the birds!"

"I hurled myself into the stairway, but at the first turning, the flames that were descending and whistling ate my skin and my hair, and I had to go back to the square. I watched the window of the aviary; flames weren't coming out yet, but the windows were all red."

"The birds! The birds!" wept Luscignole.

"Then the panes shattered, and then, in the black and white smoke and the sparks, I saw the nightingales, beating their wings. Doubtless they'd escaped from the partly burned cages."

"And they flew away! Oh, they aren't dead..."

Alas Schlemp turned his head, and continued, in a duller voice: "Yes, yes, they're dead. They wanted to get away from the fire, but they didn't know which way to flee. They fluttered, went a little further, came back, and were lost in the devouring smoke. The next day I found them at the foot of the tower, in the rubble and the ashes, little bones of little birds, all black..."

Luscignole, her eyes dry with anger, shouted: "Because they'd been blinded! Because you'd put out their eyes with needles! Villain! Villain! Villain!"

The drunkard, moved, dissolved in tears.

"Yes, yes, that's why...yes...perhaps that's why..."

But abruptly, after four gulps of Schiedam swallowed from the neck of the bottle, his rage took hold of him again.

"And as there was no more cathedral, there was no more need for a beadle. I wasn't even permitted to sleep in the cooled rubble. They took their revenge on me, the bourgeois, the professors, the judges that my nightingales had humiliated for such a long time. Not one shelter offered, in a loft or a cellar, no alms, not a morsel of bread. People even said that if I didn't quit the city, I might well be accused of complicity with the workers. The imbeciles! Burn the cathedral, I don't say no, but how could I have burned the tower where I had my nightingales, my dear nightingales who sang so well, who gave me so much pleasure?

"Anyway, it was necessary to go away. Oh, thunder, thunder of time! What days and what nights. Because I'm ugly, because I'm deformed, because I drool, because I smell bad, no one wanted to receive me; I haven't been able to be a domestic servant, nor a dish-washer, nor a farm laborer; no one wanted me to turn the spit in the kitchen! And for want of shoes I wore away the skin of my soles on the paving-stones or pebbles of the roads, and for want of straw under my head I tore the nape of my neck on the thistles of the embankment—so that, dying of hunger and more wretched than the most wretched, I made myself a beggar.

"I sat down on the steps of a church or the bollard of some coaching-entrance, I bent myself over more so that people would think me more hunchbacked, and, drooled more so that people would think I was epileptic. It's what creates horror that creates pity. But people hardly gave me anything. In the evening I hardly had enough to drink a few tankards of beer and half a bottle of Schiedam. No, that life! I'm as accursed as the Devil's dog. And that's lasted a long time, and it will last forever.

"Sometimes, yes, I have good hours. That's when I hunt nightingales in the woods, with a net I made. But when I've caught a bird, what use is it to me? I have to let it go, since I have no cage to put it in, and if I had one, I wouldn't have a wall to hang it on."

After a hate-filled glance at Luscignole, he continued, his teeth grinding: "But now I won't be alone in dying of hunger, sleeping in the mud or the stones of ditches! Perhaps you believed that it would continue, your beautiful happy life? One knows things, child. One picks up newspapers in the street, one reads the news. You had success, in the theaters, in courts, you were sleeping in good beds, eating good things. You would have been able, if you'd wanted, to drink twenty bottles of Schiedam every evening! Better still, you were the favorite of a king. It was said that he preferred you to Hans Hammer himself!

"Thunder of heaven, my child, you've given yourself too many good times, while your uncle was suffering like the stones of a road forever staved in by carts. But it's finished, for you, amusing yourself, and for me, of suffering all alone. Since I've found you again, by chance, while hunting the nightingale—a funny idea he had, your king, of putting you in a cage!—I'm taking you away. I'm your only relative, you only belong to me. To you, I can do anything I want! There's no prince or emperor who can prevent me from being your uncle.

"Anyway, we're no longer in your friend's kingdom; we've crossed the frontier. I'm your master. Oh, you'll see hardship, I promise you. I won't beg any more, me; I'll fold my arms, on the bollards of coaching entrances and the steps of churches. It's you who'll hold out your hand! And I'll beat you if they don't give you anything."

The mannish, moustached waitress with the air of a rough soldier dressed as a woman had just come back into the room. "That's twenty kreutzer," she said.

"It's twenty kicks in the belly!" howled Schlemp, suddenly standing up, and lashing out at the waitress with his knock-kneed leg.

The blow was such—for the gnome, especially when he was drunk, had the stretched of a compacted giant—that the waitress fell backwards, full length, on the tiles.

"Let's get out of here," said Alas Schlemp to Luscignole.

And he escaped, taking her with him.

III

They were beggars in the country and in the towns, asking for bread at the gates of farms, asking for sous under the windows of rich houses. They would have been able to sleep, almost every night, in one of those hovels where, for very little money, shelter is given to paupers without lodgings, for, because of the impression she gave, so sweet and so suffering, people gladly gave her alms, but the small change that fell into Luscignole's hand he employed in drinking.

He ate almost nothing; it was sufficient for him to drink, for that nourishes too. She contented herself with some crust thrown from a kitchen; but she grew thinner. She was a pitiful sight. The plumes of her garment had fallen out, like those of a molting bird, but as they had not grown back, she no longer had anything but a poor coat of clinging woolen cloth that was soon ragged, and beneath the taut fabric the frail bulges of the bones were visible.

Oh, the poor thing, so dainty, how paltry she was! Her cheeks were extinct, and her lips; but what was even sadder was her bare feet, scratched by brambles, torn by the corners of paving-stones, where grazes would have been visible everywhere if they had not been shod with dirt.

And inside her, there was even more sadness. To think that she had been received in courts, that she had worn beautiful gilded dresses, that she had been given toys so beautiful that they would have been the envy of a child-princess, that she had been the favorite bird of the youngest and most handsome of kings! Now, uncertain of shelter, uncertain of meals, she was a tatterdemalion wandering in the company of the ugliest and most brutal of gnomes.

However, Alas Schlemp, in sum, did not treat her too badly. He gladly frightened her with menacing words, but he rarely beat her, except when he was absolutely drunk. After a certain time of common vagabondage, he even stopped beating her at all, and Luscignole was obliged to perceive that he was beginning to do her little favors, such as, if they were sleeping in a grain-loft, undoing a truss of hay in order for her to sleep more comfortably, or taking her in his arms for a few minutes if the road had too many sharp stones, or pointing out to her, when they passed a wooded pathway, branches laden with green hazelnuts and mulberry-bushes bloody with mulberries.

One day, having quit her momentarily in the outskirts of a town, he rejoined her at a run and gave her some cakes; very probably, he had stolen them from a bakery, but after all, stolen or not, he gave them to her. Gratefully, she ate them with pleasure, being a little greedy, like nightingales.

As time went by, he became less cruel from day to day, almost gentle, almost tender. If he had not been so criminal, if she had not remembered the white hot needles sliding into the pale tubes, she might perhaps have come to love that poor unfortunate man.

As he became better, he became more melancholy. In his eyes, now, the malevolence was dying amid the reverie. Sometimes, as if he were experiencing some infinite dolor for which nothing could console him, he replaced his full tankard on the table without having raised it to his lips. Often, he had a haggard expression, and remained speechless, his eyes staring into the distance, with the air of a brute sick with nostalgia. Once he sobbed abruptly between his joined hands, like someone who has suddenly remembered a dead person who was tenderly beloved.

In consequence, Luscignole was scarcely surprised when, one evening when they were both sitting among the white stones and mud of a building site, he took her in his arms and clasped her to his heart, with hiccups of tenderness and tears, as a mother might have embraced her rediscovered child.

IV

It was a bright summer evening, with stars everywhere in the sky, swarming and palpitating. Hugging her more tenderly, he whispered in her ear, very softly, so softly that she could hardly hear: "Oh, I beg you! I beg you!"

For what was he begging her? She asked him, moved in spite of herself, so softly and sadly had he spoken.

"What do you want? Tell me what you want."

He repeated: "I beg you! I beg you!"

And he fell silent. There was around them the silence of desert nights, of closed windows, of the entire sleeping city, and above them the silence of the radiant sky. Why did he not explain himself? Why did she not interrogate him further? It was as if they were afraid, him of making a precise request, her of being required, after receiving it, to respond to it. And people passing by might have believed that they were asleep, side by side.

However, he went on, in a very low voice, turning away slightly from Luscignole: "Listen; I'm dying of chagrin; it's the truth, I'm dying. I can't live without hearing them, I can't live without them. It's all the same to me not eating, not drinking, to be dressed in muddy rags. What's eating me away and killing me is that I no longer have the song of the nightingales. It's extraordinary! I know full well that I'm not good, that I'm horrible, that I'm a drunkard, that I'm utterly worthless. But you see, frightful as I am, as I've always been, those birds put into me, into all my mind, into all my soul, into all my body, an infinite delight. No one can know how much love I had for them. And I don't believe that the songs of angels would be sweeter to a damned soul who had succeeded in climbing all the way to the gates of paradise than their song was to me. Oh, their voice spread within me beauty, light and goodness. It seemed to me, when they finished their song, that I was about

200

to die of tenderness. And it's finished now! I'll never have nightingales again. The smoke burned the nightingales of the tower. I'm not rich enough to keep any others. It's finished, it's finished; I'll never be content again."

Luscignole, in listening to him, became compassionate; she too had loved, so much, the singers captive in the forty cages.

Then, in a more supplicant tone, Alas Schlemp said: "But you, you, little girl, you sing as well as they sang. Perhaps you sing better! Oh, I beg you, I beg you, you're so good, I'm so unhappy, prevent me from dying. I've often been wicked with you. I've forced you to beg, I've beaten you; I won't do it anymore. It's me who'll hold my hand out to the people who pass by; instead of beating you I'll caress you all day long. But prevent me from dying. Sing for me, Luscignole!"

He had not finished when she stood up, with an anger that he had never had before.

"Sing for you? Me, sing for you? No, no, no!" she screamed.

V

He no longer dared beg her to sing. Doubtless, by the attitude and the voice of the little girl he had understood that she would not give in. To oblige her to sing, by means of threats, by means of beatings, even by the refusal of the rare nourishment that was making her thinner and thinner? He thought of that, in his evil soul. But he knew that brutality would fail, where tenderness had failed, knowing the obstinacy of nightingales, often mute for entire years in the depths of a cage.

He was not mistaken. The child, who had sung for the pretty king of the distant enchantments, would not give the torturer of her winged brothers, the horrible burner of eyes, the joy of hearing the sounds that charmed him; he would be punished for his crimes precisely by privation of the joy that he had owed to them.

Those ideas were confused in her, twelve years old, still a little girl, but what was certain that for Alas Schlemp, she would be mute forever.

For some time, their poverty had been less frightful. They no longer went from town to town, from village to village; they had settled in a village that was on the road to a grotto celebrated for stalactites and stalagmites, where tourists were abundant; so, all day long, outside the door of a hovel they had leased—the owner, by way of rent, took a percentage of the alms—they received, him deformed to the extent of seeming infirm and her dainty, with such a plaintive air, a good many copper coins and some silver ones. Then, when no one was going by any longer, when he went to get drunk in the tavern, while she ate an apple that was her evening meal, she went inside the hut of sorts, a bleak residence with two rooms and unglazed windows, with an opening in a corner of the roof through which the smoke exited of two green, oozing logs set in a cross.

It was on a pile of dry grass in the larger of the two rooms that Alas Schlemp, thrown out of the tavern, drunk, slept off the brown beer and the Schiedam. In the smaller room, Luscignole also had a bed of grass, but less faded, because every day, as one changes sheets, she renewed its verdure, and left little flowers therein, which she respired as she went to sleep.

She was so thoroughly accustomed to the staggering, hiccupping and vomiting nocturnal returns of her horrible companion, that in the end she so longer woke up; her slumber was pleasant, a refuge of her little dolorous soul, which amused itself there with dreams as if with toys. She saw herself in the cathedral again, among the saints and the cherubim; she climbed up into the tower, sought the dead eyes of a nightingale ensconced in the depths of a cage; then she rediscovered the fêtes of her glory, and the empresses and the princesses—and the king! It seemed to her that she was fluttering in the great cage in the cleft in the oak tree.

One night, her dream was fearful. Doubtless she recognized, in a dream, the presence of the enemy, crawling in the grass, who frightened her as much as when she was a little bird in the forest. But no, she heard, or thought she heard, a sound quite different from a rustle of parted leaves. There was something like a very slight sizzling in the sound that her sleeping ear perceived.

A reminiscence haunted her, which was not that of the murmur of the woods, nor a quivering of grass, but the renascent fear, anguishing, bewildered, fleeting, and also curious, of a sound that, she did not know where, had once terrified her.

And then she no longer knew whether she was asleep...

Only, perhaps, the illusion of waking up still somnolent induced her to believe that she was dreaming that which actually existed. More clearly brutal, fear took her by the throat, like a strangling hand. She thought terrifying things, or saw them.

What things? They were so formidable that it was necessary, at any price, to escape from them. She tried to leap from the bed. But no, she could not budge. Why? She was so tightly bound, as if in a tight shroud, or in the bandages of a mummy, that she thought about the nightingales enclosed, without any possible ruffling, in the narrow sheaths of tin-plate.

A prisoner! She must have been tied up, on the bed of grass, with cords nailed into the ground, fixed to the walls...

Fully awake, she widened her eyes.

Heavy, low, bumping his knock-knees, the gnome was leaning over a small table in the semi-darkness, where there was a redness that imparted to the darkness something like the smoke of blood.

Luscignole screamed, for she recognized, yes, she recognized the furnace, the frightful furnace, and beside it, the needles, and also the pale clay tubes...

She screamed, unable to move. She screamed and screamed. No, her voice was extinguished in the wadding that filled her mouth entirely, and, without movement, without speech, she looked at Alas Schlemp.

He put a needle, and another needle, into the embers of the furnace, drew them out, perceived that they were only red, and replaced them in order for them to become quite white; and he had the tranquil and busy expression of a very methodical executioner.

But since he had no cage, since there were no birds in the house, why was he heating the needles, two needles, white hot? And also, why was she bound to her bed, to the point of not being able to move, however slightly, an arm or a leg? And why was she gagged?

She opened her eyes ever wider; she watched, with more horror, the preparation for the tortures...

But in sum, was he...?

He turned toward her. He was smiling, with drooling lips. His eyes were so red, in the dense redness of the furnace, what one might have thought that they were gazing wounds. And he drew nearer, his spine curved, his neck elongated, holding a needle in one hand and a long tube in the other,

Scream! Scream! Oh, to be able to scream!

But she had wadding in all her mouth. And under the almost tender smile of Alas Schlemp she felt the coolness of the pale tube on her eyelid...

VI

Nowadays the travelers who stop in the city where the Emperor's chapel burned never fail to visit the ruins of the church. It is a curiosity, famous throughout Europe, and recommended by the best Baedeckers. A quadruple palisade prevents anyone from entering among the collapsed stones, between the ancient walls still standing. And in the bronze portal, inflated by the pressure of the fire, the cleft hollowed out by Satan's claw has been enlarged to the point that through it, beyond the ruins, one can see the sky.

People scarcely linger over such morose spectacles. The tourists say: "Good, good!" to the man charged with showing the remains of the cathedral; as they go away, they rarely fail—for one is charitable when traveling—to give alms to a frightful man, bent over and drooling, some epileptic, for whom, without moving, a little girl begs, so pale, with blank white eyes—for she is blind. It is a white wound that she has over her eyes. She cannot see. She begs. It is sad to see, in that young face, those two dead eyes.

Thus, Alas Schlemp and Luscignole have returned to the city where the tower inhabited by nightingales stood. They are stationed there all day, sitting on a bench, against the palisade. They are the paupers, as if official, of that mass of rubble, and it is only when night falls, when the passing of any stranger has become very improbable, that they return to the hovel where they have been lodging for a long time.

Before going in, Alas Schlemp stops in some tavern. He sits down; she remains standing while he drinks. She seems to be looking round, with the absence that is her eyes.

When Alas Schlemp is drunk, they go away. He can scarcely walk, totters, and nearly falls over, but she sustains him, and because she knows the way, the blind girl guides the drunkard. Oh, the poor creatures: him, for being so wicked; her, for being so martyrized.

However, they are not as unfortunate as one might think. In the lodgings, Alas Schlemp falls on to the floorboards, but he does not go to sleep, and Luscignole, near the window, in a ray of moonlight that comes from afar, which comes from the forest, which comes from the forests, sings delectably, as a nightingale, for the joy of the drunkard and for her own joy.

Never, when her eyes were open, did she sing so mysteriously, so tenderly, so recklessly!

And she attains ecstasy.

She does not lament the torture to which she was subjected, she does not regret either the skies, or the flowers, or the passers-by that one sees walking past, being resigned, unconsciously, to the implacable law that imposes as a condition of the perfect beauty of the song, dolor, darkness and, in the midst of life, exile.

Water, Ice and Fire

So pretty at the window of her cottage, a girl named Rose Lison was dreaming, a Rose amid the roses, a Lison amid the convolvulus: a dreaming flower, sister of the flowers that were blooming. And Rose Lison murmured between the climbing roses and the convolvulus, whose various colors quarreled in the sunlight:

"In truth, although such a poor peasant, I have no very grave cares, since grandmother, who is good to me, hums such lovely songs as her spinning-wheel turns, and since the young neighbor that I have rarely fails, as soon as I'm awake, to come to chat with me on the doorstep. One morning, I even followed him to the edge of the wood, to which the voice of a blackbird invited me; since then, I've always had on my lips the perfume of a strawberry, which he put there after having bitten it. However, it seems to me that I could be even happier than I am; I'd be grateful to anyone who could tell me where happiness is found."

Then, buzzing from a calyx to a corolla, a bee, who was a fay, said: "You're asking very little: and that's a service that I can easily render you. Follow the little path that emerges from this little wood into the plain. You won't take long to see a broad river, then a mountain of ice, and then a forest of flames. It's after having crossed the water, climbed the mountain and passed through the fire that you'll find happiness."

To tell the truth, Rose Lison felt perplexed; for, timid by nature, she feared the water, the ice and the fire greatly; but such was her desire to conquer happiness that she did not hesitate for long. Without saying adieu to her grandmother, who was singing and spinning, and without an adieu to the young neighbor who bit strawberries before offering them, she set off for the path, after having put into a little basket, in order not to die of hunger or ennui in the journey, an apple, a little pot of flour and an elder-wood whistle with which she took pleasure in imitating the blackbirds.

And a river appeared to her, wide and seething to the point that, if Rose Lison had known what the sea was, she would have thought that it was the sea. She was as surprised and as frightened as possible. A poor little thing who could not swim, she would never be able to traverse the vast and tumultuous river. She looked to the right and to the left, searching for a boatman; the entire bank was deserted.

Although she had never rowed, she thought that she might be able to get out of difficulty if she had a boat, and she conceived the design of making one with one of the big trees that loomed up here and there. But was that not an extravagant idea? What means was there for her, with her little hands, which would not have been sufficient to bend the hardly robust stem of a lily, and without any tools, to saw and hollow out the hard trunk of a larch?

Discouraged, Rose Lison let herself fall on to the grass and wept bitterly, thinking that she would never arrive in the place where happiness was.

But there was a sound in the basket of something round rolling back and forth. and when she lifted the lid the little girl heard the apple say: "Come on, child, I'm taking pity on your chagrin, With a sharp stone, as you have no knife, peel me entirely and, having eaten my flesh to give you courage, my skin, joined together in a long strip and fastened with horns, will make a light boat into which you'll be able to fit, by squeezing a little."

"But how will I be able to steer that fail boat through the nasty water?"

"Sing as best you can, and your voice will be the good breeze that will guide you to port."

Rose Lison did as the apple had said. Then, singing and singing, she sailed in a skiff made of the peel of the fruit between the wildly bounding waves. Oh, what alarms! But she finally landed on the other shore; in her basket there was a little pot of flour and the elder-wood whistle with which she amused herself imitating the blackbirds.

A mountain of ice appeared to her as soon as night had fallen, so vast and so smooth that, the stars and the moon already being reflected in it, it resembled an enormous crystal slope through which one could see all the splendors of paradise. But alas, how could one climb that dazzling hill, without projections, and so cold, where the fingernails, having nothing to hang on to, would be turned back, or the hands and the entire body would also become ice? It would have required harpoons, crampons and ropes; she had none of that.

Discouraged, Rose Lison let herself fall at the foot of the mountain, and wept bitterly, thinking that she would never arrive where happiness was.

But there was a little stir in the basket, like something light shaking and sliding, and when the lid was lifted, the girl heard the little pot of four, which said: "Come on, darling, I'm interested in your dolor; take all the flour into the palms of your hands, and throw it on to the smooth mountain of ice. With its help, you'll be able to hoist yourself up to the summit without your fingernails turning back and without your body being frozen."

"But the flour I've thrown will fall back as soon as I try to climb higher!"

"As soon as one of your hands has released it, you'll pick it up with the other."

Rose Lison did what the little pot of flour had said. Then, throwing the light whiteness, she used it in order not to slip, and having picked it up rapidly, threw it again. Oh, what dreads! Oh what shivers! But she finally reached the highest point of the mountain. In the basket there was the elder-wood whistle with which she amused herself imitating the blackbirds.

And in the black midnight, suddenly, a forest of flames appeared to her. It was ablaze everywhere, so leafy with red flames, so mossy with embers, that one might have thought one were seeing the park in which King Lucifer strolls on feast days with his guests, the damned souls of distinction.

Alas, what means was there to pass through that magnificent and frightful conflagration, where her hair would catch fire like golden oakum thrown on to red-hot brands, and her entire body would soon be similar to what remains of a vine-branch thrown into the broad kitchen hearth?

Full of anguish—an anguish irremediable this time—Rose Lison sat down on the edge of the forest of flames, and sobbed, and sobbed, because she understood that she would never arrive in the land where happiness was.

But there was a susurrus in the basket like a blackbird singing, and when the lid was lifted, the girl heard the elder-wood whistle, which said: "Come on, poor child, I want to help you in your despair; pick me up, put me to your lips and blow, blow, blow into me while walking toward the forest. Your breath will part the flames and make a path of sorts, in which you'll be able to pass through without being burned."

"But the fire will close behind me and ignite my skirt!"

"From time to time, turn round cleverly in order to blow backwards."

Rose Lison did as the elder-wood whistle had said. Then she advanced through the enormous conflagration, parting the flames by blowing her whistle. Oh, God, if she had run out of breath even for an instant! What anxieties! What apprehensions!

Victorious over the fire, she arrived at daybreak on a road on which there was a thatched cottage...

And she recognized the road! And she recognized the thatched cottage where the roses were climbing, where the various colors of the convolvulus were quarreling with the rising sun. Grandmother was sitting on the bench beside the threshold, and the young neighbor was hastening toward the door carrying a wicker basket full of strawberries and woodland flowers.

Rose Lison felt her entire heart melt in a tender delight. Oh, how much joy she experienced in seeing the dear flowery cottage again, and the old woman who knew such lovely songs, and the handsome boy with whom her heart was smitten,.

Happy? Yes, truly, she was happy; a thousand times more than she had ever hoped to be.

But then, what had been the use of so many perils vanquished, so many fears and so many despairs?

Buzzing from a calyx to a corolla, the bee that was a fay said: "Child, there is only contentment when one has merited it, and in order truly to possess even the happiness that one has, it is necessary to pass through water, ice and fire."

The Clear-Sighted Gold Coin

There as once a ten-franc gold coin who was a fay. She rolled and rolled over the sidewalks throughout the city.

"Why did no one pick her up?" you're thinking. "There's no lack of people willing to bend down to pick up something shiny."

It's because, by virtue of her magic power, she had rendered herself invisible, and no one knew that the ten-franc coin was rolling over the sidewalks of the city. As for the reason that obliged her to travel in that fashion, I won't hide it from you; for some misdeed, not too serious—I think it was the minor fault of having slid into a keyhole to prevent the key from turning in the hand of a husband who had come very ferociously, to interrupt the delights of an amiable adultery—she had merited, once having been a very illustrious fay clad entirely in gems, being mutated into a small coin. Such was the decree of Merlin, whose dwelling, as everyone knows, is under the third oak tree on the left after the guard-house in Meudon Wood, that she would only recover her original form and all her power when, as a gold coin, she had made the best possible charity of her own accord.

Making charity did not displease her—on the contrary—for, not being one of those nasty fays who amuse themselves tormenting people, nothing was more agreeable to her than coming to the aid of poor folk. But she felt very anxious regarding the choice that was imposed on her. The worst punishments were promised if she offered herself as alms to someone unworthy; and, very perplexed, she rolled and rolled, more rapidly, with the little sound of nutshell wheels that Queen Mab's carriage makes.

"Charity! My good Messieurs et Mesdames, charity, if you please! Take pity on a poor blind man who does not even have the wherewithal to buy a clarinet!"

She stopped. What if she were to give herself to that unfortunate man? But between the closed eyes of the beggar slid a gaze so subtle that she sensed that she was almost seen, invisible as she was. She recommenced rotating on her axis.

At the door of a bakery there was a tumultuous gathering; policemen had seized a poor old woman, weeping and struggling with children hanging on to her skirts. According to what as being said in the hubbub, the wretch was being taken to prison because she had stolen a loaf of bread from the bakery; the flour-stained owner had called the police.

The fay was on the point of giving herself to the old woman, but she thought that, with the money she was worth, the baker would be paid for the bread, and she did not want to be agreeable to such a nasty man. In any case, what good would it do that pauperess not to go to prison and to subsist for a few days more? If the children did not die of hunger, would they not be as unhappy as their mother or as cruel as the baker? It is charity, for them and for others, to allow those who cannot live happily or well to die. And the fay drew away between the shoes and the ankle-boots.

Not far from there, in front of a mercer's display-window, a little errand-girl, fifteen years old, thin and dainty, with a pink nose, patches of redness under a shock of red hair, was admiring with enviously devouring eyes a pink silk cravat bordered with fake Valenciennes. Oh, the poor child, how she would have liked to put it round her neck, that cravat, which was so expensive! And with the flame of desire, she had in her eyes the humid sadness of regret.

The fay felt very moved. With the ten francs that she was, the errand-girl could buy the cravat. But she thought that the frail and pale neck was more exquisite naked than it would be if it were veiled with silk; and soon, in any case, there would be more lace cravats than anyone could wish, and necklaces, and more necklaces. She rolled away. She did not even notice a prowler with a hungry expression gazing through the window of a famous restaurant at a pheasant with all its plumage and truffles overflowing from the carcass of the bird, the dinner of two bankers with replete bellies.

On a boulevard, momentarily moved to compassion, she nearly gave herself to one of those wanderers who speak in low voices to passers-by, wanting to take them into the shadows of nearby streets, where the corners of coaching entrances resemble the edges of an alcove; for those sellers whom beauty and amour have passed over are a lamentable disaster and in perfect despair even when they are unaware of any human ideal. However, the gold coin continued to roll.

Leaning on the parapet of a bridge, an old man was considering the somber flowing water, and because she was a fay she heard the soul lamenting within him: "So, I brought to humans the realized splendor of dreams! An inventor, I would have offered them increased wellbeing, prolonged life, durable happiness; as a poet, I would have offered their minds an infinity of exquisite and sublime chimeras. And they did not want to hear me; they chased me away. And this evening, the clerk at the hotel refused me the key to my room, the rent not having been paid for three months. It's time to die. I'll throw myself in the river, here, at this beautiful luminous place where the overlapping light of two street-lamps intersects like a splendid opening in the sky."

The little gold coin rolled to the feet of the desperate man; she was about to become visible, to allow herself to be picked up...

No, she went on her way while the man hurled himself into the river. It seemed that there were, although she did not know where, miseries more worthy of the charity that she ought to be.

In the blackest darkness, she saw cut-throats whom a windfall might perhaps spare from the crime and the scaffold; she did not give herself away.

Outside drinking-dens she saw ragged women waiting with their faces to the window for a husband or a lover to finish drinking the week's pay; she passed on. She saw nocturnal vagabondage insinuating itself under bridges, descending into the shafts of quarries; she passed on, she passed on.

She arrived before a wide open door, illuminated by a semicircle of white globes. Cries, laughter and dance music emerged therefrom: the door of some ballroom. It was not there that she would find the poverty worthy of being helped. There was nothing there but joy. She was about to roll on...

She perceived a young man sitting on a bench, who was weeping, his head in his hands, and she listened to the young man's dolor.

"She's there! She's laughing and dancing with all the others. Soon, I'll see her come out. She won't be alone. They'll go away. I'll have the sad jealousy to follow them. I'll see them both enter his house. And she would have loved me this evening if I'd been able to go into the dance-hall with her, and buy her a drink, as the rich men do!"

The fay no longer hesitated. Visible, she threw herself toward the weeping young man. He picked her up with a cry of joy, ran to the ticket-window, changed he gold coin, bought a ticket, went into the dance-hall, joyful, happy and superb, found his friend, took her in his arms, danced with her recklessly, bought her large glasses of wine, got her drunk, charmed her, took her away, and in the small room of a hotel—*beds for the night two francs*—the fay, reduced by each transaction until she was no more than a two-sou piece on the corner of the mantelpiece, heard the adorable gasps of the ecstatic lovers until morning.

It was not without anxiety that she approached the oak— the third on the left after he guard-house—in which the omnipotent Merlin was enthroned in Meudon wood. Hidden in the long grass, she waited until he appeared, and her heart was beating rapidly. Would she be recompensed or punished? Had she made the right choice? She had disdained so many lamentable or noble miseries.

She thought that the judge was about to loom up before her in terrible pomp, followed by the torturers by means of whom culpable fays were punished. Oh, what would happen? Perhaps she would be condemned to lodge for a hundred years, stark naked, between polar ice-sheets; perhaps she would remain imprisoned, for more than two centuries, in some hollow tree, full of rats and climbing ants; or she might be precipitated into profound darkness with neither a star nor a dawn...

The whole forest lit up with a delightful light, as if it had been traversed everywhere by a thousand glow-worms the color of pearls; and among his court of goblins dressed in silk, and ladies with brocade trains, and gnomes charged with gemstones extracted from obscure mines, the enchanter Merlin, king of mysterious beings, sat on his golden throne encrusted with rubies and chrysolites, his face resplendent with contentment and praise.

Another throne was beside him. "Come, come," he said, "O admirable fay. It's befitting that you take your place beside me; not only will you recover your original form and powers, but glories hitherto unknown to you will be offered to you, since, little gold coin, you have made such a judicious and fine employment of yourself."

She approached, she sat down beside the master, while around her, raising and lowering their arms, the goblins, the ladies and the gnomes congratulated her with genuflections ad prostrate praises.

"Speak!" said Merlin. "Would you like to be clad in the aurora and stars? Would you like storms and the sea to obey the breath of your little mouth? Would you like the power to make roses bloom in the snows of winter? Would you like to lodge in a sunlit palace where you would have all the queens and all the goddesses for chambermaids, glad to be your servants? For there is nothing you have not merited."

The demanding fay replied: "I accept, gladly, the glories that you offer me. But since you judge me worthy of all recompenses, there is one more that I dare to solicit, even if, for that one, I must renounce all the others."

"What is that?" said Merlin.

"It is," said the fay, "to be for an hour, only one hour, as the women sighing in her lover's arms was, in the little hotel room, when I was no more than a two-sou piece on the corner of the mantelpiece."

Jocelyne's Blunders;
Or, The Little Girl Thrice Disappointed

Jocelyne is coming to see her godmother, who is the fay who lives on the other side of the road. In those days, fays were so common that there was not far to go to find one when anyone wanted one, and more often than not it was sufficient to cross the road.

THE FAY: Good day, my goddaughter, good day, darling. What concern brings you here this fine morning, and what do you desire?

JOCELYNE Know, godmother, that I had a little dream last night.

THE FAY: Well, who sleeps, dreams, especially little girls. What was your dream? Speak.

JOCELYNE: I was traveling in the sunlight and I was very thirsty.

THE FAY: That someone who travels in the sunlight would be very thirsty isn't at all surprising.

JOCELYNE: But there was no stream in the little wood nearby. Oh, godmother, give me a gift in case I get thirsty climbing the hill in the middle of the day.

THE FAY: If you get thirsty climbing the hill in the middle of the day, there will be a cherry on the tip of a branch so large and so fresh that it will suffice to slake your thirst.

JOCELYNE: How good you are, godmother. I haven't told you all my dream.

THE FAY: Speak, then, my goddaughter, speak, my darling.

JOCELYNE: I left for a fête in which there was dancing, and I had a great desire for a pink handkerchief woven with gold, which I would have knotted as a headscarf.

THE FAY: That someone leaving for a dance should have a desire for a pink headscarf woven with gold is quite natural.

JOCELYNE: But I'm too poor to buy such things. Oh, god-mother, give me a gift in case I want to adorn myself as the local damsels do.

THE FAY: If you should want to adorn yourself as the local dames do, you will find in the ditch a hennin that the queen dropped the other morning while hunting heron and capercaillie

JOCELYNE: How good you are, godmother. I ought to tell you the end of my dream.

THE FAY: Speak, then, my goddaughter, speak, my darling.

JOCELYNE: Having seen the pigeons in the pigeon-loft peck-ing one another, and having seen the linnets and finches ruf-fling their feathers and flapping their wings, I conceived a great desire for a boy to kiss me on the lips and clasp me against him as hard as he likes.

THE FAY: That someone fifteen years old who observes the tender games of birds should have such a desire is not at all singular.

JOCELYNE: But there was no one nearby but an old beggar that I wouldn't want for a grandfather. Oh, godmother, give me a gift in case I have the desire to be kissed, because of the example of the cooing pigeons.

THE FAY: If the desire takes you to be kissed, because of the example of the cooing pigeons, you will see on a bed of flowering heather a young man so handsome that you will swoon with delight.

JOCELYNE: How good you are, godmother. I've told you all of my dream, and I thank you.

THE FAY: Go, then, darling. But by age and heart, you're very scatterbrained. Be suspicious of certain individuals who are also fays, and who will make use of adroit ruses to despoil you of the gifts I've given you.

JOCELYNE: Oh, I'll be careful not to allow myself to be duped. For, without seeming to be, I'm very clever when I want to be.

THE FAY: Adieu, then, goddaughter.

JOCELYNE: Adieu, then, godmother.

Before long, Jocelyne departs on a long journey. Where is she going? Where her dream went. Now climbing a hill in the middle of the day, she was very thirsty. She was not anxious, even though there was no stream babbling in the nearby wood. Thanks to the fay's gift, she saw, on the tip of a branch, such a beautiful cherry than none more beautiful had ever been seen in any orchard in the world. She stood on tiptoe and raised her arm; she was about to pick the fruit, but there was a little bird twittering on the branch beside the cherry.

THE LITTLE BIRD: Cui! cui! cui! cui!

JOCELYNE: What's that? What's that?

THE LITTLE BIRD: Eh! cui, cui, cui, little girl.

JOCELYNE: What's that, little bird?

THE LITTLE BIRD: Beware of eating that cherry.

JOCELYNE: Why should I beware?

THE LITTLE BIRD: Because it isn't ripe.

JOCELYNE: It's so red that it must be sweet.

THE LITTLE BIRD: That's only a vain appearance; in reality it's as acidic as a green mulberry, and you'll have a very bitter mouth.

JOCELYNE: What should I do, then?

THE LITTLE BIRD: Wait for it to ripen. Don't you have anything else to do? Follow your route and come back in an hour or two. Then it will be ripe and your thirst will be charmed by it.

JOCELYNE: Yes, but what if someone steals it while I'm not here?

THE LITTLE BIRD: For love of you, I'll stand guard. There's no danger that anyone else will touch it while I'm here, and you'll find it intact.

JOCELYNE: Au revoir, then, little bird!

THE LITTLE BIRD: Au revoir, then, little girl.

Very happy, truly, to have encountered such an obliging bird, Jocelyne continues traveling in accordance with the dream she had, and now she hears the flutes and viols of a dance in the distance, not far from a hamlet whose thatched roofs are gilded by the sunlight. Of course, she cannot go to the ball bare-headed, like a pauper. But is she sad? No; she is counting, not without reason, on her godmother's gift; and, indeed, she sees in the ditch a pink silk hennin woven with gold. She bends down, picks it up and smiles with ease, thinking that she will be coiffed. But there is an old woman there, who looks like one of the spinners that one sees at the doors of cottages.

THE OLD WOMAN: Fie! fie! fie! fie!

JOCELYNE: What? What?

THE OLD WOMAN: Beware, little girl...

JOCELYNE: Of what, old woman?

THE OLD WOMAN: Of touching that hennin.

JOCELYNE: Why should I beware of it?

THE OLD WOMAN: It's because, in the ditch, it was torn by brambles and soaked by the rain.

JOCELYNE: Such as it is, I'll be content with it, and thanks to it, I'll be better adorned than the local damsels.

THE OLD WOMAN: No! I can't abide that, dainty as you are, you put on a head-dress in such a pitiful state.

JOCELYNE: What shall I do, then?

THE OLD WOMAN: You can wait for me, a mender by trade, to restitch and repair it. Come back in an hour or two. You'll find it like a brand new hennin.

JOCELYNE: Au revoir, then, old woman.

THE OLD WOMAN: Au revoir, then, little girl.

Jocelyne, continuing her journey, feels moved by all the good intentions that are being testified to her. She swears that she will show her gratitude to the bird who is guarding the cherry and the old woman who is repairing the hennin. But now she is in the wood at the rosy hour before dusk and everything is swooning of heat and tender lassitude. The branches rustle with the slowness of arms and everywhere whispers, sighs and perfumes are dying away delectably. Jocelyne feels so troubled that she thinks she is about to faint. Fortunately, her godmother has refrained from refusing her the last promised gift. Jocelyne sees, on a bed of flowering heather, a youth as handsome as an angel, who is dressed as a nobleman of the court. He is asleep, his mouth half-open, his eyes half-closed; his mouth is like a rose that is about to blossom, and each of his eyes is a cornflower veiled by a petal of a white rose. And Jocelyne...

But there is a strange woman there, dressed in golden rags and skillfully faked jewelry, like a gypsy, who has bare breasts; one might think her a pauper who could be a princess.

THE GYPSY: Oh! oh! oh! oh!

JOCELYNE: Why these cries?

THE GYPSY: Beware, little girl...

JOCELYNE: Of what, Madame?

THE GYPSY: Of kissing that youth.

JOCELYNE: Why should I beware of that?

THE GYPSY: Don't you see that he's still very young? Scarcely fourteen, I imagine. Such as he is, caressed and caressing, he'll only give you furtive delights.

JOCELYNE: Young as he is, and although the birds sing for a long time about amour, I'll accord myself an enchantment that's a little too brief, as long as it's extreme.

THE GYPSY: No! I can't abide that, smitten as I see you are, that you should disappointed by such a novice lover. Haven't you left on the road, at the tip of a branch, a cherry that pleases your thirst?

JOCELYNE: Yes. A bird is guarding it for me. It ought to be ripe by now.

THE GYPSY: Have you not left on the road, near a ditch, a pink hennin woven with gold?

JOCELYNE: Yes, an old woman is mending it for me. It ought to be repaired by now.

THE GYPSY: Go and eat the cherry, then, and put on the hennin. During your absence this boy will have time to become a valiant young man, and you'll have all possible satisfaction when you return.

JOCELYNE: But what if someone other than me comes to take him away?

THE GYPSY: Am I not here to defend him? I've conceived a sincere amity for you, and I'll conserve intact for you the man who will be your wellbeing.

JOCELYNE: Se you soon, then, Madame!

THE GYPSY: See you soon, little girl.

Jocelyne is no longer walking; she runs. She runs so rapidly, along a lateral path, that she soon arrives at the place where the cherry was ripening. But the cherry is no longer there, and the poor little girl, raising her head, sees the bird, who is mocking her—Cui! cui! cui! cui!—its beak still pink with the fruit it has eaten. Oh, the traitor! The villain! Alas, what is the point of lamenting?

She retraces her steps, still running. She reaches the ditch where the queen's hennin lay. But the hennin has disappeared, and in the distance, amid the flutes and the viols, near the hamlet with the thatched roofs red and gold in the dusk, she perceives the old mender, laughing and dancing coiffed in the hennin woven with gold. Oh, the sly individual! Oh, the hypocrite! Alas, what is the point of lamenting?

At least, while she was returning for the cherry and the hennin, the youth ought to have grown enough for her to have all pleasure imaginable, and it is worth more than a fresh fruit to be eaten or a golden head-dress to put on to be kissed by the lips of a vigorous lover. She hastens toward the bed of flowery heather.

To tell the truth, the young nobleman has not disappeared, but he is lying in the arm of the pauper with the airs of a princess, and whereas her breasts were naked before, the rest of her is no less so now. Jocelyne, utterly crestfallen, returns to her godmother, who is the fay on the other side of the road, and she cannot talk, so much is she weeping.

JOCELYNE : Ai! ai! ai! ai!

THE FAY: What did I say, my goddaughter? What did I tell you, darling? However, console yourself. Tomorrow I'll give you new gifts. But let today serve as a lesson, and don't leave your cherry to be guarded by a sparrow, your fine attire by an old coquette, or your lover, even very young, by a beautiful young woman who undresses quickly!

The Poet and the Pearl

A fay gave me a pearl, saying: "Most people think that pearls form in mollusks. Nothing of the sort: pearls are the tears, which fall into the sea, of young Elect scolded for playing truant along the Milky Way by Saint Gudule and Saint Veronica, the schoolmistresses of Paradise."

"I've always suspected it," I affirmed.

"In any case," she said, "that's not the issue. Look carefully at what I've given you. It's the brightest, the purest and the most exquisite of the tears that were wept by the heavenly schoolgirls. Neither Theocritus nor Banville would be able to find an image worthy of depicting the miraculous soft splendor of the pearl. In a word, it's quite perfect."

"How I thank you, good fay, for such a present!"

"You'll thank me even more! To that pearl, so marvelous that nothing can equal it, by touching it with my hazel-wood wand encrusted with rubies, I have accorded the miracle of mutating, in accordance with the wish that you form, into no matter what being or thing, and retaining its incomparable beauty in its new form, which you will determine. Choose, then, between your desires; if you want it to become a star, it will immediately become more radiant than Sirius, Venus, Orion and Aldebaran."

"Oh!" I cried, recklessly. "I want it to be..."

"A woman?" the fay interrupted. "I expected such a wish of you, knowing that you are not one of those—rare, in any case—who make a horror out of the lively rose of young feminine lips. Don't be in such a hurry to make up your mind, though; one often repents of hasty decisions. Take your time. Reflect, and above all, dream...I'll come back tomorrow to ask you what choice you've made. Is that agreed?"

"It's agreed."

"Until tomorrow then, poet!"

"Until tomorrow, fay!"

To tell the truth, I was certain that neither reflection nor dreaming would modify in any fashion my instinctive and so reasonable desire. The most beautiful of pearls having become a woman while remaining as beautiful—what treasure is worth as much as that?

Already, the delight that suddenly makes all the roses on earth bloom, sets the day ablaze and tints the profound sea blue when Aphrodite looms up outside a fleeting robe of foam, was enchanting my heart and my soul, and—you could bet on it—my body as well. I would see, I would embrace, and I would possess the chimera of perfect beauty, eternally hoped for and never seized: the perfect beauty that made the likes of Phidias and Cleomenes sob with ecstasy and laugh with despair.

Religious transports toward the infinite sky of eyes in which strange stars rise! Adoration joining hands—soon opened—toward the divinity of the breasts, one and double! The fervor of masses celebrated before the white sheet of the belly! The intoxication of calices drunk at the main altar that radiates between the august colonnade of marmoreal limbs! I would know all of those joys! And I raised my forehead proudly.

But at that moment the young person who is tender to me leaned over my shoulder, curious about my pensive silence, I had the soft breath that is the precursor of a kiss close to my moustache. Alas, how pretty she is, the dear! Would the pearl-woman charm me to that degree, perhaps more beautiful…but no more delectable? What! For the love of perfection, it would be necessary for me to renounce such exquisite and adored imperfections? Perhaps I would lose by it. Besides which, contrary to the example of great Lovers trailing after them an innumerable troop of Elviras, I have always had, I blush to admit, a horror of change…

How agreeable it would be to live in a palace where, as in the one that Pierre Corneille evoked for Psyche, everything is made for the pleasure of the eyes. The nobility of architectures has the wherewithal to please souls smitten with well-ordered poems as white as princely vestibules. I thought that it would not be so foolish to mutate the pearl into a superb edifice.

What if it were to become a sumptuous domain, with long avenues, extending my seigneurial reveries toward the horizon of the sea? What if I made of it a horse as fast as a storm wind, with a mane of lightning, which would carry me toward the vertigos of dream? What if I were to make it into garments so resplendent that Sardanapalus could not have had their like on his triumphant pyre; or a feast whose odor, universally spread, would rejoice the resuscitated hunger of Brillat-Savarin and Monselet; or a sacred carriage amid the enthusiasm of crowds, or the mantle of a emperor; or a crown so arrogantly fulgurant that all diadems and tiaras would be humiliated before it?

Those various metamorphoses of the pearl had much to tempt me. I could also wish that it might become the throne of lightning and cloud on which God the Father sits, where I could sit in my turn...

In truth, I remained as perplexed as one can be.

The next day, however—after so many reflections and dreams—there was no longer the slightest hesitation in me. When the fay came in, I was considering with an untroubled gaze the pearl that she had given me, which I had put among the papers on my table, in a bronze cup, between a volume of Léon Dierx and a volume of José-Maria de Hérédia.

"Well, is your choice made, poet?" the fay asked.

"Yes, fay."

"Definitively?"

"Yes."

"You don't retain any regret for the good things you've had to renounce?"

"None."

"You won't ever believe that you've used the privilege that belongs to you poorly?"

"Never."

"Speak, then," said the fay. "What do you want the destined pearl to become, in its new form, which will be yours, while retaining its incomparable beauty?"

"A sonnet," I said.

Prince Lys and the Wave of Snow

I do not have a clear memory of whether I have taken the tale I am about to tell from the legend of Saint Armentarius, where mention is made, as early as the year 1300, of a Provençal fay named Esterelle—the same one, no doubt, who put all the gifts of poetry and charm into the cradle of our dear Paul Arène[18]—or whether it has stuck in my memory for having once read Olaüs Magnus, who was a very savant historian of fades and formosas, of which, in his day, there was a great multitude in Sweden.[19] It might also be the case that I had invented the story.

Imagination or memory, I cannot help being moved, not only by compassion for Prince Lys but by a personal sadness, and you will be moved in the same way, for is not his adventure still our adventure too? But for us, it does not end so happily...

Here is the tale:

---

[18] The Provençal poet Paul Arène (1843-1896) published "Deux légendes de la mer," which mentions the fays Esterelle and Morgane in the literary supplement of *L'Écho de Paris*, of which Mendès was the editor, on 13 March 1892.

[19] *Historia de Gentibus Septentrionalibus* [A Description of the Northern People (1555; French version 1561) by the Swedish Catholic clergyman Olaüs Magnus was a patriotic work that is the source text of much information about Scandinavian folklore, including stories of sea-nymphs, although he does not use the exotic terms *fade* and *formose* [formosa], here recruited by Mendès to refer to supernatural creatures. *Fade* appears in the English romance of *Gawain and the Green Knight*, apparently as an English equivalent of *fée*. *Formose* is derived from the Latin, meaning "beautiful."

There was once, in kingdom in the North, all white with snow and all luminous with frost, a young prince who was known as Prince Lys because he was whiter than the purest of the country's snows, and also because he had in the face the impression of a strangely candid soul. Although he had attained twenty years of age with the first snowflakes of last winter, he did not want to hear any mention whatsoever of marriage. It served no purpose to show him the portraits of the most beautiful princesses of the earth; he did not deign to cast his eyes upon them, to the great chagrin of the king and the queen, whose only child he was, and who were naturally very desirous of seeing their lineage continued.

The ladies and damsels of the court were also in the greatest melancholy for, more handsome than it is possible to say—as handsome as young Esplandian was when he appeared in white armor of Oriane's island—he had no less coldness toward them than toward the daughters of foreign sovereigns. If by chance, at some fête he passed between the double row of marquises and countesses, he hastened as much as he could, not without an air of disdain, or, when etiquette obliged him to walk less rapidly, he kept his eyes lowered toward the carpet, as if to avoid seeing the shoulders and cleavages of so many beautiful women in low-cut dresses.

The most common opinion was that Prince Lys was the victim of an enchantment. Yes, a spell must have been cast upon him. But who had done that? On the day of his first smile in his royal cradle, his parents, as was the custom in those days in that country, had not failed to invite all the most powerful fays. Urgèle had come in her robe the color of jasmine spangled with silver, so that she seemed to be wearing a fragment of the Milky Way; Abonde had come, clad in golden convolvulus,[20] with a bee tintinnabulating in every flower; and Mélusine, who, for having been a serpent, leaves behind the

---

[20] Abonde is a Gallic derivative of the Roman personification of abundance, Abundantia, who appears in the thirteenth century allegory *Le Roman de la Rose* as "Dame Habonde"

fugitive gleams of narrow and supple garments; and Titania, very small, all around whom flew ribbons of pearl and chrysolith, and whose train was carried by a fat man with an ass's head braying amorously, as comically as possible.

The last to come, but not the least radiant, was one who does not always deign to come to the celebration of royal births, Madame Holda, a little less pouty for having been made into a goddess, but so marvelously beautiful, and, in addition to her lunar or auroral satin robe, allowing the sight of a breast more miraculously sublime that the one that made the old men marvel when the Argienne appeared on the rampart with a lily in her hand. Madame Holda was particularly amiable toward the newborn prince; as he was waking up from his first slumber, she took him in her arms, and cradled him momentarily over that adorable breast...[21]

Truly, the child who had had such powerful and radiant godmothers ought not to have had to fear either enchantments or spells,

However, the young prince because increasingly antisocial. He did not want even the portraits of princesses to be shown to him; he no longer consented to appear at court. As soon as no one was looking, he escaped from the palace, and his sole joy was to wander all alone in the whiteness of the Northern country.

---

[21] In German folklore Frau Holda or Holle was a protective spirit of agriculture and female crafts, demonized by the Catholic Church, who associated her with the imagery of the Sabbat, and partially redeemed by Jakob Grimm, who tried to establish her as an echo of an ancient Teutonic goddess—the redemption to which the story refers. Argiennes (female inhabitants of Argos) were said in some Classical documents to have special privileges with regard to the temple of Hera; the specific reference here is to a poem by Mendès, "Ballade de l'amant fidèle" which invokes the appearance of one with a symbolic lily in hand to frighten white-haired old men.

Prince Lys often remained motionless for entire hours, his gaze and his arms raised toward some snowy mountain, whose summit, in the evening, was gilded by a star, or, in the morning, tinted roseate by the dawn—and slowly, tears ran from his eyes toward the ecstatic smile of his mouth. Then he resumed his route, the road of Dreams, which goes no one knows where; and he staggered as he walked, like a man carrying an excessively heavy burden.

At other times, in some path scintillating with frost, he picked one of the flowers, so white, known as snowdrops, and he kissed it for a long, long time with bewildered lips...

But then he shook his head, dropped the flower, and sighed profoundly, his head between his hands.

Sometimes, too, with untrodden snow taken from the slope of a hill, he tried to make between his hands a roundness of splendor and candor, but he doubtless did not find it splendid enough or candid enough, for he let the snow fall from his fingers, and sobbed desperately...

One day, he went much further than usual. He had traversed plains and climbed mountains and, from the height of a rock, he saw the sea in the distance, bristling with icebergs, where the iridescent daylight was dazzling, and much closer, so soft, so purely profound, slowly fading away in delectable swellings, the sea that had once given birth to Venus, now named Holda, the goddess become a fay, as beautiful and mysterious as itself.

But the waves, in that country, because of the reflection of the snows, which add further whiteness to the whiteness of the foam, swell more delectably than toward any other shore. And Prince Lys experienced a joy unknown until that day, the never-realized presentiment of which had caused him, after cruel hopes, so many torturing disappointments...

One wave, in particular, enchanted and attracted him, rising so exquisitely, so round, so smooth, so white so reminiscent of...he knew not what.

And, his arms forward, he slid deliciously toward the wave, the wave similar to Madame Holda's breast...

The Flowers' Carnival

One evening in April or May, or perhaps July—what I remember very clearly is that it was last year—as I was leaning out of my window, around which convolvulus and wisteria were climbing, one of the convolvulus flowers leaned toward me and whispered something in my ear. I was not at all surprised, and I cried: "Aha! There you are, then, little fay Elvine!"

"Good," she said. "I see that you're not forgetful, and I'm glad that, without seeing me yet, you've recognized me merely by my voice."

At the same time, she leapt out of the calyx on to my wide open hand; and it was indeed, speaking with the frisson of a dragonfly skimming the water, the little fay Elvine, no larger than the little finger of a little girl, but entirely clad in golden satin, with red shoes that were made from a ladybird's wing-case, and a diadem in which twelve specks of adamantine dust were scintillating, looking just like the Princess of Lilliput's doll.

"Finally, here you are!" I said. "I haven't seen you for a long time!"

"Oh," she said, "that's because, for several months, you've been behaving badly. More than it's possible to say. Haven't you taken it into your head, for instance, to speak well of a sonnet with fifteen lines and a ballade without an envoi? Fie, Monsieur, fie! Who can one trust henceforth? Fortunately, last week was better, in eight days you've written a little ode in which there as a new rhyme, admired a fine piece of music, adored a pretty woman, praised a true poet and insulted an imbecile. That's worth a recompense, and bonjour—I've arrived!"

"Oh, the sweet pleasure!" I said to her. "I've always cherished fays, but I cherish them much more since real people came to seem so wicked and stupid."

"And I'll give you another pleasure too," she said.

"What's that, little Elvine?"

"We're going to a ball."

"Don't mock, I beg you, the ancient rhymer that I've become. Don't you know that I can't walk without the aid of a stick on which to lean, unsteadily? And that I cough. And that if I possessed anything and had heirs, for a long time they'd have had every right to reproach me for my tenacious survival? They're not for people of my age, the amusements of dancing."

"It's certain," she said, "that you're strangely old. But I know you, good apostle! Let's wager that you'd still be capable of one or two turns of a waltz, if your dancing-partner promised, afterwards, in some solitary path or an almost-dark boudoir, the dress having slipped from her shoulder, to let you lick the two or few drops of dew that warmth had put in the golden flower of her armpit?"

"Ah!" I said, cheered up by that amiable thought.

"Furthermore," said Elvine, "it's a matter of a ball at which you'll only have to watch others dance."

"And where is it being held, this ball?" I asked.

"In your garden," she said.

I went downstairs, the fay sitting on the stone in my ring; the flower-bed, in the moonlight, was delightful.

But great gods, how agitated it was. Although there was no great wind, the branches, rattling their leaves, were leaning over, rising up, swaying to the right and the left, with little leaps and sometimes with languor, depending on whether the vague breezes, like an invisible and very quiet orchestra, were blowing to the rhythm of a polka or a waltz. The branch of an eglantine, in the distance, also moving, gave the impression of beating time.

"Oh!" I said. "What magic is making all these flowers jiggle like that?"

"It's not magic," said Elvine, "but my kindness. As a fay, am I not able to give them the illusion, once a year, thanks to their rapid or slow movements, that they're no longer fixed to the ground by their stems? And it is, so to speak, the carnival of the garden. In any case you're not at the end of your surprises. Lean over and tell me what that flower is."

"I know what it is, little fay Elvine. It's a white rose, the most beautiful in my flower-bed."

"Lean over a little more and look a little harder."

"What do I see? The white rose is red!"

"And that other flower, a little further away?"

"It's a lily."

"Look again."

"It's blue."

"And this one?"

"A jasmine. It's violet!"

"And this one?"

A rhododendron. It's yellow!"

"And this one?"

"A China aster. It's black!"

"And this one?"

"A cluster of lilac. It's tricolor!"

You will divine my astonishment.

"Nothing is simpler, however," said the fay, "since it's the carnival! White roses become bored with having been white for such a long time, and lilies and jasmines are also bored with being white, rhododendrons with being red, lilacs with being lilac and China asters with being pale; and for the ball, they dress in new colors; it's their fashion of disguising themselves."

In a grave reverie, I said: "How many things humans don't know!"

"Fortunately, fays are here to inform poets of everything."

"But how do the flowers succeed in changing color?" I said, while all the perfumed jiggling redoubled under the livelier allegro of the breeze. "That can't happen without some magic."

"No magic!" said Elvine. "When young women of the human race, and old ones, for they often…"

"Alas!"

"…want to disguise themselves, who comes to their aid?"

"There are hirers of costumes."

She made me a sign to walk toward an enormous bush of azaleas, where all the shades that the gaze can hope to see were flourishing.

"Well," she said, "there it is, the hirer of costumes, or colors."

"That azalea bush?"

"Yes, of course."

"No, plants can't walk. How can the calices choose and take the colors they want?"

"Oh, how you lack imagination! At any rate, that's the opinion that everyone has of you. What! You haven't divined that the azalea bush has eager and rapid salesmen: the hornets the butterflies, and the bees? On the eve of the ball, those insects go from calyx to calyx, making offers. 'What tint would you like to take this year, Madame White Rose? We have a bright violet that would suit you marvelously. But perhaps you prefer pale green…? 'Ah Monsieur Lily, we have a vermilion that would give you a very fine look. It's the finest bloom, and the latest. We refused it to the jasmine in order to reserve it for you… In your place, Queen Aster,[22] I'd decide for the azure with blue dots!" And, the orders having been placed, the bees, butterflies and hornets bring the desired colors."

I had no further objection to raise. Nothing was simpler, nothing more natural, in fact, than the flowery carnival that had appeared so complicated and so strange, and for long hours, there was an exquisite charm for me in watching the

---

[22] The French term for the China aster is *reine-marguerite*.

flowers dance beneath the half-veiled moon: all the flowers, glad no longer to resemble themselves.

But the fay said: "Let's go, let's go! We're leaving now."

"But why, little Elvine."

"Come, I tell you. There's nothing sadder than the day after a ball…"

I wanted to stay longer. I was wrong. Under the commencing daylight, the breeze was no longer singing polkas or waltzes; the melancholy flowers ceased to lean over and rise again, the branches were disentangled, and now, swarming from the azalea bush, the agents were already coming, with a sullen haste, to reclaim the hired colors and the fees that were due. What fees? A little of the perfume of this calyx, a little of the pollen dust of that one. And the white roses became white again, and the pink roses pink, and the lilacs lilac, languidly. Yes, all the flowers became themselves again, so sadly, under the light of day.

"You were right, little Elvine, let's go, let's go," I said to her.

As I went back into my house I darted one last glance at the flowers. They were all moist. Dew? No, their tears. And I saw a little daisy, so pale, which was fading with chagrin, about to die because she was no longer blue.

Azure, Gold and Crimson

Although the time is past when the poets of Hellas sang the divine marvels, the dazzlement of humans, when every little stream, a momentary mirror of the mouth or breast of a nymph, carried to the sea a fragment of the all-beauty that she had given to the earth, when the world was still oscillating from being passed from the shoulders of Atlas to those of Hercules; and although the time is also very distant when—as Aristomenes relates,[23] who was a merchant of honey and cheese—a certain Meroë, a magicienne as well as a tavern-keeper and an overly gallant old woman, changed advocates into rams, who continued their speeches bleating, innkeepers into frogs, travelers into tortoises and prevented pregnant women from going into labor for eight years, with the result that their bellies were finally as enormous and taut as if they were about to give birth to an elephant, it is necessary to refrain from believing that prodigies, large or small, are no longer seen in Attica, the Peloponnese, Macedonia or Thessaly, and that there are no fine stories of rare adventures there. I can tell you a few, either by virtue of remembering having read them once in very scholarly books, or by virtue of remembering having heard them once when I was, in a dream, the guest of shepherd storytellers half way up Mount Liacoura, which is the whitest of the summits of Parnassus. But it is not with snow that is white, as one might think, but with settled swans.

Commencement of the tale: Bonsoir, company!

---

[23] This Aristomenes is a character in Apuleius' *Metamorphoses*, also known as *The Golden Ass*, to whom his friend Socrates tells the story of the witch Meroë, who turns her former lovers into animals.

A king who had many nations and many wives was, in those days, very avaricious. In order to keep all the oil for himself he forbade the lighting of lamps in the houses of a country he had conquered by treason and possessed by violence. He wanted all its oil to fill his own lamps, to anoint his wives, and to render the blades that cut off heads more trenchant.

Now, in that country there were three daughters of a very poor old woman, who would not have been able to nourish their mother, or subsist themselves, if they had not worked in the evening. They therefore lit a candle in spite of the prohibition, after having taken care, in order that no one would see it, to block all the holes and cracks in the doors and the shutters—there were a lot of holes and cracks, for it was a wretched dwelling in such a poor fatherland—and they worked. But the salary they were given was very little, and while they worked they wept with fatigue and misery.

One of them, who was named Matin, because she was born near the sea where the sun rose, said as she was cutting the cloth: "If I were to marry the king's baker, I'd be quite content, for I could eat small loaves of bread that were still warm. But I'd rather be the wife of the king himself, because I'd give him a child the color of azure."

The second, whose name was Midi, because she had come into the world in the hottest climate in the country, said as she plied the needle: "If I were to marry the king's cook, I'd be quite content, for I'd be able to eat good meat, delicately prepared, and the most appetizing creams. But I'd rather be the wife of the king himself, because I'd give him a child the color of gold.

And the third, who was named Soir, because she was born in the west, said as she cut the thread: "If I were to marry the king's tailor. I'd be quite content, for I'd have magnificent garments of silk, brocade, velvet and fur, but I'd rather be the wife of the king himself, because I'd give him a crimson child.[24]

Then the old woman, who was their mother, got annoyed. "Bad daughters, unworthy daughters of the man who came back to the house one evening with a wound in his throat, from which all his blood ran; be cursed and consecrated to the Lord of the Subterranean World for the thought you've had! It would be better for you to become pregnant by a goat or a dog from the farm than the king who has many nations and wives.

But the three daughters said: "Don't grumble, old woman. A man who is alive knows that he isn't dead, but one who is dead doesn't remember having lived. Turn the spindle, thread the distaff. And if we have children of the king, you'll do well out of it."

Now, the king, who was walking in that city of the conquered country to see whether his orders were being carried out well, had noticed the light in the cracks of the shutters and he holes in the doors; in consequence, he was very angry; but he had heard the three sisters, and he had seen them; in consequence, he conceived a great desire to have them for wives.

He therefore summoned them to his palace the next day. "Ah! Here are the insolent women who light a candle when I've forbidden it." But he couldn't help laughing, because they were very beautiful.

He asked the one named Matin: "Isn't it you who boasted about giving me, if I married you, a child the color of azure?"

"That's me," said Matin

"And who furnished you with that assurance?"

"It was the little red mullet sorcerer, who isn't unaware of anything that happens in the sea.

---

[24] The actions of the three sisters liken them to the Greek Moirae, or Fates; their mother was supposedly Ananke (Necessity), so they were presumably sired by her consort and father Chronos (Time).

He asked the one named Midi: "Isn't it you who boasted about giving me, if I married you, a golden child?"

"That's me," said Midi.

"And who made you that prophecy?"

"It was Tzetzinaena, who, because she understand the language of the crickets and the blades of grass, knows all the things of the earth."

He asked the one named Soir: "Isn't it you who boasted about giving me, if I married you, a crimson child?"

"That's me," said Soir.

"And who swore you the promise?"

"It was the Winged Horse, who, because he flies through the clouds, knows everything there is in the sky."

The king burst out laughing.

"Well, I want the proof off it. I'll marry all three of you one after the other. But if the children you have aren't such as you say, all three of you will be precipitated from the summit of my highest tower."

First he married Matin. She did not take long to become pregnant. Everyone was astonished because the young woman's belly, which was strangely wide and high, moved and swelled and undulated as if, instead of a human fruit, it contained a sea wave.

Having gone away in order to combat a fleet that he destroyed with cannon fire and drowned in the gulf, asked as soon as he returned whether his wife had given birth to an azure child. His ministers refrained from telling him she had; malevolently, they had given the new-born child, who was indeed all azure, to an old woman sitting outside the gate, who had offered to take charge of it, and they told their master that Matin had brought into the world a nasty little white dog that had been thrown in the river. The furious king had the mother imprisoned in the dungeon of the highest tower.

He married Midi. Soon she became pregnant. Nothing was more surprising than her belly, from which emanated, through the skin and the fabrics, radiant light and metallic flashes. One might have thought that, instead of a human fruit, it contained a miraculous treasure.

In fact, while her husband was away, having gone to burn a few neighboring cities, she gave birth to a marvelously beautiful child the color of gold. The ministers gave it to the old woman who had already taken charge of the azure child, and when their master came back they told him that Midi had given birth to a little black monkey, which has been hanged from one of the apple trees in the orchard. The king, full of chagrin and rage, ordered the mother to be imprisoned beneath the tower, in the blackest dungeon.

He married Soir. As soon as she became pregnant, there was question of sending for the most expert midwives in the realm, for from the soon-to-be-maternal belly emanated, as if among the glorious clashes of swords in a tourney, an unknown crimson splendor, the like of which has never been seen.

The king would dearly have liked to witness his wife's childbirth, but he had to go away to preside over the decapitation of three thousand prisoners that had been taken in a recent war. When he returned, his ministers told him that Soir had brought into the world a sort of large gray mouse, which had been given to the palace cats. In reality, a superb crimson child had been born, whom they had given to the old woman at the gate. But the king knew nothing about that, and, crazed by wrath—for as a miser, he had hoped, truly, to have a son of sapphire, a son of gold and a son of ruby—he commanded that the three sisters be precipitated simultaneously from the summit of the highest tower.

The executioners took them to the extreme platform, from which they could see the whole sad country. They embraced one another and spoke to one another in low voices, after having looked around. They did not appear to be frightened by the imminent and certain death. They only advanced with anxious expressions...

They were precipitated.

They uttered a triple cry—a cry of joy.

For, in falling, they saw surging forth and rising toward the king's palace—one from the Orient, one from the South and one from the Occident—the three children that the old woman had received and enabled to grow: the child of azure, the child of gold and the crimson child: marine inundation, conflagration and carnage.

I wasn't there, nor were you, and you can believe what you please.

CLASSIC FRENCH FANTASY

Marie-Catherine d'Aulnoy. *Tales of the Fays* (2 vols.)'
Honoré de Balzac. *The Last Fay*
Gabrielle-Suzanne Barbot de Villeneuve. *The Naiads / Beauty and The Beast*
Chevalier de Béthune. *The World of Mercury*
Jean Carrère. *The End of Atlantis*
Charlotte-Rose Caumont de La Force. *The Land of Delights*
Comte de Caylus. *The Impossible Enchantment*
Félicien Champsaur. *Pharaoh's Wife*
Jacques Collin de Plancy. *Voyage to the Center of the Earth*
Gaston Danville. *The Perfume of Lust*
Comtesse D.L. *The Tyranny of the Fays Abolished*
Marie-Antoinette Fagnan. *The Enchanter's Mirror*
Paul Féval. *Anne of the Isles*
Charles de Fieux. *Lamékis*
Judith Gautier. *Isoline and the Serpent-Flower*
Nathalie Henneberg. *The Green Gods*
Gustave Kahn. *The Tale of Gold and Silence*
Edmond Haraucourt. *Dieudonat*
Nathalie Henneberg. *The Green Gods*
Françoise Le Marchand. *Florine and Boca*
Marie-Jeanne L'Héritier de Villandon. *The Robe of Sincerity*
André Lichtenberger. *The Centaurs; The Children of the Crab*
J-M. & Randy Lofficier (eds.). *The French Fantasy Treasury* (3 vols.)
Charles Lomon & P.-B. Gheuzi. *The Last Days of Atlantis*
Maurice Magre. *The Marvelous Story of Claire d'Amour; The Call of the Beast; Priscilla of Alexandria; The Angel of Lust; The Mystery of the Tiger; The Poison of Goa; Lucifer; The Blood of Toulouse; The Albigensian Treasure; Jean de Fodoas; Melusine; The Brothers of the Virgin Gold*
Marie-Madeleine de Lubert. *Princess Camion.*
Camille Mauclair. *The Virgin Orient*